Dec. '05

On Thin Ice

Waking up every morning and
Thanking God for another beautiful day

Meena Lawrence
&
Gilbert Lawrence

Dedicated to the many cultures
that add spice to the American way of life

10-Digit ISBN 1-59113-826-4
13-Digit ISBN 978-1-59113-826-6

Printed in the United States of America.

Booklocker.com, Inc.
2005

Table of Contents

>>> Foreword <<<

On Thin Ice is a story in which East meets West in the scenic countryside of upstate New York, a social microcosm, one which is replicated in cities and towns across the North American continent. The tale narrates the interactions between Americans and their Asian-Indian neighbors. An Indian-American physician and his family weave and link together the various ethnic communities and residents of this mid-sized American city. In “The Ballad of East and West,” Rudyard Kipling, the British author born and raised in Colonial India, claimed, "East is east and West is west; and never the twain shall meet...when two strong men stand face to face, tho' they come from the ends of the earth!" This novel negates his well-renowned stand.

Asian migration to the U.S. and Canada has been significant over the last fifty years. Asians have been well absorbed into their new environment, adding to the two countries’ rich cultural tapestry and achievements. **On Thin Ice** is a contemporary fictional novel depicting the many winter activities available in this part of the country, including ice-hockey, downhill and cross-country skiing, snow-shoeing, snowmobiling, curling and all of the pleasures associated with them. The story enlightens us about ourselves and our environment in a touching narrative, laced with different brands of humor - American, Indian, medical and sports-related.

New York City has been the traditional eastern gateway for various immigrant groups to the U.S. From there, they have transplanted themselves across the vast country. The paths of these groups continue to intersect, both for the émigrés and their descendents. Hence a few centuries later, “the twain" do meet and interact on the North American continent, and both achieve the American dream. The story presents everyday challenges and triumphs. The narrative reflects the tenuous nature of new émigrés as well as those well-settled. Our strength lies in how we work together to overcome challenges. We enrich one another in mutually beneficial relationships, often without realizing it.

Through its humor, **On Thin Ice** cuts through the stereotypes of peoples and situations. It reminds us that a dead-end always has a side street that can lead to new opportunities. Success can be found if one can look forward with excitement, a smile and a desire to succeed. We travel on thin ice, which often guides us to exciting discoveries.

New York State The land and its history

&

On Thin Ice on and off The Ice Rink

Upstate New York - God's Country
> 1 <

Whiteface Mountain in the North Country region of upstate New York is one of the higher peaks in the Adirondack chain. The mountain is a skier's paradise, and aptly named, as it is one of the major ski resorts in northeastern U.S. Among the multitude of skiers enjoying a cold, crisp mid-December morning in 2003 were Dr. Atul Reddy, his wife, Anita, and their two teenaged sons, Ajit and Anil. The absolutely splendid majesty of mountains always impressed them, even more so in the winter. The breath-taking Adirondacks had the same effect on the Reddy family as mountains did on naturalist, explorer, lyricist and writer, John Muir, who said, "Mountains have the power to move us."

The sight of the snow-clad peaks and vistas was so deeply moving that the Reddys were often at a loss for words to adequately describe the spirit of the moment. The Reddys were proud to call upstate New York home and were quick to distinguish that region from the City. "We do not live in New York City," Atul pointed out to the uninformed skiers on more than one occasion. "We live in Utica - a city between Albany and Syracuse. Utica is a city in New York's countryside."

On this Saturday, the mountain was at its height of glory with six inches of fresh white snow. The air crackled in the cold temperature. The slopes were dotted with skiers schussing and gliding, snowplowing, poling and stirring the powder with parallel turns. Watching the more experienced skiers was like witnessing poetry in motion as they went free skiing and snow boarding, carving their giant S turns on the wide open runs. Extreme skiers leaped off cliffs and bluffs, challenging the meanest slopes on the mountains with death-defying techniques, daring gravity with surreal agility. Those who practiced their freestyle techniques of ballet, aerial and mogul skiing seemed to be having much more fun than the rest.

The Gen-Xers (born between 1980 and 1989) formed homey groups whose members preferred snow skating and had mastered pop-shove-it, kick-flip techniques as well as 360-degree flips. For some, the heart-pounding, muscle-shearing thrills of skiing provided adventure. Quite a few people believed in pushing their physical abilities to the limit and surviving on bare instincts. For the Reddys, skiing down the spectacular rock formations and drops was a liberating experience because they were also able to take in the natural beauty. It was an action packed and exhilarating event that began when the parents said, "Let's go, gang!"

The Reddys' skiing prowess required some serious sweat. They enjoyed skiing because it challenged them to be the best they could be and feel the energy. The Reddys were avid skiers who could hardly be considered fool-hardy when it came to testing their skills. They were health-conscious and physically very fit - the epitome of lean mean muscle machines with flat abs. Their idea of a relaxing weekend involved enjoying the great outdoors, always taking pleasure in doing something different, yet not-so-wicked. These activities were "an attitude boost." The parents were self-confessed overachievers. "You must be persistent, determined and work doggedly to excel," dad repeatedly advised his children.

Mom would add, "You've got to push yourself. There is no such thing as a routine attempt. Doing things perfectly is its own reward."

Whiteface Mountain is a hot spot on which to be on an icy cold day. The ski slopes which extend over two mountain peaks are among the top ranking ski resorts in the eastern United States. The mountains, famous for their varied terrain, cover more than 220 ski-able acres, as well as miles and miles of snowmobile paths. Crisscrossing this ground are 75 trails for all levels of skiing and riding abilities. The base of the mountain is 1,220 feet above sea level and receives an average of 190 inches of fine powder annually. The highest ski terminus is 4,386 feet high with an additional skiable terrain about 240 feet above. From here, standing on the mountaintop of serenity, one can appreciate and enjoy the radiant sunlight. *(Ski resort's print and electronic brochures*).

On this day nature allowed the skiers to share the thrill of its bounty. After adjusting to the change in altitude, it was time for the Reddys and others at the summit to ski downhill in whatever pattern their hearts desired. Nobody was sloughing off and the action was pretty intense. On reaching the bottom, the skiers called it, "an energy boost."

The Reddys always remembered the warning given to them by their ski instructor, Speedy Eddie. "When tackling Whiteface, or any other mountain, injury is only a misstep away," he would say. "This isn't a forgiving terrain. Have fun yet be cautious."

Like the other serious skiers at these altitudes, the Reddys had both form and function. They carefully assessed the situation, always keeping in mind the need to anticipate the unknown. This was the only way to safely experience the thrill of a lifetime. From certain vantage points, viewers could take a break from skiing, snow-shoeing or snow-mobiling to enjoy the rugged topography of the Adirondacks and the surrounding scenery. Up here, the air is thin and it is easy to immerse oneself in the serenity of one's surroundings and completely escape from responsibility. A stretch of the arm and one might very well touch the sky and the gods, or so it seems. On this clear day, the Reddys could see Montreal's Mont Royal to the north; Vermont's rolling Green Mountains to the east, McIntyre range to the south and St. Lawrence River to the west. Closer at hand at this height, they could see rime ice on trees - perfect for photographs of panoramic views and magnificent vistas. The ice reflected the morning sun, dazzling all those who ventured into the cold. Clearly, a winter lover's enjoyment is determined by the amount of precipitation and sunshine; and the day's view was the best spice to warm the body. As dad put it, "Mountains embody the spirit. It's a picture-perfect moment."

On the slopes, the Reddys saw islands of evergreen pines weighed down heavily with snow. Some trees that had shed their leaves had two inches of snow outlining their wooden skeletons. Ten ski-lifts and gondolas of various sizes took the skiers to the peak. The most challenging of the downhill ski trails led to the famous 3,430 foot drop - the highest in the east. This is just one of two vertical drops of greater than 3,000 feet in the eastern U.S. Skiing the slopes was heart-pounding exercise but the Reddy family enjoyed the thrill. In this encounter, they lived Muir's axiom: "One must labor for beauty and pleasure as for bread."

Waiting at the base of the ski slope was the Welcome and Recreation Center where visitors and skiers relaxed around the warm fire and listened to live music of a Zydeco group. Children were entertained by magicians. On the deck surrounding the Center, parents watched the skiers or read. Some bundled up in blankets and sat a comfortable distance away from the outdoor fire.

The region is surrounded by summits with names like Whiteface, Marcy, Colden and Algonquin; cradled in its midst is the town of Lake Placid. The town, with its International Winter Sports Center, hosted the Third and Thirteenth Winter Olympics in 1932 and 1980 respectively, the Winter Goodwill Games of 2000 and the National Alpine Championships in 2003. Lake Placid is a quaint town with museums and art centers, and is reminiscent of Old European ski towns. Its population of 2,500 plays host to 1.8 million tourists annually. During the Olympics, Lake Placid welcomed athletes from 37 countries and coordinated 38 international competitions.

The town's main street is dotted with cafes, confectionaries, bistros and signature connoisseur restaurants serving sinfully decadent desserts and wine selections. Lake Placid is an epicurean's delight - gourmet food and freshly brewed specialty coffee served at the finest restaurants. Additionally, there are hotels which pamper their guests with spas, saunas, and massages; numerous attention-grabbing boutiques with Adirondack-themed designs and treasured antiques satisfy the most discerning of skiers and visitors.

After a full day of skiing, the Reddys relaxed at their cottage in the evening, giving their muscles a break. However, their cerebral neurons continued to be in over-drive as the family planned the next day's activities. "Let's go skiing on Gore Mountain tomorrow; it's only a short drive from here," Ajit suggested. The plan was unanimously agreed on. Yet now, rest was their priority. The day's strenuous activities had left them happy but tired. The family was primed for a peaceful restful sleep which came easy as they snuggled under down comforters; their cozy cabin was warmed by crackling sweet-smelling pine which burned in the fire place.

Early the next day, after a delicious breakfast of hot chocolate and blueberry muffins, the Reddys stepped out into the freezing cold. Most of their cabin was buried up to its eaves in snow. They cautiously began the always-challenging winter drive in their 4-wheel vehicle.

Dad commented, "Today we are going to get our money's worth from these new snow tires." Ajit added, "We'll soon know if those 'sipes' of the tires can bite into slippery surfaces for max-traction."

Mom replied, "If the tires keep our four-wheeler from skidding, they'll be worth their weight in gold and will have done their job."

The Reddys were prepared to be pitted against nature. They were determined not to be bogged down by snow in this lonely wilderness. A heavy overnight snowfall, coupled by a brisk wind made it imperative for dad to carefully maneuver the vehicle over powdery roads and past grown-over timber. Though the drive was slow and precarious, excitement ran high as the family anticipated excellent skiing conditions. Their route circled the mountains of the Adirondacks. One road sign reassured them as well as made them laugh. It read, "If this sign is completely covered with snow, the road is impassable."

The evergreens were cloaked with snow. As it was early in the morning, the family was on the lookout for foraging wildlife. In the distance they spotted a deer crossing the road and then galumphing to the open fields on the other side. Finally they arrived at North Creek, home of the Gore Mountain Ski Resort.

Blue skies and frosty-sunny weather greeted the Reddys. For them, it was the closest thing to paradise. North Creek is rated as one of the ten top ski resorts. The slopes are spread over three mountains with a summit elevation of 3,600 feet which includes the 3,200-foot summit of Bear Mountain. Taking in the views, dad announced, "We are one with nature, relying on our primal instincts."

For skilled skiers such as the Reddys, Gore Mountain offers twelve black or double black diamond trails. There are also cross-country trails on which amateurs can enjoy a wide variety of winter sports.

On reaching the summit, Mom said, "Let our spirits harmonize and our bodies synchronize with nature for smooth exhilaration."

Dad reminded the family of the words of humorist and philosopher George Carlin: "Life is not measured by the number of breaths we take, but by the moments that take our breath away."

With that, their bodies shifted into instant acceleration. They challenged one another to faster speeds and trickier moves as they improved their techniques and prowess on the slopes. Other skiers were tearing up the ski slopes with freestyle mogul skiing. Along the way, Ajit encountered some competitive Olympic skiers zipping past and stated, "Looks like they're equipped with boosters." The Reddys were there to have family fun, not to practice for the Olympics. So, they allowed themselves time for horseplay to make their skiing enjoyable.

The plan was to begin with a few hours of downhill skiing and then to switch gears for some cross-country skiing. As the day advanced, it became bright and brilliant. The family had a fun-filled time scrappin' and stampin'. It was mildly windy and the sunlight made the snow glisten. This day was one of the season's best.

Above its entrance, the local Coffee Shoppe had a large sign announcing its logo: "Eating Healthy Never Tasted So Good." At the noon hour, the Reddys decided to taste the healthy fare, and at the two sons' behest, the family indulged in some "Fondue Fun."

Then it was back to skiing. The cross-country trails were narrow and covered with fresh white snow. The air was clean and refreshing. Along the way, they saw tracks of deer, rabbit and other wildlife, and the foot-prints added to the excitement. After a few hours of cross-country skiing, the Reddys called it quits. Mom and Dad planned to unwind, rev up the romance and spend a heavenly night together after making time for some spiritual reflection. The boys anticipated playing their favorite computer games and relaxing until bedtime.

The Reddys and others descended to Peaceful Valley Road for their drive back to Lake Placid. They had so much of fun that dad said, "If we are going to walk on thin ice we might as well dance." The family looked forward to returning to their warm log-cabin, a rustic-living cottage. In this deluxe lodge, the parents and kids could indulge in the art of snuggling amid comfy pillows and down comforters. It was the perfect setting for silent nights and sweet dreams.

As Atul Reddy, affectionately called AR, drove back to Lake Placid, he spotted a Super-Buck - the whitetail deer that even experienced hunters rarely see! These handsome bucks are between four and seven years old, loners who outfox hunters and live to be huge. They sport giant racks and don't appear in the open during hunting season. Their home range is small, and during the hunting season they tend to be like hermits, hiding under thick cover. The enormous body bulk and the thick mass of antlers - 16 to 20 point racks - are indications that these creatures are survivors who avoid becoming mounted trophies.

"Quick! Give me the camera," dad said as he slowed down.

He pulled off the road and came to a stop on the shoulder. As he captured images of this rare sight on film, a few others stopped to admire the creature and take photographs, too.

AR was not a hunter but he had learned a lot about wild animals and game from his neighbor, whom all called Bull's Eye Billy. "Bears, for example, hibernate at this time of the year," Billy had informed Atul.

Atul shared with his family what he had learned about the white tail from Billy and other sources. "To conserve energy in the winter, the animals live in low-lying areas behind wind-deflecting cover, and on south slopes to absorb the winter sun. If you look in the right places it's possible to spot these elusive animals. This stud survived the hunting season. In a few weeks it will be time for him to shed those racks."

During the winter, deer feed on acorns of all types, beach nuts, and the tender tips of aspen, maple and white cedar. Secondary foods include ash, aspen, green briar, red maple and honeysuckle. As they pulled back onto the road, Ajit turned to take another admiring look at the animal and remarked, "It is One-deer-full and a Wunder-Stud!"

And in another play on words, AR said to the family, "The buck does funny things when the does are present."

On the way back, AR told his family that the untamed wilderness is also home to the black bear, beaver, fox and coyote. The family enjoyed taking in the sights of the winter wonderland. The skeletons of the tree limbs, bare vines and picket fences were blanketed with snow which accentuated their discreet, understated elegance and quiet beauty. The passing scenes were like a slide show depicting the paintings of Thomas Kinkaid in real life. For all those who admired nature, as the Reddys did, this was Seventh Heaven found.

Arriving safely at their cottage, the Reddys unwound. Then it was a retro-style cocktail supper of jambalaya with shrimp and andouille sausage, chickpea curry with yogurt, and banana pumpkin smoothies. Over supper, the Reddys reminisced about the day's adventures. "We sure had a great time today yet I'm not ready to call it quits. I think we have all earned the right to indulge in calorie-riddled desserts," Ajit said. Their late night snack was a triple chocolate mousse pyramid.

Dad summed up the day. "It was delightful and we can splurge on all these calories, guilt-free." The decadent treat spiked the Reddys' level of endorphins even higher and they felt more than just content. As Anita watched the three men in her life relax in their chairs, she decided, "Life is wonderful and so rewarding!" She truly believed that, "Happiness isn't having what you want, it's wanting what you have."

Most skiers to the Lake Placid area come from around the Adirondacks where residents can get unrestricted views of the mountains from their front and back yards. Other skiers come from the eastern seaboard - city dwellers from the Big Apple (New York City), Bean Town (Boston), from cities in Connecticut and New Jersey, and from small towns scattered across the eastern United States and Canada. While most ski downhill, cross-country skiing has become increasingly popular. Skiers gambol and glide as they somehow make it through the kick turns. Some go radical on the trails, throwing tricks on jibs and rails. In keeping with that spirit, enjoying each moment is easy for the skiers. By day's end, the most avid of the bunch will have experienced trails from long flats to short and steep surprises before returning to the parking lots.

Among other activities that the Reddys enjoyed in and around Lake Placid was visiting The Verizon Sports Complex and the United States Olympic Training Center run by the Olympic Regional Development Authority (ORDA). The site attracts America's winter sports enthusiasts, including athletes skilled in bobsled and luge, speed-skating, Nordic and cross-country skiing, ski jumping and the Biathlon. It is the only training site in the U.S. for luge. ORDA also manages the Mount Van Hoevenberg Recreation area, the Ski Jump Complex, the Speed Skating Oval, the Whiteface Mountain Ski Area and the Whiteface Mountain Veterans Memorial Highway. (*ORDA's print and electronic brochures*).

While visiting these venues, the Reddys re-lived the highlights of the 1980 Winter Olympics which they had followed closely. They visualized Ingemar Stenmark, the Alpine legend of Sweden, win the men's slaloms. In the women slaloms, Liechtenstein's Hanni Wenzel did the same, earning the smallest country a win. The Reddys remembered cheering Nikolay Zimyatov as he won his three gold medals in cross-country skiing. And of course, there was American Eric Heiden who won all five speed-skating races (500m to 10,000m), breaking all records. The family relived the "Miracle on Ice" – the unforeseen victory of USA's ice hockey team over the Russians.

In the northeastern part of the Park are the rugged "High Peaks," with 43 mountains rising more than 4,000 feet, including the 5,344-foot Mount Marcy, the highest point in New York with Whiteface being 4,867 feet tall. Here, the Reddys once again experienced the awesome grandeur of nature. AR remarked, "In the summer there are awe-inspiring views of rugged ridges with heavy wooded valleys and waterfalls, which attract hunting, fishing, hiking and mountain climbing." Within the park are 3,000 lakes and ponds, and 36,000 miles of rivers, streams and brooks which contain the headwaters of five major basins - the source of water for numerous major and minor cities in the state. (*The Park's print and electronic brochures*). These surroundings allowed AR to be the "energizer," and Anita, the "energizer-recharger." Their kids were always "supercharged" for fun.

After spending the week in Lake Placid and taking in all the attractions in the environs, the Reddys made their way home along Route 30. They passed Tupper and Long Lakes and then Blue

Mountain Lake where they took a short break to enjoy the Adirondack Museum. The exhibits chronicle the relationships between human beings, wildlife and this untainted wilderness over the last few centuries. A relief map of the Adirondacks and dioramas of the park display the character of the mountains and people who made it their home. Through old and new, still and cine-photographs, this open air museum gives a 200-year account and historical perspective of the mountains, their breath-taking scenery, and activities of the people of the region. The museum's brochure boasts of the "largest collection of rustic furniture and inland watercraft as well as the work of local artists and artisans." The museum itself is spread over 22 buildings located on 32 acres. Blue Mountain rises to a height of 3,800 feet with beauty and serenity as far as the eye can see. The Adirondack Park has about 120,000 year-round human residents, and is also home to thousands of trees - spruce, beech, birch, maple; 300 species of birds, 35 species of reptiles and amphibians, and 82 species of fish. The park is certainly a place that invites visitors to take the long scenic route. *(Museum's print and electronic brochures).*

While enjoying the lake, the family talked about the upcoming week.

"It's going to be hectic with mid-term tests, mid-week ice hockey practice and weekend games," Ajit said.

"I also have to proofread the student newspaper," Anil complained.

As a piece of advice on how to get things done, Mom quoted Einstein: "Make everything as simple as possible, but not any simpler."

Academics were always a top priority for Ajit and Anil. Yet the boys were also immersed in ice hockey, playing the forward line as they excelled at stick handling and shooting a variety of levels. They talked about "the fixable flaws" and ways to get ready for the upcoming game in which their team was considered the underdogs. This would be an opportunity to learn more. Ajit and Anil were "All American" boys; their interest in sports was nurtured by their dad's coaching and their mom's encouragement. Though he grew up in the tropics - far from an ice-rink - AR found himself intimately drawn to ice hockey. As his sons grew up, they practiced the sport, which is very popular in the upstate region. And, as in any high school sport, the boys became extremely competitive and learned how best to play the puck and position themselves on the ice. Their team's aim was to be the league's new leader in high pressure tactics. In Utica they were considered the best show in town, with moves that ranged from the basics to do-as-you-dare type of action.

On their return trip, the Reddy family stopped at a café with a wood-burning fireplace. AR had an aversion to fast food and sugar-loaded sodas. His medical training taught him that they were "heart attacks packaged in Styrofoam."

Yet with their week's intense physical activity, this was a guilt-free time-out. As endurance athletes they needed to do some carb-loading.

They requested, "Two lemon teas, two hot cups of tea, four sub sandwiches and an apple pie, please."

As he filled their order, the attendant replied, "With delight!"

"No! With ketchup and mustard," AR quipped, winking at his wife.

He had a good sense of humor and believed that laughter is good for the *atma* or soul. He deemed that "laughter reduces stress and perks the immune system."

Refreshments completed, the Reddys thanked the attendant for making them very satisfied customers and continued along Route 30. They passed well-groomed snowmobile trails and cross-country ski paths. They made their way to Indian Lake where they watched adventurous locals ice-fishing. AR was both amused and befuddled by this hobby. "They obviously want to get away from their wives pretty badly," he said. "It looks like their priority is to bring-out the warm clothes and keep the worries at home," Anita countered. Anita was a lady of the lakes, in the winter and the summer. The sight and sound of water had an especially calming and reassuring effect on her. The family reached Route 8 in Speculator, near Lake Pleasant. Here, the Reddys were 2000 feet lower than the high peaks of Whiteface and Marcy, where the forest changes to reflect the altered topography from high mountains to rugged foothills. In the summer the forests display every shade of green. The Reddys made another stop to complete the spectacular day by taking in the sights of the glistening lake with the snow-covered mountains in the backdrop. This was heaven 'n earth, both gorgeous and romantic.

The good thing about these solitary paved roads is that one cannot get lost and like most visitors to the park, if you don't care where you are, then you aren't lost. To break the silence of long drives, dad developed the habit of keeping the kids amused with humor. Never at a loss for a good joke, AR told his family this story: "A distraught patient phoned her doctor's office. Was it true, the woman wanted to know, that the medication the doctor had prescribed was for the rest of her life? She was informed that it was. There was a short pause before the woman continued, "I'm wondering then, just how serious is my illness? The prescription says 'no refills'."

As dusk was setting in on their journey home, AR knew he had to be careful to avoid hitting the deer that ventured out in search of food at that time of day. The creatures paw at the soil along the highway in search of bits of edible greenery, especially when the winters are severe and the fields are snow-covered. Oblivious of oncoming traffic, they bound across the roads in search of greener pastures. In a local body shop, AR had seen the twisted and dented remains of cars that had run into deer. He found it hard to believe that the damage had been inflicted by these delicate animals. A fully-grown buck can weigh 150 pounds, enough to cause major dents and shatter wind-shields. Injuries to the driver, passengers and the animals were always possibilities. So, as always, AR was cautious.

To continue with the fun of the week gone by, the family played mind-games as they made their way back to Utica. They came up with a list of interesting vanity plates on cars which possibly described the owner's profession. Yet, underlying his humor was AR's optimistic creed: "Challenges are opportunities and opportunities will be challenges." AR was self-confident with a positive attitude; he gave his best to the project at hand. He had zero tolerance for wasted opportunities and his favorite adage was: "There's no better time than the present." AR loved quoting proverbs as they were short sentences based on long experience.

As they continued along, Anita caught sight of a family of deer; a little later, a red fox sprinted over the glistening lake. It had been a long day as the family made its way home. The trip through the scattered one-light or no-traffic-light hamlets and villages was a welcome cool-down after a hectic week of traversing snow-covered mountains. As they drove past the small towns, they recalled knowing a few of the residents, some of whom were never too busy to share a local tale, swap recipes or reveal the best fishing spots for visitors wishing to return in the summer.

In the spirit of the Christmas season, the family played carols on the car's CD. Outside, the stunning scenery and the stillness of the evening made it a Currier and Ives kind of moment. In such a setting it wasn't hard to experience peace. It was a soulful experience.

Mohawk Valley (MoVa)
> 2 <

The Adirondacks were formed at the end of the Paleozoic era when a major upheaval in the earth's crust raised the mountain chain in the northeastern United States. In addition to the Adirondacks, the chain includes the Catskills, Green and Great Smoky Mountains. The Mohawk Valley (MoVa) and the Mohawk River lie between the Adirondacks and the Catskills and were carved out as the ice age was ending 10,000 years ago. This waterway, from the Atlantic seaboard to the west, inspired the early pioneers to connect the northeastern coast of the United States to the Great Lakes. The Erie Canal was built through this gap to connect the Hudson River with Lake Erie while bypassing the St. Lawrence River, Lake Ontario and the Niagara Falls.

At Lockport, just northeast of Buffalo, a set of five locks built in the 1840s lifted the boats in stages over the forty-nine-foot Niagara Escarpment. Then ships sailed with their cargo and passengers to the rest of the Great Lakes and through them to Canada and the Midwest. Later, with the dawning of the Industrial Age, railways and roads which ran parallel to the Erie Canal pushed through the MoVa. A century later, Interstate 90 was built parallel to the prior routes of transportation. Lockport, in Western New York, is one of eight regions of the Empire State. The others include the Finger Lakes, North Country, Mohawk Valley (Central New York), Catskills, Hudson River Valley, New York City and Long Island. The Adirondack Park lies mainly in the North Country. Just south of the Adirondack Park, on either side of the 161-mile Mohawk River (and Erie Canal) lies MoVa. The town of Utica has always been the commercial center of MoVa. About six tribes formed the Iroquois Confederation when the Native Americans settled this land. This fertile land and river made the area the leading settlement territory for all newcomers. The valley is also very scenic; the rolling foothills of the two mountain ranges are blessed with abundant moisture, forests and wildlife, highlighting the four seasons in all their natural grandeur.

The region of MoVa around Utica was made famous by the August 6, 1777 Battle of Oriskany - one of the decisive battles of the Revolutionary War. British forces under General Barry St. Leger came down from Fort Ontario in Oswego, laying siege to Fort Stanwix at

Rome. They marched east and had proceeded barely four miles to the town of Oriskany, when they were ambushed. They were defeated by American patriots and county militia led by General Herkimer from Fort Dayton (located in the town of Herkimer) and their allies, the Oneidas. The British red-coats retreated north leaving intact the bread basket of the American Revolution.

The Iroquois Confederacy was split in this battle The Mohawks, led by one of their own - Mary (Molly) Brant, sided with the British loyalists who were led by Sir William Johnson (Molly Brant's husband). The Oneida tribe, led by its chief, Hanyery, joined the Tryon County Militia. After the battle at Oriskany, the Oneidas galloped east to Saratoga. Once again, they helped the rebels defeat the larger British force which was led by General Burgoyne who had come down the Champlain Valley from Quebec. For the Americans and their Oneida allies, these were two major victories in one year – and just a year after signing the Declaration of Independence in 1776. These were the early stages of the successful eight-year Revolutionary War (1775-1783). The lack of support from General St. Leger's troops led to the British defeat at the famed Battle of Saratoga later that year. This was the start of recurrent events in the Revolutionary War which led to liberty and the birth of the new nation.

Evolutionary changes in the upstate region continued for the next 225 years and still continue today. MoVa has also been a source of (sometimes unexpected) humor over this period. In 1783, General Washington toured the area and suggested a transportation canal to help with inland navigation in the "Western Country," the bread basket of the nation. Yet in 1809, then-President Thomas Jefferson refused to provide Federal help for the seven million dollar Erie Canal project. President Jefferson, known for his foresight, called the project an idea "a hundred years ahead of its time...and a little short of madness to think of it at this time."

The "Great Ditch," also called "Great Western" or "Erie Canal," built between 1817 and 1825, was 363 miles long, 40 feet wide and 4 feet deep. The canal's 83 locks connected the Hudson River and Atlantic Ocean (same level) with the Niagara River and Lake Erie at 570 feet above sea level. The deepest lock is 40.5 feet, at a town called Little Falls. The canal, which some called the Eighth Wonder of the World was built by the Irish, mainly with manual labor. The canal was enlarged in 1862 to accommodate larger ships (the Lakers) which measured 96 feet by 17.5 feet (wide) by 12 feet. The towns along the canal and their economic activity made MoVa a thriving region of the country. *(Erie Canal's print and electronic brochures*). The American population at that time was less than 10 million. Despite Jefferson's concerns, the Erie Canal paid for itself within a few years as a result of the increased barge traffic and trade between the Great Lakes states, Canada and the Eastern Seaboard. The main canal also led to the development of scores of lateral and side canals in western New York and Pennsylvania and greater barge traffic. Consequently, Pittsburgh (in landlocked western Pennsylvania) and beyond were linked by a waterway to the Hudson and the Atlantic Ocean. The canal spurred its own commerce with boat building and dry dock repairs.

The third generation of the canal which has 35 locks survives today as the Barge Canal. It is used by pleasure crafts which take the same route as their predecessors did. In the fall, "snowbirds" sometimes sail their boats from the towns bordering the Great Lakes down the canal to spend the winter in warmer climates along the southeastern seaboard or in the Caribbean islands and then return north in the spring. Along the way they stop at the many small ports-of-call to enjoy the charm and the festivals of the upstate region.

About fifty-five years after it was built, the value of the canal was superseded by the railroad, which was built and operated by Italian immigrants and other pioneers in the 1880s. This progress could have occurred earlier had not the energies of the country been diverted to the Civil War, which started on April 12, 1861. After the war, Utica and MoVa were economically and politically vibrant, with their native, James S. Sherman, serving as vice president under William Howard Taft from 1909 until his death in1912.

MoVa was the home of the Native Americans. The first colonists – Dutch, English and Welsh - came to trade fur in the seventeenth century. The construction of the canal brought the Irish pioneers to the area (1817). They were followed by the blacks (1820), Germans (1832) and Jewish settlers (1847). These émigrés made MoVa an important link between the Great Lakes and the Atlantic Ocean. Later, the Italians (1883) and Poles (1900) arrived during the Transportation (road and rail) and Industrial revolutions, respectively. In keeping with U.S. immigration trends, MoVa has seen its share of Syro-Lebanese (1888), Ukrainians (1945) and Asians (1970s). In the late twentieth century, people arrived from war-torn countries of the Americas, Africa and Europe. A Refugee Center in Utica serves as a training and transition point for the refugees. After they adjust to American ways, many decide to settle locally. They help to revitalize and reconstruct the city and region in the same way preceding immigrants did.

Like the rest of the country, MoVa's economy has changed from farming to labor-intensive industry, and more recently to healthcare, technology and related fields such as information technology, fiber-optics and other connectivity technology. A good example is PAR Technology (Par Tech) which is a high-tech provider of information technology, and organizational skills with technological solutions for the hospitality trade. Started by an Utican, the company's expertise extends from hardware to software, including professional services to businesses in the restaurant, hospitality and retail industries. Par Tech has installed more than 35,000 systems in 95 countries. *(Company's print and electronic brochures).*

With 250 years of settlement history, many residents in MoVa are older, wiser and relaxed. New settlers, sometimes referred to as being FOB or "Fresh-Off-The-Boat," work hard at getting a toe-hold in American life. They labor like worker-bees round the clock, at any job, for the experience and the ability to make a down-payment on a car, buy a winter coat, or repay a personal loan. Like immigrants who preceded them, and those who will follow, the new émigrés are ambitious and determined, like butterflies out of cocoons. They are driven by a force which compelled them to make that long, arduous and uncertain trip to the U.S. in the first place. Most compensate for their broken and accented-English with a smile, gusto and determination. Enthusiasm marks every effort, whether at establishing a career or setting up a home. Though their homes might have a ruler of the cozy castle, there was no king of the couch.

Like their predecessors, immigrant women in their quiet way accept the roll of the dice without regrets. Even without a course in home economics, they are masters at Budgeting 101 and live gracefully on a shoestring paycheck. While the wives continue to learn about U.S. customs, they have mastered Marriage 101 in the old country and know "what every wife and mother should know." They work hard to climb the prosperity ladder and sooner rather than later achieve their goals. They assimilate into American society through friendships with their neighbors, co-workers and the parents of their children's classmates. As mothers, they are the "sweet" in Home Sweet Home. As the world knows, "never underestimate the power of a woman."

Every settler has a tale! In the first two decades, there isn't time to tell it. Days are spent squeezing the best out of every hour - earning a living, learning the U.S. ways by socializing with friends, making contacts or nurturing the children. Most émigrés left home and the security of their immediate families "for a dream, to ensure a better future for their children and to get a little more out of life." So, helping their children with homework and projects are an important part of an immigrant's daily routine. Old timers warn the new arrivals: "Now you are the driver and there isn't any rear view mirror." New arrivals have exciting skills to learn. At times, the experience is painful. This is not difficult for immigrants to accept, as the desire to experience, explore and try new avenues is part of human nature.

Recent émigrés ask many questions, some practical and some philosophical. Since money is limited, new-comers want to know about the hidden expense and the bottom line before making any major purchase. They are new to America, but they weren't born yesterday. They are fast learners and always try to implement the right solution to achieve results quickly. When they immigrated, they had already taken a great step in the right direction, wide-eyed with excitement. The émigré's philosophy, after overcoming the culture shock, becomes one of managing and struggling to adapt, of taking the bitter with the sweet. When daunting decisions present themselves, most take courage from the popular adage, "Nothing ventured, nothing gained."

Learning about American culture can be humorous. Émigrés find it is possible to listen to AM radio stations in the evenings. Most take the culture-shock and funny incidents in stride as just another lesson learned! They say good-naturedly, "You learn a thing or two everyday."

Invariably, one or more American families "adopt" an immigrant family and lend a helping hand in teaching them the basics of American life - how to start a lawnmower, or get rid of weeds in the lawn, and that dandelions are not flowers to be admired and preserved, (though some make them into wine!). The help and advice are graciously and eagerly accepted. This "adoption process" is just one of the numerous examples of the incredible kindness of strangers.

These situations also lend themselves to immigrant-related comedy: A newcomer envied her American neighbor's large red tomatoes. One day she plucked up enough courage to ask him, "What is the secret of your success?" The man obligingly told her the brands of seed and fertilizer he used. Then he shared his secret ingredients: "I sing to the plants daily and flash them weekly, which make the tomatoes really blush." The woman followed his advice diligently to the last detail. At the end of the summer season, she confided to her friends, "All my love and care for my tomatoes were a total waste. But for some reason, the cucumbers flourished."

Having left their native lands, émigrés are quite literally an outgoing, smart group of survivors with a modern day frontier spirit. They realize that even calamities can be advantageous and can bring people together. Yet, laws of probability dictate that a few newcomers will not land on their feet and will unfortunately find themselves unable to cope. Some return to their homelands.

With so much uncertainty already faced and still more looming ahead, new immigrants tend to be pack rats and penny pinchers. So, amassing utilitarian items, especially during special sales, is the norm. The first home must have a basement to store and increase the collection. In their new home, émigrés maintain their native and sometimes brightly-hued home décor along with Americana. This same mix is also seen in their wardrobes. They exhibit true flexibility and fall in love with their adopted country for all the right reasons. They are Americans by choice! They believe that it is better to pursue something than nothing! While adopting the best of American ways, they also discover new ways to relieve their stress. They share their old and new character-building experiences to the delight and amusement of their listeners. Since immigrants start life from ground zero, they have no unmet expectations. Like the fixer-upper first home that they invariably buy, the newcomers realize their tremendous potential through patience, elbow grease and muscle power.

After a hard week's work, when the men get together over a beer, they share their native proverbs: Try and try again like the ant inching up the wall...The road to success is under construction...When a man gets married he gets a spokeswoman...There are two kinds of women - those you dream about and those you marry...The best way to knock off a woman's sexual desire is to feed her wedding cake.

When the women meet socially, they swap advice: Smile, it makes people wonder what's on your mind...The best way to get a man to do something: suggest he's too old for it...A sense of humor does not mean you tell him jokes; it means you laugh at his... Bachelor - a man who missed the opportunity to make some woman miserable.

When the adults socialize, they reminisce about their youth. "Back then, until I was thirteen, my older sisters convinced me that my name was 'Shut Up'." They educated each other on American ways: The side of the shirt with TGIF does not mean 'This Goes In Front'; a bag of chips which says, "You could be a winner! No purchase necessary. Details Inside," is not a shoplifter special.

Émigrés have no time to tell their history and no one who would listen to them anyway. They often met on weekends for emotional and spiritual nourishment. They shared their new stories and experiences. Some of these are funny, such as the tale of the newcomer who was at his job for three years without a day of personal leave.

One day, he called his manager and said, "I'm having a splitting headache and backache and please requesting a day of sick leave."

"We do not have a sick leave policy for your work level. So, I really would advise you not to take the day off," the employer said, and then he continued. "Let me be helpful. When I'm very sick like you are, I make love to my wife. Gee, my aches and pains disappear; I am enthused, rejuvenated, and feel fresh and ready to go." Then he added, "I suggest you try that, and give us a call in an hour."

An hour later the new immigrant called his boss. "Sir, I tried exactly and precisely what you said, Sir, I thank you, Sir, for that helpful advice and your kind generosity... I will be to work in an hour, Sir!...Thank you very very much, Sir!...Very thoughtful of you, Sir!...And Sir, I have to compliment you on your beautiful million dollar house."

Beyond the humor, immigrants follow the suggestions of the experts without necessarily reading their advice or realizing it. These include: "Keep an open mind," and "maintain a 'rearing to go' attitude," as well as "lose past inhibitions caused by family or events." The recent arrivals focused on their dreams and more importantly, put in the effort to achieve them. Failure wasn't an option. They realized that there was no other way but to move forward in this new land of new hopes.

Immigration was an end to one phase in their lives and also the fresh start of a new chapter, one which they began with more experience, maturity, hope and determination. For the émigrés this was a dramatic change which would evolve, as the status quo just would not do. They all knew or were told, "Innovation doesn't come easy." New settlers realize there is no pleasure in apathy; it is imperative to do what is right rather than what is convenient. Émigrés believe in pushing their efforts to the limit and achieving success with the support of family members and friends. This is just as true today as it was yesterday. The Reddys remembered these lessons even after they became "weathered residents." As Atul would advise his sons and other new émigrés, "While America is the land of opportunity there are no easy steps to success."

Half of all U.S. residents can trace their roots to one of the twelve million immigrants who entered through "America's front door" at New York's Ellis Island from 1892 to 1938. After that, millions including Anita and Atul flew into JFK Airport. Many of the descendents of immigrants try to reconnect with their heritage by returning to the eastern seaboard to explore their genealogy through family records and tombstones. Each immigrant group added flavor and diversity to U.S. culture, including its cuisine, music and dance.

When the Reddys first came to MoVa, the seasoned and well-settled immigrants advised the newcomers about the subtle aspects of life in Utica and in the U.S. in general. Ray and Kristine Dujac, for example, became the Reddys' adoptive parents. Ajit and Anil had a third set of grandparents! The Reddys still reminisce about the day when Ray, tugging at his waist band, swaggered over to their recalcitrant lawn mower and said, "Hi, neighbor! What's the problem?"

Atul recalled that Ray first cleaned the spark plug with an air of confidence and gave it a generous squirt of the universal WD-40. Then he tugged on the start cord and that second-hand monster just sprang to life and roared like a lion. "Why didn't I think of that?" he recollected asking Ray. "What are neighbors for?" Ray replied, waving away any expressions of thanks. From then, AR joined the millions of Americans who were members of the "Saturday Lawn Ranger Company."

At that time, the relationship seemed to be a one-way street with the Reddys on the receiving end of the Dujacs' intellectual largesse, counsel and kindness. Yet an unwritten bond was being forged. Ironically, when the Dujacs' grandkids visited their grandparents, it was often partly to play with Ajit and Anil, which allowed the old to teach the new a thing or two. And just like children who never forget who helped them with their first steps, the Reddys, like other émigrés, never forgot who guided their paths when they first arrived. Soon, the Reddy and Dujac families were sharing a lasting and fulfilling relationship. It was a tale of two mutually adopted families.

Indian Babus and Biwis
> 3 <

Atul Reddy (AR) was from Bombay, now called Mumbai. He received his medical degree there before emigrating from India to the U.S. in 1984. After completing his residency in a hospital in New York City, he received his American board status from the College of Radiology in Radiation Oncology. This field includes the art and science of treating cancer patients with radiation therapy. Dr. Reddy derived great satisfaction from his work. Although he worked very hard, he also enjoyed living life to the fullest and had the right balance between career and family. In 1988, when it was time to choose a place in which to settle down, the Reddys chose Utica. Both husband and wife excelled in music and sports; the couple also served as the "social-secretaries" of the Indian-American community.

AR was a handsome and charming *babu* (Indian man). He was a forty-five-year-old with the body of a twenty-five-year-old. When he was with his family, medical staff, colleagues and friends he exuded an air of knowledge and confidence with never a hint of stress, even under pressure. His positive attitude and winning smile were in keeping with his dictum that he shared with others: "You'll run just as fast with a cheerful disposition and with more hope in your heart." While AR was a take-control type of guy, he did not go overboard. He always sought family counsel and friendly advice. He led a busy life, yet took the time to kick back and develop close relationships with those on his wavelength. AR imagined the possibilities, but kept things simple so that he had time to pursue a broad scope of projects.

Anita was talented and beautiful, the devoted *biwi* (young Indian wife) and *mummy* (mother) who, like many Asian-Indian women, fell in love with her man after their marriage, rather than before. To AR, she was physically attractive and had an endearing personality, a "can't help loving that gal" type of lady. Atul was Anita's rock of strength and soul mate, a man she trusted implicitly. They were each other's greatest fans who often spoke through subliminal messages. For them, marriage was a true union, one *atma* (soul) shared by two bodies. Their closeness was reflected in the way they bonded with each other and spent time with their sons. Her adage was: "You don't have to be big to think big."

Their *bacche* (sons), Ajit and Anil, were 15 and 13 years old, respectively. The sons, like most of their contemporaries, were gadget freaks. Their rooms resembled Tech Mecca and they were hooked on weird hybrids and infinite boundaries. With their dictum, "Don't let another moment slip by," the boys were not couch potatoes. Their alarm went off at 6:00 AM, and they didn't even think of hitting the snooze button. That kind of commitment calls for a trophy, and the two had plenty on display. They were competitive between themselves and with their peers. To them and to their parents, winning wasn't everything, yet it often seemed that way because they tackled any project with the determination to give it their best. They were taught at an early age to overcome setbacks and to do nothing sub-standard. The boys did not speak in grunts and groans like most boys of their age did. Their parents encouraged them to voice their concerns and then listened to what their sons had to say.

The family represented a dynamite team when they worked on any project. Individually and as a family, the Reddys went out of their way to be helpful. They practiced random acts of kindness long before the phrase was popularized. Anita, for example, had the habit of giving little gifts for no particular reason other than to reinforce her thoughtfulness and the bonds of friendship. The Reddys were a private family, whose "home-coming" kisses were shared at home rather than at the airport. The mother followed the mystery path to hassle-prevention. The well-behaved boys reduced her mommy-stress. Anita enjoyed a close relationship with each of the three men in her life. She could lie in bed, contemplating ways in which she could bring rainbow colors into their lives, share with them her homemade happiness or brighten a bad day. She had mastered the art of bringing it all together around the hearth.

Grandma Reddy lived with them and was the matriarch of the Reddy family. She was the family's story-teller and its compass. She was non-interfering and reinforced the advice the children got from their parents. Even when the boys were toddlers, grandma drilled into them some valuable pearls of wisdom and proverbs from "the old country." Grandma was considered "a hidden benefit" to the family, a person of few words who took life philosophically, having experienced both great joys and sorrows in her lifetime. Like the hub of a wheel, she kept all the members of the family connected while they went their different ways, pursuing varied interests. For the young parents, she was a role-model; and for the kids, a powerful ally. When the kids or adults returned home, grandma issued her first order – "Eat."

Both young and old held grandma in high esteem, as one who must be obeyed. Her watchful eye and experienced mind taught her to believe in an ounce of prevention. "When in doubt of what is right, consult your pillow overnight," she would say when weighty decisions had to be made. To her, proverbs were the daughters of experience. At her station in life, there were more important pursuits than stressing over the inconsequential. Grandma Reddy was in touch with things that really mattered and easily let go of things that did not.

The Reddy home was a harmonious blend of eastern and western décor. Their house was a comfortable, warm home that matched their life style. The Reddys didn't believe in having a "never-lived-in" living room. The furniture invited relaxed entertaining and family life. Leather sectionals hugged three sides of the room. A cream and red silk carpet covered most of the parquet floor. In the center stood a circular coffee table with delicate *chinar* leaves carved on the top and sides – typical artwork from the northern Indian state of Kashmir. A corner show case held objects d'art the family had collected during their travels – a crystal vase from the Czech Republic, a lace fan from Spain, an etched ostrich egg from South Africa, and a turquoise figurine from New Mexico. These were heirlooms with a contemporary global flair.

One wall of the family room was lined with framed photographs - the Reddys smiling on their wedding day, with their newborns, school pictures of the boys in their younger days, and action shots of them playing ice hockey. And, as was in most Indian households, there was a prayer room. In keeping with tradition, this was the family's "protected space." The family knew the healing power of prayer and made time for spiritual exercises. In the hallway, photographs of Atul's father and Anita's deceased parents were draped with orange and white garlands. The pictures, though faded, made the Reddys feel they were honoring their ancestors who seemed to watch over the day-to-day happenings in the home. The rest of the house was designed to make life less stressful.

During the Christmas season, the house was decorated with traditional holiday trimmings. Each year, on a reasonably pleasant day in the first week of December, Dad and the boys would string the outside lights. Between shouts of, "Hold the ladder," or "hand me the hammer," and "next string of bulbs," followed by the final, "turn on the lights now," the exterior would blaze with color. Inside, the boys draped evergreen garlands and festooned the hallway with white lights held up by red bows. Decorating the tree was a much-loved family ritual. The house was alight with Christmas cheer; a home in which they could celebrate the joys of the season as a family as well as with their relatives and friends. Christmas was one time of year when Anita abandoned her "less is more" philosophy of interior decorating and trimmed with gusto. Their theme for this year's celebration: "Be a peace maker. It is hard to shake hands with a clenched fist."

Everywhere one looked there were Christmas angels and other festive decorations. The parents had carefully chosen Santa's surprises for their sons, though the lads were well aware who Mr. and Mrs. Claus really were. All that was left was to hope for a White Christmas, which would add charm to the scenery. Anita had worked out the menu, including her exotic cuisine and other Indian hot chunky, crunchy and crispy dishes for the series of special occasions during the holidays. Nobody was better organized than Anita.

She always had a Plan B. Indian spices are notorious for staining table linens, yet Anita had at hand the best stain busters for clean-ups. Her dinners were occasions for giving thanks for the friendships and achievements of the year gone by. She even had her Christmas treats ready for the Christmas cookie exchange. The Reddys were ready for celebrating...making memories...lighting the lights...decking the halls and celebrating the season...by sharing the joys of Yuletide. For the immediate family, they limited the gifts to three per person to help maintain their sanity through the holidays, and ensure a stress-free Christmas. After the holidays there were the usual "happy returns."

The family room held a hand-carved, hand-rubbed, hand-polished mahogany table; for the holiday season, it sported a wondrous rose wreath. The room's décor was conducive to drop-in guests and informal entertaining; it reflected warmth and convenience, with form following function. The home was not designed to flaunt money, art-deco excesses or architecture; instead, it fulfilled the family's needs and dreams. The family worked as a team with the father as a can-do type of a guy who thought inside as well as outside the box; the mother was the kind who would move heaven and earth for her family and believed in giving a home a heart. Anita had the recipe for a happy kitchen and happy family. She learned to cook meals that were delicious, nutritious and quick to prepare, with her love as a consistent ingredient. Nobody did it better. It was a comfortable home, a source of happiness. To the family, home was where the heart is.

The Reddys decorated their home with many family heirlooms. Every item had a story to tell - how, where and by whom it was acquired. The exhibits were just a part of the tale. For example, their dining room was decorated in a Chinese theme. On one of their out-and-about trips to Bouckville, the antiques capital of America, Dad had picked up a blue ceramic Chinese plate. Anita was not excited about adding another curio to their collection. "Just another item for me to dust," she complained.

Atul pleaded, "I didn't spend much on it. Maybe we can enjoy it for six months, and when we do the spring cleaning, donate it with our other stuff to the local thrift store. Our trash will become another person's treasure." The bargain was agreed on as Anita knew the plate represented Atul's "thrill of the hunt" and all was well. Just before spring cleanup, the Reddys decided to have the plate appraised.

"I'll buy it," the antique dealer said. "It's 150 years old!"

The plate still hangs in the Reddy's dining room four years later - at Anita's insistence. It has become "cool junk."

Utica's cold winds, freezing temperatures and several feet of snow from December to March do not permit year-round outdoor horticulture. "Why don't we build a glass-paneled Florida room just like our neighbors have? We have the perfect location for such an addition. All winter long we can relax in the heated room and the plants will thrive year- round," Anita suggested. The others agreed it was a great idea. For the Florida room, Anita chose plants that she enjoyed seeing even while snow hung from the roof. She had dwarf banana and palm trees, sweet-smelling jasmine as well as red and yellow hibiscus. Anita believed in "flower power" and art in the garden room. The bright sunlight was perfect for her orchids and Christmas cactus; the shadier areas of the room housed her colorful, delicate African violets. Chinese fan palms added an oriental touch to the medley. Even in the summer, she liked to be able to see the large, brightly hued dahlias blooming inside; the Florida room allowed her to do just that. Here she could indulge in a little time for herself and feel rejuvenated.

Anita understood the importance of being part of the community, of contributing to the good of all, especially the less fortunate. The Reddys realized that people who are wrapped up in themselves make very small packages. Anita enjoyed the vast array of cultural opportunities available in Utica; she volunteered and helped out at many school events and local charity fund-raisers. For her school-aged boys, she served as a chaperone for out-of-town events and was a typical "soccer mom." She was just as comfy playing with her children, addressing their tummy troubles or packing their soccer and ice hockey gear, as she was fixing one-pot wonders for her husband's social events. In spite of having a physician in the house, it was Dr. Mom who was the Wound Wonder, Skin Saver, Sleep Inducer and Stomach Soother. This was all part of her day. She practiced both waist-management and waste-management. She called her own shots with behind-the-scenes and behind-the-seams work.

The family occasionally considered it perfectly fine to be imperfect, yet for the most part, the boys were well disciplined. Non-compliance usually resulted in a gentle reprimand: "Why don't you want to do it, my *choto-beta* (young-son)?" The reprimands for the kids would include: "difficult to get good help...don't bliss out...be forever known as bullhead...chill out...let this be a lesson...knock off the blame game...this is your opportunity; draw the line...don't monkey around...stop splitting hairs...take it easy...stop tearing each other down...chalk this up...where there's a will..."

As they got older, the kids were reminded that childhood came with an expiration date. There was to be no talking back, ignoring, dishing or sassing! Even as kids Ajit and Anil did not display temper tantrums.

Dad would counsel the boys: "There are no short cuts in life or instant glamour." Then he'd show them and their friends the real deal, know-how for DIY projects. AR was the problem solver with an air of self-confidence and a do-it-yourself maven.

As the youngest in this three-generation family, Anil was the baby elephant in the herd and was given the pet name *Tinu*. The 13-year-old was loved and protected by all, especially by the matriarch. Anil enjoyed the best of all worlds. He was mummy's boy, yet could also hang around with the big boys. As he grew older, there was a role reversal between him and his aging grandmother. Often, he held grandma's hand protectively as they walked, just as she had held his when he was just a child. The grandparent-grandchild bond and relationship were precious. Grandma had her own way of thanking Anil for his considerate ways. "If *chacha* (grandpa) could see you now, he'd be proud of you," she'd say. With such words of encouragement, Anil was proud to help others, too.

Ajit, the older sibling, was affectionately called *Bantu*. He had the air of confidence of a firstborn and was a good role model and mentor for his younger brother. At 15, Ajit had important things on his mind, including owning his first car. He consulted his friends and Consumers' Digest on which wheels were hot and what was in style. Then he shared his findings with his dad.

"These cars have the legend, design and are retro. These others need to be revved-up for power and hyper-style; and those are just souped-up versions," he said, as he pointed to the various models. He focused on the hot cars which would make him look cool. "Dad, let's go for power and road performance as well as looks!" he exclaimed.

Dad encouraged his sons. Fuel-injecting his thoughts, he said, "You need to do some more research on concept vehicles like the Firepower and MX-5 Miata." He wanted Ajit's interests in car mechanics, electronics and computer systems to continue, yet a word of warning was in order. "A car is not designed to be a babe-magnet for sixteen-year-olds. Besides, you need to give your dad's wallet a break." Anita was even more pragmatic and down-to-earth. "The car is just a mode of transport from point A to point B," she said, matter-of-factly.

The Reddys believed in living life to the fullest without being extravagant. The boys did not overdo the trend to own every single new-fangled piece of technology. They were model students and were encouraged not to be tempted to take the easy way out. They didn't play hard to get. They were hard to get because they were busy with their lives. Their parents' challenge was to figure out what made the boys tick, and often it was their grandmother who knew the answers. Like their classmates, Anil and Ajit belonged to Generation-Why. They thought digitally and liked to network to garner helpful information.

The family always insisted on "checking it out" before embarking on any plan of action. Dad's words of caution guided their choices. "Give my wallet a break," he would declare. The one that had them laughing was dad's classic line: "Don't get your cortex caught in a vortex."

The adults and children alike believed that laughter could be therapeutic. However, it was not always fun. At times, dad did the heavy-lifting as he counseled the boys. The three "men" in Anita's life were her pride and joy. Her friends would tease her and say she was always on "male-call." As the estrogen-driven minority, Anita knew when to take her leave from the boys-only Turkey Club. The Club's meetings did not last long. It just was not much fun without her, the general secretary, and Anita liked it that way. Simply put, the men did not accomplish all the necessary tasks without the unconditional support of the missing member of the Reddy team.

When the Reddys socialized with their friends in MoVa, there often was an identification of "newcomers" and the older "early settlers." Asian-Indians arrived in Utica in the early 1970s. Today, the entire group comprises about one hundred and fifty families, mainly professionals. Indian-Americans (Ind-o-US – Indians of U.S.) are physicians, engineers, technically-skilled workers and college professors. Like most prior settler groups in MoVa, most Ind-o-US first landed in the Big Apple, (though not at Ellis Island) and then made their way to the valley. MoVa provided a perfect location for those with ties - family and emotional - to New York City. Most did not want to sever these ties in their first major re-location within their adopted country. Once these families moved to Utica, most found a welcoming local population as well as fellow Asian-Americans and a smorgasbord of ethnic groups. The new arrivals made Utica their new home, one in which they would live *La Vie Americaine*!

"Immigrants are the blood transfusion of this country," AR would sometimes remark to his family and friends, using a medical metaphor. He'd continue, "That pint is only 20 per cent of the patient's blood and a fraction of the body's fluid. Yet, that pint of blood makes the difference in the individual's quality of life by increasing the pep, vitality, energy and oxygen-carrying capacity; in some cases it may save the person's life."

The Indian-American community in Utica was comparatively small, although the families came from nearly all parts of the subcontinent. So, within this group of one hundred and fifty families, there were about thirty Indian and international languages (of the former European colonies in India) spoken and understood. This is not unusual if one comes from India, which has 35 states and union territories, 24 officially recognized languages, as well as about 1,600 dialects. As settlers in a new country, with no "godfather" to provide them advice, support or a monetary loan, immigrants find themselves always on the go and are compelled to think afresh. Without quite realizing it, they were multi-tasking even before their arrival in their new country.

This Indians of the US (Ind-o-US) as a group traveled widely both within and outside the country. Being émigrés, they had an international outlook, exposed as they were to a lot of ideas and information at work, from the internet as well as other sources. There were no brow-beaten *patis* (husbands) in this crowd. The *patnis* (wives) functioned as super-moms. They developed an attitude and an expression of pleasant determination. Having survived in India in a very competitive academic environment, (there are hundreds of applicants for every college seat) nobody was sloughing off. As a result, they were primed for success. A few experienced the angst of a new environment; and on occasion, events overwhelmed them. Even though their religions and customs varied, they all had similar values, which served as a compass to guide them in their adopted country.

Sometimes, in keeping with their culture, three generations lived under one roof. In rare cases, both sets of elderly grandparents were part of the joint family. This is clearly a situation of the-more-the-merrier, with grandma's hands to help and grandpa's ideas to inspire. Of course, at grandpa's age, most of his thoughts are idealistic. It isn't unusual for a grandpa to engage everyone, including total strangers, in the eternal dissertation on "The Philosophy of Life." Some add a touch of humor to their freely-given advice, with gestures and fingers pointed for emphasis: "Trouble in marriage often starts when a man gets so busy earning his salt that he forgets his sugar." Elderly Asians can rarely be accused of being vain. One octogenarian put it best when he said, "Some people try to turn back their odometers. Not me. I want people to know why I look this way. I've traveled a long way and some of the roads were bumpy."

Like any other group, there were the "problem solvers" and the "hopelessly confused." At parties, the conversation usually turned to what was in style and how to sort out computer glitches. Regular social get-togethers kept the community united and the culture alive. These events often served as the forum for a discussion on the new and improved tangibles and intangibles in life. The men shared the screw-ups while the women dished it. The kids were full of surprises! There was humor all around but there were no nincompoops in this crowd.

New Year's Eve plans were underway with a menu full of snacks that satisfy and a special toast with the best of the bubbly. In addition to "Curry with a Flavor" there would be sautéed chicken and mango salsa, seaside prawns and pineapple kabobs, and the regular vegetarian dishes in the "Spice is Nice" category, with luscious desserts to go with the fiery food. This was one time of the year when, like all Americans, they were determined to indulge in the best.

This medium-sized Ind-o-US crowd in Utica was growing-up. There was no more baby-mania or talk about pregnancy. The days when the social gatherings were a maternity Mecca were long over and the *patnis* had forgotten that lingo. While adapting to their new country, the matrons broke some traditional rules. To one still with bibs and cribs they would unabashedly say, "Thank God it is not my turn anymore." Since the ladies no longer did diaper duty there was a lot of mom-to-mom sharing of advice such as, "You don't have to be twenty to look good." The women enjoyed ladies' nights-out, speedy suppers, the exchange of secrets to staying youthful, and gardening tips. The *yoginis* (yoga-practicing women) formed a Miss Congeniality crowd.

There were working moms, some with home offices. Yet, traditions die hard. Up-to-the-minute scoops on prices, sales and hunt-down-a-bargain-nirvana delights were quickly shared. The *devis* had days when they felt like tearing their hair out but they also learned that a little planning goes a long way. They knew how to sort through conflicting facts. This was a group who knew the bottom line and doled out their all-time favorite tips to those in their coffee klatch, diva-2-diva.

There were tales from the self-appointed divas – goddesses - of smart shopping and the coupon queens. And all eyes and ears were on *rani* – the queen of Sensible Chic. She was the lady with smart advice on how to "spice it up" and who provided tips on how to make wrinkles a thing of the past. The ladies, including the timid souls, enthusiastically prodded the knowledgeable ones for details about midnight madness sales where they could browse for the perfect combination in designer clothing and get BOGO (Buy One Get One free) deals. There was the *ustad* (teacher) who disclosed to her closest friends her secrets of being feminine, beautiful and flirty. Also, there was advice from the super-divas – the style gurus - who preached to those mini-divas who wanted to be fabulous at fifty. There were the new *avatars* of style - Western, Indian, Hot or Cool. A proverb claims, "An Indian woman lies only about her husband's age, to make her appear really young."

These ladies were not keen just about beauty topics. Besides addressing tummy troubles in their families, these *padma lakshmis* (wife goddesses) were interested in healthy eating, as well as developing their creative talents. Each *mem-sahib* (lady) had a perfect plan to masterfully juxtapose herself between her husband and her children who were her pride and joy. She did not just make their dinner, she made their day. Some had westernized their cooking to create dishes such as curried chicken with mango and cantaloupe. Others swapped Indian recipes from different regions of India. In the summer, friends would organize pickle exchanges. There was a lot of togetherness during which time they traded tips on everything - good stocks to invest in, great deals from airlines, and the newest novel in Oprah's Book Club. For these mothers, real love meant real care. Some were high-pressured parents, especially those who were multi-talented. "Life is full of ups and downs. So, we must make time for spirituality," the matrons in the group would admonish the younger set. Both groups found it humorous and nostalgic to listen to anecdotes about those who had recently arrived in *Emrika*.

Along with humor and informative chit-chat, these *desis* (Ind-o-US) knew their priorities. They did something sweet for their kids who were their top priority, and made sure they didn't stray. These mothers learned from their parents that marriage is like a garden - the more you put into it, the more you get out of it. They created a plan for happiness and health for the family. They shared their lessons learned, along with words of wisdom. They took care of themselves, too; these *patnis* (wives) practiced a blend of yoga postures with breathing techniques, self awareness and other routines of the five-day *panchakarma*. In their own quiet way, these *biwis* and *mem-sahibs* had "girl-power."

When the *desi* (Indian) company was mixed, the group talked about travel and the world in general. They swapped notes on their experiences in the countries in which they had lived. This globe-trotting group came up with, "Ou est le bade Zimmer / bathroom?" to get directions to the rest stop in all EU countries of Europe.

To them, Princess Diana's death was the epitome of globalization. One recounted, "This English princess and her Egyptian consort toasted each other with French champagne, feasted on Indian cuisine in an exclusive Viennese garden café and drank Australian Shiraz. Then they sipped Bailey's Irish Crème. Later they were driven by a Belgian who was inebriated with Scotch. He drove a German car and crashed into a Parisian tunnel wall. These events were recorded on Japanese film by French paparazzi working for Italian magazines and riding Harley-Davidson motorcycles. Even a fiction writer could not come up with this scenario. Is this reality or fantasy?"

They also expressed their opinions on the issues of the day. On the controversy of prayer in public schools, one said, "As long as there are tests, there will be prayers in public schools. So why are these folks causing such confusion?"

At parties, the *pundits* (wise men) freely doled out advice: "Leave your worries behind,"..."Adjust your rear view mirror,"..."Some have photographic memories but often no film," and other *crappola du jour.*

One said, "It's not a great buy if you don't need it in the first place."

Another *gharwalla* (home owner) would admonish others with his usual mantra, "Love your-self enough to say 'No'."

A *maharishi* (sage) offered lofty advice: "Think mission, think goals!"

A *swami* (teacher) was more down-to-earth: "You'll have trouble putting on your pants if you keep your feet firmly on the ground."

An *ustad* (teacher) advised, "Always keep your words soft and sweet, just in case you have to eat them later on."

One jovial *babu* added, "Alcohol is not an answer, it just makes you forget the question." The get-togethers included the know-it-all and the win-it-all types who could tell the ins-and-outs of every situation - or at least they thought they could. Every absurdity had a champion who would defend it. The well-settled talked about trendy restaurants and fast-paced night-life. Some shared tried-and-true facts to help others stay ahead; they gave newcomers information they could rely on instead of having to learn through hit-and-miss attempts. Soon, the new arrivals developed an autonomous mind.

None claimed rights to the "perfect parent syndrome," though some parents did double duty. *Pitajis* (dads) had no problem saying to their kids, "Now knock it off." Most of the *sahibs* (men) were even-tempered but some were dour and humorless; a few were even crotchety. There was rarely a slap-happy comedian in the crowd. The "he-men" worked hard and played hard. Their parties were characterized by excitement, enjoyment and riding high, especially after a few rounds of beer or Scotch. AR was a party hit, as he was a take-control-with-fun type of *babu*. While the *devis* liked to pump-up-the-passion, the *babus* were eager to pump-up-the-fun, but tone down the craziness and temper the tantrums. Most *sahibs* will admit to a sweet tooth, causing the *gurus* (educators) to advise: "Because you are overweight, you need to aerobicize the *charbi* - belly fat." Another *ustad* (teacher) related this joke: Jay Shah was the Managing Director for Corporate Research and Planning. His business card read: Jay Shah, MD, CRAP.

The jovial and intellectual types were constantly imagining the possibilities, where everything had to be optimally formulated, even though no one expected instant success. They argued endlessly on implementing the right solutions to achieving results. This was the "I pod, You pod, and Everyone pods" group. They invariable had projects-around-the-home lists. They encouraged each other to turn "Not me, I can't," to "Yes, I can." And they admired those who were creative. A few had the gift of the gab, which they believed was good for the body and soul. Some touted what they deemed their talent for "circular reasoning."

One *babu* recounted this story: "Three brothers who were originally from India settled down in Scotland, Canada and the USA. On a family get-together in India, they were involved in a fatal car accident. Their Maruti (India's mini-car) became a *chapatti* (flat bread). The brother who survived was the one who lived in the U.S. Everyone in his town was amazed that he alone survived. A month later, the surviving brother divulged the events following the accident. He claimed he, too, had died that dastardly day. The brothers went to the Pearly Gates and met St. Peter. They complained loudly that they were just too young to die, even though they admitted they should not have been driving so fast under those road conditions. They requested special consideration because of their good deeds and their youth. St. Peter, persuaded by their arguments, agreed to settle for a fine of $100.00 for their poor judgment. The American brother whipped out his wallet and paid the fine; he was instantly returned to earth. The last thing he recollected was his Scottish brother insisting that the fine be reduced and his Canadian brother arguing that the fine was fair, especially by Canadian standards, but his government should be made to pay it!"

As the Ind-o-US community has the highest risk for coronary artery disease among all ethnic groups in the U.S., there is an acute awareness of the need to keep one's cholesterol levels and weight down. Smoking is frowned upon and most are determined to "lose the weight we hate." The Young Turks (both guys and dolls) take up aerobics; some *devis* have personal trainers help them achieve physical fitness. The aim is to be heart-smart, snack savvy and achieve a trimmer torso. The Ind-o-US invariably had a garden. New York's four seasons permitted the ambience to change about every three months. As in nature, the spring and the summer were always the busiest months for those with a green thumb. Once winter was over, spring-related activities began; all gardeners realized that a great garden does not grow by itself. As New Yorkers, they were aware that blooming May flowers such as peonies and lilacs heralded spring. In the summer, hobbies and outdoor activities brought extended family members and friends together.

The crowd of chachas and chachis, nanas and nanis (grandpa and grandma on the dad's side and mother's side, respectively) would invite fellow retirees to *Chale Chalo* (let's walk). Their logic was that a half-hour-a-day of brisk exercise would keep their cholesterol, tension and stress levels down. After they nodded their *namastes* (hellos) and began their walk, they would advocate their preference for walking. Invariably one would reveal, "Walking is the simplest, safest, cheapest, easiest and most effective exercise that can be done anywhere and at anytime with no expertise or equipment required. It breaks the monotony of staying indoors. How much simpler can it get?"

This aging group was in their twenties during the early 1940s when Mahatma Gandhi led the struggle for India's independence. So, rain or shine, the *chachas* and *chachis* would wake up after their afternoon naps, enjoy a cup of *chai* (tea), and start the round robin phone calls: *Chale Chalo*! Tennis shoes on, they'd meet in small groups and hit the road around their neighborhoods. They walked off the little *charbie* (belly fat) they had. They also practiced their one-day-a-week fast from food as a penance to get ready for the afterlife. This religious edict and custom of fasting started many centuries ago and has therapeutic effects - it lowers the caloric intake of senior citizens when their metabolism slows down with age.

On their walks, the seniors talked about fats - facts and fiction. Many of them could quote the latest studies: "The Nurses' Health Study from Harvard has shown that walking perks memory, attention and other measures of cognitive function." They always had something to laugh about, as they believed that "Laughter reduces stress and perks the immune system." One *chacha* (grandpa) with a sense of humor said, "One advantage of walking every day is that you die trimmer." A *chachi* (grandma) smiled and countered, "I'm in shape. Round is also a shape."

The grandparents' ambitions and prayers were to see the success of their children and grandchildren as well as to be promoted to great-grand-parents! They proudly showed off their grey hair and felt they had no time to think about wrinkles. These *Sita devis* (common Indian woman's name) were very comfortable with their grandmotherly appearance, which they wore as a badge of honor.

The Zamboni
> 4 <

Living in the snow belt of upstate New York made the Reddy family want to take up the usual winter activities. Because New York has four distinctive seasons, the family was determined not to hibernate all winter long. Like others of their generation, the boys became easily bored when they were not busy. For both the parents and the kids, being fed up was worse than a physical injury. The family looked for a break from the predictable, and the attentive parents tried to keep things interesting by finding better, faster and easier ways of doing things. They had a wide variety of winter activities in which they could participate. So, like prior generations of New Yorkers, they made the best of the winter season by skiing, snow-mobiling and snow-shoeing.

"It's difficult to excel in more than one sport. You boys need to choose your favorite, and channel your energy and enthusiasm into it," their dad advised. Without hesitation, both boys opted for ice hockey. So, ice hockey it was.

With the unwavering support of their parents and coaching from their dad, the boys focused on ice hockey and became players for the Grizzlies - the high school team. That was no small feat in this part of the country, where the sport is popular and considered hip among the adolescents, each wanting to show off his metal and prowess. Ice hockey demands that players be calm, collected and unflappable even under pressure. To be really good, the players need to demonstrate dexterity, coordination and speed in ice-skating as well as in stick-handling. Practice sessions were hard and required a lot of discipline. Before the Grizzlies reached the final rounds of the season, they had to play competitive games with other high schools in the region where ice hockey is virtually a religion.

Upstate New York kids, the Reddy boys included, often learn to skate during the first winter after they learn to walk. When they start school, they join youth ice hockey teams to learn the basics. Before long, the Reddy boys were learning offensive and defensive strategies, mastering new skating styles for which versatility is a must. The sport requires never-ending drilling in the fundamentals of the game as well as anticipating the unknown, responding rapidly, moving fast and hitting hard when seconds count. It was one continuous season of practice, improve and adapt. Only the most adept make the team.

Often the Reddys had to leave a party early, to the dismay of their hosts and friends. "The boys have an out-of-town hockey game tomorrow morning and we have to leave home by six," AR would explain. The Reddys' devotion to the game baffled their friends. "How did you become a soccer mom?" Sonia, one of Anita's friends asked. "You don't look the type who knows which end of the hockey stick meets the puck." Anita took the ribbing good-naturedly. "When your children are excited about a sport, it rubs off on you, too. You get to know the other boys and their parents. We scream and shout whenever any team member does well. The game is really quite exciting," she explained.

The parents did a lot of driving and chauffeuring. The drives to out-of-town games presented perfect occasions for the family to relax together and chat about sports and life in general. While driving was a chore, it gave them precious personal time. Their car was not loaded as a "mobile entertainment center" which would permit family members to be immersed in their own little worlds. Instead, the long drives were designed to allow for quality time together. The tone of the dialogue was an eclectic mix but generally leaned on the humorous side.

Ajit said, "Last summer, Mrs. Snoggles used her daughter's minivan to drive the boys' soccer team to a game. The guys decided to have some fun and changed the NEW DRIVER sign on the back of the van to NUDE DRIVER. Several drivers on Interstate 90 pulled up alongside the minivan and smiled as they strained to look at the driver. In those two hours, Mrs. Snoggles had more smiles from motorists than she had received in all of her high school and college years combined. Both she and the weather were sizzling hot!" Anil joked, "Her cool, strapless outfit on that hot day may not have helped the situation."

"The things parents have to go through for the sake of our angelic kids!" Mom told herself, shaking her head.

Once they were on the rink, Coach Brian Dicks' regimen began with drilling the basics, followed by key strategies. The players responded by focusing single-mindedly on the game, whether they were at practice games or at tournaments. They worked like dogs, because of their competitive spirit and their earnest interest in the game. Like most boys their age, the team's main topics of conversation were games and girls – not always in that order. Yet as serious and competitive boys, they believed in being constructive. On the rink, the Grizzlies were a storehouse of pure energy; they were here, there and everywhere. With their coach's guidance and parents' encouragement, each player was extremely spirited. They all knew that when it came to getting ahead, homework and presentation were everything. The Grizzlies were in Division II, which included schools from the big cities of the upstate region. The team successfully completed the grueling tasks of playing their home and away games and had risen through the ranks of their division. The Grizzlies were now high up on the ladder of success, and could realistically aspire to reach the top.

The semi-final match was an away game against the Arctic Seals in Cooperstown. The town is named after Judge William Cooper, father of author James Fennimore Cooper, and both are buried in this quaint resort area on Lake Otsego. Cooperstown prominently featured in several of James Cooper's literary works; his 1826 novel, "The Last of the Mohicans," reflected changes in this part of the "new country." Cooperstown is best known as the home of the National Baseball Hall of Fame and Museum – a sport started in 1845 when Alexander Cartwright formulated the rules. The town has numerous other attractions unrelated to baseball, including European micro-breweries and the theater. Last summer, the Reddys had visited the Glimmerglass Theatre and the Brewery Ommegang (O-muh-ghang) which produces Belgian-style ales from Belgian malts, hops and spices. More than a century ago, eighty percent of hops grown in the U.S. came from Otsego County. So, Brewery Ommegang represented history, good taste and skill.

Baton Rouge, the Bier-Meister, told the Reddys, "Depending on the desired flavor of the ales, the spices used - sweet orange peel, coriander, ginger and others – are varied to produce some unique flavors without making the beers over-hopped." The Reddys found spiced ale a hot and refreshing drink. AR told the family, "The Belgians, unlike the Italians, Dutch, French and British did not go halfway across the world in search of spices. Yet they clearly knew a good one when they tasted it."

After winning at Cooperstown, the Grizzlies were eager and pumped up for the championship game. It was a golden opportunity for the Uticans to get into the finals. Every time the team scored, the Aussie exchange-students at their school yelled, "Boy-Oh-Boy!" At school the next day, an Aussie said to the players, "Better men never stood in two shoes! No worries chums...Nope, oi can't do what y'a do!"

The upcoming championship ice-hockey game at Utica's Auditorium, affectionately called "The Aud," was the final game in the Division II East. It pitted Utica's Grizzlies against the Syracuse Ice Pilots. The Grizzlies did not practice on Friday before the weekend match. They wanted to be well rested for the biggest game of the entire season. So, along with their coach, they studied reruns of prior games and prepared their strategy for the Saturday competition. The team's most important letter of the alphabet was E - for effort, enthusiasm and excellence. There was no "big-bang" game plan.

AR's advice never wavered. "This is a team game played by individuals," he would remind the players before each game and added; "Attitude is everything. You have to believe you can do it."

Coach Dicks had innovative game plans. He encouraged his offensive line to turn around and shoot or just bull their way to the goal. His ultimate directive was always "pass first and shoot second," especially during a nerve-wracking period when the opponents might keep attacking. "If they keep coming, be tough and fight back," the coach advised. The Grizzlies knew the contest was going to come down to the wire. It was a battle every week, with some weeks better than others. This time, the Grizzlies were determined to win.

The Reddys, other parents and many high school friends loudly cheered for the Utica team. The friends were mostly Gen-Xer dudes (dude = dud plus attitude) and chicks. Some had friends with benefits (dates), and a few were self-proclaimed PHAT (pretty hot and tempting). In the parking lot there were cars with hot wheels, which of course belonged to hotties. The "in-crowd" was clearly present.

Al, the exchange-student, saw one of the hot cars and exclaimed in his Aussie accent, "Grouse! That's a beaut!"

The corridors leading to the rink were filled with families and posses of friends spotting out the metrosexuals (kids with hyper-style). The conversation included a lot of, "wazz-up...yo, yo, yo...yo' y-all...what the dilly yo'?...yo' movin' and groovin'...and...what's crakin'?" While some were getting hooked-up, others ended their short conversations before heading for their seats in the stands. The buddies sat together doling out advice: "Don't worry what people think; they don't do it very often," and "Don't be too open-minded; your brains will fall out."

There was the continuing talk of "endless possibilities." Some used trash talk, shouting "Yo' Mamas...Wazz-up Dog!" Yet, make no mistake, this pack was just like the rest of the adrenaline-pumped crowd. At the drop of a hat they would scream, "Let's go Grizzlies! Let's go defense!"

Because Ajit was doing so well in the sport, an unusually large number of members of the local Ind-o-US community turned up to root for the home team at the championship round. The groups were split by age. The baby-boomers (born 1944-1963) were sitting in the lower stands; the Gen-Xers and Gen-Zers (born 1990-1999) were higher up in their separate cliques. Chachas and Nanas (grandfather on dads' and moms' sides, respectively) were present in full force. Chachis and nanis (grandmas) were conspicuously absent because of the weather as well as their baby-sitting duties for Gen-Alpha (born after 1999). After the usual "What's up?" and "Kea rre?" and "Kea Hora?" the adults proceeded to talk about "sumpin' sumpin" in Hinglish - a widely used lingo combining Hindi and English. Everybody had stories to share.

The Grizzlies were ranked number two, and that was the disappointing reality. No team was harder to conquer than the traditional division favorite - the number one Ice Pilots. In the past several games between the two teams, the Ice Pilots had won, and so they came to this game with optimism. However, this time things were different. The Grizzlies had fine-tuned their pressure defense, added an aggressive offense, and had a game plan. Under Coach Dicks' direction, the Grizzlies were good at every aspect of the game. The players were better trained and better equipped. They could be the new leaders of the Division II East Games. The current leader was under pressure! The Ice Pilots had lost two games in their run-up to the finals. This could make them even more dangerous, as the last thing they wanted was to fall three games behind in the standings. To bolster the team at this important game, there was a large contingent of students, alumni, parents and fans from Syracuse - a big city 45 miles west of Utica.

In the stands, the teenage girls in the crowd surveyed the guys and zoomed in on those who were pretty cute, "for a guy." The boys eyed the cool-looking girls. A non-Asian girl spotted a good looking Ind-o-US guy and asked her girlfriend for an intro. "I'll check him out to see if he has a thick accent," the girlfriend promised.

Indian chicks would wonder if an Indian dude was "an FOB" (fresh-off-the-boat). The Ind-o-US fellows wondered if the attractive girl was Tandoori (natural Indian) or ABCD (American-born, confused *desi* - Indian). An American guy might have different qualms: "Are her parents pretty liberal?" While all these considerations were going on in the stands, the championship game was about to begin, with the fans' enthusiasm at an all-time high.

The Zamboni (ice spreader) readied the ice. The commentator requested everyone to rise for the playing of the National Anthem.

The Grizzlies, cheered on by the home crowd, took the lead in the first few minutes by scoring from the crease with a shot the fans called, "the wicked fast." That quickly extinguished the bravado of the Syracuse Ice Pilot fans and lit the fuse in the Grizzlies' own supporters. Both teams looked on this game as a must-win event, so they played aggressively from the start. The Ice Pilots scored some dramatic tying goals. By the end of the second period, the score was a tie at 4-4.

At the break, the Grizzlies' coach Dicks told them, "Nasty goals son...good play...keep it up." Then he added, "Put the first two periods behind you and go into the third thinking about what this victory would mean for your school and your city." AR warned the team, "The opponents have a way of intimidating you and giving y'all the big squeeze. The Grizzlies will have to bring the trophy home by fighting hard, skating harder and focusing on winning."

In an attempt at boosting the team spirit, one mother advised, "It's your attitude that determines your altitude and success."

A dad hollered, "The Ice Pilots are playing as if their belts haven't gone through all the loops at their waists!"

The team reviewed the strategies they had developed during the practice and film sessions; they planned to execute the defensive and offensive tactics during the third period. They knew that once they got off to a good head start, they could stay ahead. Then, they could make the final stretch to victory with the loud and tireless support of their raucous home-crowd. The Grizzlies returned to the ice rink realizing that an even stronger effort was required.

The Ice Pilot's coach told his players, "Put your poor start behind you and start hitting and passing...If you can't outsmart them, then confuse them." He reminded them that in the past, in spite of being notoriously slow starters, they did win their games. He hoped history would repeat itself. His final words before they went back on the ice were: "It's all about timing and team work. Don't panic; rally for victory."

Everything about the game between the Grizzlies and the Ice Pilots was big. Morale was high; the crowd was enthusiastic and loudly chanted, "Let's go...Let her rip...Ice it." The game attracted the biggest crowd - 3,500 screaming fans packed the Aud to capacity. Both the players and the fans were on edge. The Grizzlies just wore down the opposition by rolling four lines down the rink every time they got the chance. Even little players made big plays. Clearly, they had more energy. Although the Ice Pilots made dive-bombing raids and had the upper hand several times, the Grizzlies kept coming back. There were numerous twists and turns, great saves, big hits and efficient penalty kills. Both sides were mining-for-trouble and were prepared to expect the unexpected. Yet it was the Grizzlies who were primed to transition from mobilization to devastation. And for the Ice Pilots and their coach, that meant "Grizzly Problems."

Mid-way into the third period, the Grizzlies began presenting a concerted, unified effort. They definitely played like a very skilled team. They were composed and unruffled. The Ice Pilots had to face a determined team which had the chance to take the lead. There were a few potential flash points. The Grizzlies killed both penalties without allowing a goal. They had their own fair share of tough moments but these just created a needed rush of adrenaline. The team was now a bunch of "prowling Grizzlies." Their mistakes just made them more determined and primed them for some major action. The pressure brought out Ajit's killer instincts. After beating the defense, Ajit scored with a backhand snapper. A few minutes later, with agile control of the puck, he made another Grizzly-kill to give the Grizzlies a 6-4 lead in the finals of the Division II East game.

Any hope of an Ice Pilots' comeback was crushed. They were not used to playing behind so late in the game and were woefully unprepared. Their goalie was rattled by the Grizzlies' lead. The Ice Pilots' coach tried to encourage his players, "Put the swing back into your game!" he called out. The fans kept yelling, "No guts; No glory!" Yet, after that point-spread, the game went south for the Ice Pilots and kaput in the face of the marauding Grizzlies. The self-esteem of the Ice Pilots went from inflation to deflation. The final goal was a huge confidence-builder for the Grizzlies and they made it happen for their fans. In the final five minutes, they were relaxed and a little showy in front of the home crowd that kept singing, "Make our dreams come true." The final horn sounded to thunderous shouts as the Grizzlies whipped the Ice Pilots. The crowd was proud of the shot-making abilities of their home team and roared, "It's amazing!...Nobody does it better, nobody!" and "You richly deserve this!" For the Grizzlies, their coach and fans it was a great victory and a "Whoa!" The red-clad Grizzlies' school crowd stood up and cheered, as did the boisterous band of loyalists behind the goal and in the balcony.

All the Ice Pilots fans could do was to shake their heads and shrug their shoulders. The ghosts of the two lost games reappeared to haunt them. They consoled themselves: "The game could have gone either way, but our players didn't execute as well as they could and should have." They chided their players who had picked up fouls and forced the coach to alter the player rotation. This team had made too many small mistakes, which added up to a big loss. One of the Ice Pilots players had earned a seat on the bench. During the traditional round of handshaking at the end of the match, Ajit said to his worthy opponents, "Keep your chins up. This was just a bad luck streak."

As he walked away, the Ice Pilots' coach turned to one of the equally disappointed parents and complained, "It's exhausting. You go over the game plan repeatedly. You think they've got it down. Then they go and make mistakes. It feels like I've failed in getting the strategy across to them." This could have been a huge win on the heels of embarrassing losses for the Ice Pilots. In the coach's opinion, "They had frittered away their victory and went from boom to bust." He hoped they were not a spent force. His assessment of the day's outcome: "Another game of missed opportunities and a month of disappointment." His assistants were more upbeat. "This was an impossible mission. Now there is nowhere to go but up."

With his two goals, Ajit was undoubtedly a valuable player for the Grizzlies and their coach. In the locker room, the Grizzlies admired how far they had come as a team. One member had an interesting analogy. "We moved from being lemmings to Mario Lemieux clones," he said. Another responded, "Teamwork makes the competition look easy to beat." This was one sweet finale and the players were ready to walk the red carpet. While the school was in contact with recruiting gurus, a few players were already hoping to meet the college draftniks.

After the contest, Coach Dicks, AR and the other parents congratulated one another on the success of their team. The sweet smell of victory crowned the season's hard work. None doubted that the team would be playing for keeps.

After the game, the fans made it to their cars and headed for the food and fun. They certainly had a lot to choose from - bars with beer on tap as well as many ethnic and social clubs – all well known for great food and good times. At the upper end of the epicurean scale were Utica's beaucoup elegant restaurants, where "nothing but the best" is served - succulent steak, juicy prime rib, delectable shrimp, and a wide choice of "pastabilities and sauces" – guaranteed to satisfy any taste! For the weight conscious, many of the restaurants provided menus that were light on calories but loaded with taste. Regardless of their choice of food, for the fans it was non-stop "Salute!" The spectators received their money's worth and had expended as much energy as the players did. They all congratulated themselves saying, "Whoa! It doesn't get any better...This was the season's best and brightest...it's a winner...the longer you wait, the sweeter it gets."

The Utica Journal's report was euphoric, just like the ones of the other newspapers: "The Grizzlies played like a well-oiled machine with miniature Dicks all over the rink. The team played above the radar and should be complimented for its remarkable offensive and defensive attacks in the face of a more highly skilled team." The sports editor wrote, "At every stage of the game the home team carefully assessed the situation and used every tactic to overcome the competition."

The newspaper had its critics. Yet, everybody agreed that the reporting did justice to the team this time. Some senior citizens met regularly for breakfast and to discuss the news as well as the quality of their local newspaper's reporting. Today, they were unanimous in their assessment. Regarding the Utica Journal's story they said, "Today, the Utica Urinal got it right." The Grizzlies were "The Adrenaline Guys."

Coach Dicks and AR savored and rehashed the highlights of the Grizzlies' championship game. The coach also had a proposition for AR to consider: the coach wanted to duplicate his success with the youthful team by forming a slightly more mature group. He suggested putting together a team of men, those born between 1955 -1979, to play as the Baby Boomlets. Well! AR was buoyed by the exuberance of Utica's recent victory and volunteered to be on the new team. He looked upon this as an opportunity of a lifetime! He told Anita and his sons, "This special opportunity does not come along every year."

The Big League
> 5 <

The Baby Boomlets began practicing the following week. After his first encounters, AR moved from being a spectator in the sport of ice hockey to being an active player in the game. Now there was a role-reversal between the father and his sons. It was the sons' turn to coach and encourage their dad every step of the way. They yelled admonitions just as loudly as their dad used to do: "Get your act together...don't be a turkey...get moving...no loafing around...be aggressive...no pain, no gain...nice and easy...focus on the moves."

There were many evenings of practice which always started with a power stretch; the sessions lasted two or three hours with everybody going Dutch on treats after practice. AR had to learn to stick-handle, control the puck and other essential facets of the game. In time, AR bettered his speed, agility and consistency. He learned that defenders stall and contain the attack; that passes add speed to the attack. In an "attack role," he learned that if he saw an opening in the defense, he should make a break. The sons taught their dad the art of shoulder and stick deke in order to fake the opponent. They also taught AR that the puck-carrier is helped by other teammates and so he should transition from defense to attack and be one of several possible pass-recipients. Coach Dicks drilled into his team's psyche that everybody was expected to multi-task and that teamwork was what made the game look easy. Sometimes, though, they acted like adult goof-balls. At times like these, Coach Dicks good-humoredly said, "These guys need a transfusion." The coach was unfailingly even-tempered and glib. He made each player realize that he was an integral part of the game plan and had his own unique contribution to make. Coach Dicks often admitted that he had more fun than anybody should be allowed to have. AR had to cope with his less-than-proficient talent in ice-skating because he had learned the skill as an adult. On a few occasions, AR muttered, "What am I doing on this frigid ice? I am from India where the weather is warm, hot or rainy, with peak days of sizzling and sweltering."

Yet that did not deter the practice and rehearsal routine. Coaching his sons had taught him that every player on the team had a job to do. There were days when AR called himself, "The stupidest of the smart guys!" On other days he felt, "This stuff is cool." At this stage of the practices, he and his teammates were well ahead of the curve.

It was one thing to critique from the stands and to be a "Monday Morning Quarterback;" it is another to be down in the trenches. Loud observations were replaced with training and workouts. The new squad had its good days and bad; rarely, there were moments of angst and inspirational flash. Gradually, they began working as a team and gaining control by mastering and overcoming the complexities of the game. Though many dads were rookies, the seniors decided to call themselves the "Utica Blizzards."

On the whole, the players were warm, easygoing and self-effacing with a constant demeanor of pleasant determination. There were no smooth-talking rakes among them and none were listed as "no-shows" for practices. Even though the action was on ice, the players perspired profusely under their many layers of warm clothing and from their intense physical activity.

AR shared his medical information on good nutrition and hydration techniques with his teammates. His advice included the need for carb-loading before the game and the bio-availability of protein. He explained, "Fluid intake prior to, during and after the game is a must. Liquids, called the 'elixir of sport', improve the endurance and performance of athletes." After the players learned the basics of the game's moves, the survival guidebooks were no longer needed. The dads were beginning to feel a quiet inner strength. AR looked forward to breezing through the practices and being a standout. He was poised to learn the key strategies and anticipate the unexpected. In the summer, practice sessions ended when the players groaned and exclaimed, "We just can't do anymore!" They worked hard, played hard and had fun in the process. While they rested, they analyzed the pitfalls and pratfalls of the game with humorous comments like, "You did great!...Man, you were about as useful as a one-legged man in an arse-kicking competition." And, on occasion, "You were so tight that you wouldn't shout if a shark bit y'a."

AR knew how to skate and had coached his boys in ice hockey. Yet skillfully playing the game himself was a different experience. He relearned what he had already taught his kids and focused his efforts on moving swiftly. The boys trained their father to be a driving force for the team, in addition to making the right decisions at any given time. It took hours of practicing his back shot, snap shot, slap shot and wrist shot before AR was confident about himself. Yet it was not enough. Shooting practices followed, with careful application of the body stick and shoulder checks. AR tapped his mental and physical abilities to help him get through the grueling practices. His only consolation was that other dads faced similar challenges. They all supported one another. These were not a bunch of dimwits and nobody was a snooze. Soon they had their hockey smarts down pat. They also learned that the game looks easy when every player multi-tasks and works together as a team.

Team members sometimes got on one another's nerves but they generally got along well. They developed an incredibly close working relationship and made sure nobody felt left out. There always was someone to pick up the slack or to start a do-you-dare maneuver. Part of the routine included a "prepare and practice" regimen. After much turmoil, the team was finally learning to enjoy the game.

AR's skillful handwork with the stick made him a natural for the position of center forward in the attacking zone. By the fall season, he had a much-needed feel-good and get-moving attitude. He could capture the moment and get his puck moving. He excelled in the art of wrist shots in addition to the usual slap shots. AR also learned techniques such as back-checking, working behind the net, making centering passes and blind passes to other team members. He had to be reminded how to avoid being offside, and handle covering, charging and checking by defending players. AR's sons cheered and advised their dad - a clear task turnaround. Several other boys also devoted what seemed like endless hours to instruct and coach their dads.

To cope with the stress of competitive play, the Reddy family allotted the weekends for the practice of yoga and tai-chi as well as relaxation in the various hamlets in the Adirondack Mountains. Colleagues and friends of the Reddys considered it their honor to offer words of encouragement and advice. The range of suggestions was as wide as the skies of Montana – special diets, exercise, home remedies and nutritional supplements "to build inner strength of mind and body."

The 2004 winter season began with an early blast of the white stuff. The Reddys belonged to the Utica Snowmobile Club. This activity was a good change of pace from ice hockey. The snow-mobiling season is obviously weather-dependent and usually lasts until March. Snowmobilers prefer having at least eight inches of compact snow to cover any hazardous stones or debris on the paths. Members would meet at the fire-house on a Saturday morning; each one was clad in heavy duty windbreakers. After downing some doughnuts and hot coffee, the convoy of riders was all set to go. Sometimes, the conditions were perfect – bright sunshine, an inch of fresh snow overnight, and the temperature just around 20 degrees Fahrenheit. Below-zero Fahrenheit temperatures were uncomfortable for the riders; above the freezing point, the riders would sweat and the trails would break down.

The Reddys donned their boots, helmets, arctic wear pants, jackets and gloves before going to the clearing where the snowmobiles were parked. Almost all of the club's 100 members were present. Some were feisty senior citizens; the youngest member appeared to be around ten years old. No doubt he had passed the mandatory safety course meant for those younger than 18 who did not have a driver's license. To the Reddys' surprise, a third of those suited up were women. "The gals have the newest models and best brands of equipment," one dude moaned. Another empathized with him, "Look! The gals have the sleek Ski Dogs, and Skippy Dos snow mobiles. We fellas have to make do with ditch pickles!"

The ride was sponsored by a local charity, and a highway patrolman led the way to the outskirts of the town with the riders lined up behind him. At the starting line, the pecking order was evident: the faster riders led the pack. One rider in that group, a friend of the Reddy boys, forewarned the family, "We are usually with the leaders and we sometimes have turned around to catch up with the rest of the group. Since this is your first time we'll be considerate and just stay with the average Joe, around 30 miles per hour." The Reddys were relieved.

Besides raising funds for charity and indulging in their favorite winter sport, snowmobilers have the satisfaction of knowing they can help in emergencies. When snow storms necessitate the closing of roads to regular traffic, snow-mobilers are permitted to travel on those roads to help stranded and injured travelers as well as shut-ins.

Though the organizers could not control the weather, they had done everything to ensure the safety of the riders. From 11 p.m. the previous night to 3 a.m., the day of the event, some members were responsible for "maintaining" the trail. This involved using grooming machines to remove bumps in the trail and widen it to measure at least eight feet to allow two snowmobiles to travel alongside or cross each other. A 12-foot wide trail is ideal. Some summer meetings are earmarked for clearing the trail of downed trees and brush in cooperation with the property's owners.

The assigned route that morning took the riders over smooth, frozen expanses along well-used tracks. Sunlight hit the crusty snow and it glinted like a bed of scattered diamonds. After they were well within the wooded areas of the Adirondack Mountains, the riders spied turkey, white weasels, squirrels, deer and coyotes. The deer showed no signs of fear; they stood still, mesmerized or perhaps used to the sight of the snowmobiles whizzing by. The riders had to pass over some streams which involved crossing over cracking ice. The highlight of the day came when they spotted a pair of foxes. The creatures, at first startled by the sound of machines, found safety on higher ground, and continued to watch as if the parade was in their honor.

AR appreciated the snowmobiling outing as a welcome change from his work. For the young boys, it was an enjoyable break from the other winter sports. As the dates for the scheduled ice hockey matches neared, it was back to practicing daily for the upcoming competitions.

The Utica Blizzards' first challenge in 2004 was a home game in late November. Practice sessions were in full swing with the Grizzlies serving as their opponents. The youngsters nearly always gave the older gobblers a break. After all, they had to be kind to their dads and their friends' dads. The Blizzards' team members had now gotten the bug. The coach's catch phrases and comments kept them inspired: "You can't help but get excited...seize the moment...be exceedingly clever...it's not what you're expecting...improve...adapt...overcome."

The players helped each other with their observations: "Change up...back check, there's a man behind you...fore check...shoot...let her rip." The Blizzards were a fun and friendly crew that enjoyed the thrilling experience of playing a sport they thought was usually reserved for the young and the swift. The days when they had the heebie-jeebies and felt they would be eaten alive by the opponents were long gone. They soon became the fastest, smoothest, safest and the best team - for their age. They referred to themselves as "heavy duty." Soon it would be the dress-rehearsal before show time.

The Utica Blizzards' ice hockey techniques were staple topics of conversation for Uticans at their dinner tables and at social functions. The evaluations were positive. Many nurses pointed to AR's physical fitness as being a role model for their husbands. Some wives endorsed a strict "no dessert" rule solely for their husbands, some of whom humorously protested, "Now you know why I call you my princess. You are a royal pain!"

At Indian social get-togethers, appetizers were no longer served, in the hope of losing *charbi* (fat). Few *patis* (husbands) remonstrated, "Sweetie! We don't live any longer! We only look younger and die fitter-looking." One humorist added, "With all this dieting, we will be sad but die looking healthy." AR's participation in the Blizzards and the Baby Boomlets tourney was the talk of the town among the Asian-Americans, as he was the permanent social secretary of the Ind-o-US community. At get-togethers, he received plenty of free advice: "Master the techniques and be ready for the big game." AR would smile and reply, "I am ready for the fast pace, the pressure and the fluctuations. The team is ready to rumble."

AR's diet was discussed and his stamina attributed to yogurt made from goat's milk. A well-wisher suggested, "A special body massager could really work your muscles and joints to make your body nimble." The theory was that if the body was like a wet noodle, it would offer no resistance, thus preventing fractures. Another theorized, "What Atul-*bhai* (brother) needs is the body of a piano wire – strong and flexible with a spring-back action." His buddy, Rao-*bhai,* suggested, "Let's hire a well-known contortionist-massager from the state of Mysore."

After an hour's discourse at a social event, AR's devoted fans agreed: AR needed a reflexologist who would give him a rubdown together with manipulation of his joints and kneading of his back. The challenge was where to find one with all these skills. The internet, they agreed, was a good resource. A few phone calls to New York, Los Angeles, and of course, to Addison, New Jersey - Little India - would definitely narrow the search for "the best."

At the first match, the Ind-o-US were in full force to cheer their favorite – *ahmara babu* (our guy) at his first game. Grandparents showed up for their first live ice hockey game. After the usual '"Kea rre...and Kia Ora?" the adults and seniors settled down in groups and continued their usual chit-chat and repartee. The Gen-Xers turned up in large numbers. The news about a *babu* who plays ice-hockey was out on college campuses. Asian-American students from the nearby colleges, including the FOB (fresh-off-the-boat) post-grads from SUNY-IT (State University of New York – Institute of Technology), attended en-masse. For some, this was their first social outing where they did not have to BYODKM (bring your own display key board and mouse). There were Hindi-babes and Bindi-babes. A few showed off their bling-bling (flashy jewelry) and all had the flair of webinair. The college in-crowd was tech-savvy and Netizens, fully familiar with www – the World Wide Web!

Before the game, the conversations between the undergrads centered on DEEP (department education evaluation program), and BULL (basic understanding lecture list). The techies began a heated discussion of BIG (boss in general) SHIT (special high intensity teaching). After nodding their hellos, the senior-most of the techies counseled the freshmen, "The opportunities always look bigger going than coming." The seniors advised the juniors: "Hiccup and shake off your old grudges and misconceptions." They knew that when it came to getting ahead, homework and presentations were everything.

After graduating from India's casual clothing, the under-grads and post-grads sought out fashionable wear. For the most part, they were in a league of their own. Because of their youth, they portrayed their sense of individuality, both through traditional and contemporary styles. They understood the limits of science and technology but these young people also had their lighter moments. The story is told of an FOB techie who took his first American gal out to dinner. While the young lady was perusing the menu at the formal restaurant, her date tried to impress her with an order of appetizers. "We'll have a quickie to get us going," he told the waitress. Both the women were embarrassed! The quick-witted date immediately reworded his order, "We'd like a quiche, please."

The hip-talk in the auditorium was a distraction from the male collegians' main pre-game action – to survey the hotties and just chillaxin. Their classmates, Carol and Dianne, had to remind the techies that the chicks they were ogling were "blondes with or without hair dye." To this the thinking geeks would respond, "Go-fish! She could be more than just another pretty date!" and, "She has the power of 2." The FOB females excelled at critical thinking. When Tupperware became the topic of conversation during a date, the tandoori (young Indian lady) techie responded: "I'm a new immigrant. I don't know about Tupperware, but I can tell you anything you want to know about hardware and software."

This was a crowd of internet trailblazers, software and program developers. Anybody who did not belong to this pack but overheard their vernacular and lingo might think that these young adults were perverts. The standard vocabulary included terms such as: hard-drive, joysticks, mother-load, floppies, controlled shift, explore the slow-downs, connect my PC to your PC, float the mouse, boot-it, laptop's hard drive, speed, hard grinding noise, Go-daddy, just surf, Google, slash-dot, clickers and internet junkies. This group, called bloggers (Blog = web + log), spoke Blingo and belonged to Blogosphere, a.k.a. Blogland or Blogistan. The best the technophiles could do for pickup lines were, "My PC is more than just a pretty interface" and "I am being realistic and accurate without being technical."

The Indian hubbies - mostly baby boomers - all huddled together. One *chacha* (grandpa), a retired military old-timer, had a conspicuously enormous mustache. But regardless of age, the crowd keenly analyzed the players and their strategy. This was most noticeable during the two intermissions when the could-have-beens and might-have-beens were analyzed. Ghosh's opinion: "There's a possibility for a big-bang win."

Those spectators who did not understand the game socialized, opined about life in general and freely doled out advice: "Eat well, exercise, stay fit, and die anyway." One grandpa added, "The older I get, the fewer things seem worth waiting in line for." They all agreed on one thing: that AR had ACE - Attitude, Courtesy, and Excellence! A few muttered about this inscrutable new sport. Most said, "Sometimes it is good to try somethin' different."

The wives sat separately - for a change! Several traded in their conservative Benares nine-yard sari for a new pair of perfect-fit dream jeans. With the excitement surrounding the impending debut of the *babu*, the more conservative husbands either overlooked or ignored the change in the women. The ladies enjoyed the evening at the Aud and swapped opinions gleaned after years of living in the U.S. One was overheard saying, "No, no, no! It isn't the jeans that make you look fat. It's the laddoos and Indian sweets we order from New Jersey." But another added, "Those jeans make you look forty-five and foxy." Invariably one woman would ask, "Is it possible to develop a diet which allows us to eat more and yet lose weight?"

Then they shared news about the best sales in town and which Indian stores in the Big Apple and in Little India had "60 percent off, cut to the bone" sales. Some ladies would have preferred to go shopping instead of being at the Aud. Others were the team's staunchest supporters. The grandmas were peaceful and content having learned that middle age broadness of mind and waist go together. There were no TWIXTERS (adult kids staying at home) or KIPPERS (kids in parents' pockets eroding their retirement savings).

For the first official game, the players were rearing to go right from the opening bell. This was a match-up on home turf against the Arctic Seals, a neighboring team. The Blizzards won 6-2 as they crushed the competition. Every goal was met with "McNifiq" or "Oh, no!" depending on which side scored. After their first competitive game, the Blizzards yelled out a collective, "WHOA!"

After the game, the crowd dispersed for pasta-fasta. The Ind-o-US went for their *desi* (Indian) cuisine where "Spice is Nice." The favorite choice was chicken *tikka masala* and an assortment of other Indian dishes, all washed down with cold beers. Other ethnic groups went to their favorite haunts: pizzerias, bistros, trattorias, cafes and gourmet restaurants. There again, the Blizzards' talents were hashed and rehashed. The execution was described as "Precise and accurate!" The local newspaper featured the game on the front page! Half of the sports section was devoted to describing the game in glowing terms: "Exactly...Correctly...Unerringly...No Mistakes!"

The next game was going to be critical. It would be a match-up with a team which would target the most gifted player. In such a situation, the defendant is likely to resort to board-checking with the body, elbow or just downright tripping, even if it is a minor or major penalty. A power play is little consolation to any skilled player intent on scoring a fair goal with an even-handed opponent. The away-game against the Snow Ploughs was scheduled for two weeks later in Albany. All the players knew it would be arduous, demanding and needing precision performance. The Utica Blizzards appeared fearless and would be dressed in their on-the-road uniforms for the game.

When that day arrived, many Uticans made the hour-and-a-half long drive on Interstate 90 to attend the game. With a little time left before the game started, they organized an impromptu party in the parking lot. One reveler had a beer in one hand and a digital video camera in the other to preserve the details of the celebration for those who couldn't attend. Cars entered the parking lot and honked to "Here we go, Blizzards," to show off their hometown pride. A handful of the

Ind-o-US group joined the party and attracted even more people from Utica and its neighboring towns. Clearly, all were having a grand old time before the game began. Some *desis* found the partying scene captivating, with plenty of spirits. In spite of the freezing temperatures, there was drinkin', dancin', sweatin', and callin' 'em both in the parking lot and in the stands.

Other *desis* who ranged from the elderly dadas and nanas to tiny *bintus* (grandkids) made it to the stands *jaldi* (ASAP). They were equipped for the bone-chilling cold and looked more like Eskimos in the winter, bundled up as they were with woolen scarves, gloves, and ear muffs. The few who wore knitted ski caps appeared more like terrorists in Asian Indian garb than like sports fans.

The adults had their MoSoSo (mobile social software) to keep the folks back home informed of the play-by-play action. Though they were a distinct minority behind enemy lines of the hometown Snow Ploughs fans, the Uticans were animated and knew that nothing could beat that winning feeling. As cars crammed the parking lot, they had little to complain about. The temperature, in the upper 20s (Fahrenheit), made for a chilly rather than a freezing reception. In true Utica spirit, they would stand up and cheer loudly during the game even while they chowed down on their treats - nachos, hot dogs, pretzels, and pizzas.

The teenagers from Utica were out in force to support all the dads on the team. The game was also a good reason to get out of town. The few who lingered in the corridors wound up their banter hurriedly: "See y'a later." Using instant text messaging, it was, "GTG (got to go), TTYL (talk to you later), BRB (be right back)." During the game the messages would read, "LOL (laugh out loud), Cool, Sweet, Awesome." And for the few not in the game, the text messaging included "CYL (see you later), NVM (never mind), BBL (be back later), OK (Oll Korrect)!" Undoubtedly, the kids and adults alike were energized!

The Snow Ploughs' devotees packed the Albany Auditorium. The Capital City looked forward to making chicken-feed of these small town Utica Blizzards. The fans were prepped for some real action on this cold winter night. The atmosphere around the ice rink became serious and tense as the minutes ticked by. The announcer asked everyone to rise for the singing of the National Anthem.

Both sides played well with spot-on passes and faithful executions. Yet the Blizzards were generally "on the dot" - they made it look "sooo eazy!" The home team delivered an inspired performance in the first period. There was a lot of board-checking and the usual body checking, elbowing and tripping. The players were keen on sweeps and scrambles. The forward line was under pressure. It was not uncommon for three-on-two and two-on-one breaks leading to screen shots at the goal, while the fans screamed, "Dump and Chase." There were also episodes of slashing and spearing. The Blizzards' attack line had the first strike by scoring from the slot with a slap shot after a succession of stick deking and flips shots.

The Albany fans went berserk over their hometown players. A spectator on the north stand screamed at the goalie, "You don't have enough brains to give yourself a headache!" Another targeted the defense: "You guys wouldn't go two rounds in a revolving door."

The Blizzards were focused. Their fans screamed, "Go Blizzards! Rip It! Let's go defense...Let's go Utica!" Both teams wasted a few opportunities when they played short-handed as a result of power plays or penalties. The stands were packed and, as expected, most were hometown fans giving the Snow Ploughs the psychological advantage. The Ind-o-US from Utica were a tiny minority in this sea of ice hockey diehards. Yet they made their presence felt, at least to the group around them. Those who heard their remarks were very pleasantly surprised by the good nature of the Ind-o-US group even though some were desperately trying to figure out whether the puck was coming or going. Others did not grasp the violations, fouls, off sides and frequent face-offs. Those watching ice hockey for the first time were carried away by the speed and agility of the players. Coming as they did from a country known for its philosophy of non-violence, a lot of Indian spectators were taken aback by the intensity of physical contact and aggression. Still, they joined in the chanting, "Let's go, defense," and "Ice it!" One *patni* (wife), failing to grasp the humor, inquired, "Why are the fans saying 'kick their butt'?" During the break, the fans analyzed the plays in great detail.

In the second period, there was a flip pass and AR scored the second goal with a wraparound shot. This came after a series of superb shoulder and head dekes to fake the defense and bamboozle the goalie. The puck hit its mark as the fans screamed, "Wrist it!"

The Snow Ploughs began to slip on their defense and did not execute their offense effectively. The two-goal lead squelched the initial exuberance of the Albany fans. After a rather dismal shot, one of them commented, "You must be the world's only livin' brain donor."

The game had its usual Bang...Whack...Boom...Crash...Jolt...and bruises. The spectators cheered, jeered and protested. The decibel level was so high, little that was said could be understood even by those near the speaker. All this made for some hilarious misunderstanding of *desi* comments. A *gadha* (a dim-witted person) was heard as Buddha – the Enlightened One! *Buddhu sala (*unintelligent fellow*)* was construed as brother Sal, and *mar-golie (*shoot the goal*)* was interpreted as marigold.

The third period began in earnest. The Snow Ploughs immediately underwent a transformation and scored a dramatic goal, making it a 2-1 game. The tension increased but it did not last long. There was a third goal for the Blizzards when Coach Dicks was fed a forehand pass. He converted the flat pass to a flip shot, lickety-split, to take a snapper and pass the goalie. The Utica fans were ecstatic! The Albany fans, on the other hand, gave the goalie the thumbs down sign. One rabid fan screamed, "If I had a head like yours, I'd circumcise it."

The Snow Ploughs were desperate. They did manage to get a goal in during the last few minutes. The Blizzards kept up the pressure in the final stretch and went on to a 3-2 win. They were on a winning streak! The Snow Ploughs and their fans had to be content to lick their wounds and salve their pride. A bitterly disappointed fan addressed one of the Albany players, "Pull your lip over your head and swallow!"

In the final hand-shake after the game, AR said to his worthy adversaries, "Stick to the fight, buddies; when things go wrong, that's when you mustn't quit." The Snow Ploughs were upset with their performance and their consequent defeat at the hands of a small-city team. They still could not understand why they were left reeling or how they were outscored. When they had stepped onto the ice, their impression of the Blizzards was, "they certainly do not instill fear into any of us." Once they saw the Blizzards handle the stick and the puck, their impressions changed rapidly. And in the third period, in the words of the Snow Ploughs, "The Utica team just swung the momentum."

The Snow Ploughs' coach, a tad desperate, muttered to a friend, "I talked to them about their individual talents, the importance of speed and precision as well as working as a team. Failures like this evening's just don't happen without a breakdown – mental and physical. We just didn't put a hundred percent of effort into the game." He evaluated his team's performance: "In the three periods, the players' energy went from get-up-and-go to gone and then to passed-on." The coach conveyed these feelings to his team. He stressed that he expected a change in pace for the next game. One of the players griped, "It's just a game." The coach retorted, "No one says 'it's just a game' when they are winning." The Snow Ploughs' fans were beside themselves and tried to analyze where their team slipped. They drowned their sorrows with a lot of drinkin', fightin', dancin', sweatin' and callin' 'em.

The Ind-o-US attendees were delighted with the game's outcome and praised their *babu's* "grace in motion." After the game, a few chose to celebrate in style by relishing *shish kabobs, tandoori and tikka* chicken, sesame chicken wings and of course, cold beer. For other Uticans, the hard won victory called for the best in dining - filet mignon! Later, the Utica fans and team departed for home with farewells: XOXO, Ciao, TTFN (Ta-ta for now), Big Kiss, Bisoux (French good-bye), Cheers, Hit me on the hip (call me on the cell phone) and BCNU (Be seein' you).

When he arrived home, AR ached all over and moaned in pain. Dr. Patel, a colleague for twenty-five years, stopped by. He was a family friend and a source of strength to the Reddys ever since they made MoVa their home. Dr. Patel told Anita: "Give him two aspirins and put hot packs over the bruised areas and sore joints. He should be fine tomorrow. Call if there are problems." Anita could have figured out the treatment on her own, having taken care of two sons who were also ardent sportsmen. The phone rang incessantly with friends and relatives calling for information about the game and the prized player. Numerous calls were fielded by Dr. Patel, who subbed as the answering machine. In between the telephone calls, Dr. Patel made himself at home by helping himself to a glass of bourbon. After the commotion subsided and Atul went to bed, Dr. Patel took his leave. On his way out, Dr. Patel had a final piece of advice: "When Atul gets well, tell him he is running low on bourbon."

The word was out that the small-town Blizzards, like the diminutive David, had trounced the Goliath-like Snow Ploughs and that the Indian *babu* was the star, albeit an injured one. The phone rang constantly with callers giving Anita motherly advice on how to take care of bruises and joint pain "the way we do back home." One woman suggested a poultice made with turmeric powder as "the best wet paste."

Others sent e-mails describing the benefits of Epson salt soaks, or better yet, sea baths. Some called with suggestions of "compresses of arnica, marigold, witch hazel and yellow sweet clover."

Their next-door neighbor, Mrs. Lee, offered her special remedy. "I am sure a meal of barley, mung beans, sprouted grains and millet will have the good doctor quickly fit again." Mrs. Kaplan, a few doors down, suggested, "A regimen of fruits, cabbage and sprouted beans is best."

Mrs. Sen, an old family friend from Kansas, gave the Reddys a buzz. "I swear by a diet rich in garlic, onions, pepper, sesame seeds and ginger," she said. Every *desi* caller had a piece of advice on how to care for the doctor. The evening's advice could have been compiled into a book of home remedies or a text entitled, "Miracle of Spices."

As night approached, Atul downed a couple of extra-strength Tylenol tablets for his pain and decided to get a good night's rest. Anita, after her nightly *Satyanarayan puja,* rounded up the boys and with Grandma Reddy said the family's involved set of evening prayers.

Ind-o-US from Utica who knew the Reddys, fielded questions from out-of-towners: "Yea-rre, Yea-rre, you can talk to me. I know all about Atul *bhai's* physical and mental condition." Another offered a piece of news: "AR's been nominated the MVP – *Maha* (very) Valiant Performer." Yet another tried to sound decisive, "With the goal and the assists, he's approximately and more or less the best all-a-rounder. That's my exact estimate." When there were questions about Atul *bhai*'s physical condition, the response was, "Roughly in pretty good shape...something like black-and-blue with expected full and near-full recovery by next week." The friends conveyed their advice to the friend of the friend that Atul should "persevere with it" and "stick with it."

The Utica newspapers were proud of the home team. One paper bragged, "The Utica studs outfoxed the Albany jocks." It went on, "The team started almost from scratch. Now they played with grace under pressure and deserved their sweet success." The reporter wrote, "The Blizzards were the best thing that happened to Utica since the invention of the salt spreader." The sports writer opined, "The Blizzards should keep on, endure and continue!"

This was a moment that made Utica women proud of their sons, husbands, cousins, brothers-in-law, ex-boyfriends, and classmates. Some still had a difficult time believing the amazing truth about the Blizzards. Any way one sliced it, the team was an over-night sensation in the city. The players had achieved mega-star status and had become irresistible. Wherever they went, they were the "Android men."

The Beam is On
> 6 <

The next day dawned bright and cheery at the Reddy residence. Atul awoke at his usual early hour, with no time to coddle his bruises and blisters. His personal practice of physical fitness included a daily regimen of Vinayasa yoga and Yoga-Lattes (yoga with Pilates). Pilates strengthen the core muscles in the abdomen and back; yoga increases flexibility and balance. Twice a week, AR practiced yoga-robics for weight loss. The exercise routine was followed by a cold shower and meditation to renew his body and soul for another productive day. And Dr. Reddy had a busy day ahead. Fortunately, he was a super-organizer. Today, he had his morning rounds of patients to see in the hospital before he made it to the Radiation Oncology Department where he spent most of his day. Years of living in New York had taught him to schedule a little extra time in the morning for the winter ritual of shoveling snow. That morning, the snow blower worked like a charm.

The Reddys did their best to have breakfast as a family. While they ate, Ajit and Anil wondered how sore their dad felt after his physically taxing ice hockey game of the previous night. They debated whether their dad, in spite of his excellent physique at his age, could take the beating to which ice hockey players were accustomed.

"How did you sleep, daddy?" Ajit asked. "Do you hurt?"

Their dad assured them he felt fine; then he left for the hospital. After the boys heard the garage door shut and knew their dad was out of earshot, they discussed their fears with their mother.

"It can be pretty dangerous, you know, mummy," said Anil. Ajit's assessment of the situation was a mixed bag. "Sure there have been injuries, some of them serious, and even some deaths in ice hockey. But Dad's tough and fit. Besides, he loves the sport!" That day, the family breakfast time was short on dialogue and long on thought. Breakfast did not last very long.

Grandma Reddy deemed breakfast time to be the young family's opportunity for private conversation at the start of the day. This was the Reddy family's quality time together. As was her routine, she skipped breakfast, but she had heard that morning's conversation loudly and clearly. She hid its message in the silence of her heart.

After the kids went to school, Anita busied herself with her chores. She started her activities with her daily *Asana*, followed by one of the five forms of Yoga – non-competitive exercises: Bhakti yoga (emotions), Gyana yoga (wisdom), Raja yoga (meditation), Karma yoga (actions) and Hatha yoga (physical) as well as breathing exercises. *Surya-Namaskar* (prayer) yoga sessions followed. Even during her exercises that day, her thoughts reverted to the previous day's events and the morning's breakfast conversation. Anita was convinced that her husband was entrenched in ice hockey but she also wondered if the sport was more than he could handle. Her challenge was how to broach the topic of reassessing his interest in the sport without bruising his ego.

Dr. Patel, too, had sleepless nights, worrying about his friend. Ice hockey can be a strenuous sport. In his practice he had found many men who thought they were ten years younger than they really were, and took up vigorous sports to reassure themselves and their friends that they indeed still retained their dexterity and youthfulness. Like Anita, Dr. Patel mulled over how he could convince Atul to re-evaluate his fascination and involvement with the game. At the back of his mind, Dr. Patel understood that an acute injury could incapacitate the doctor and his practice; even a minor hurt could lead to chronic problems. Dr. Patel decided that perhaps in a week he'd take Atul out for a drink and, as he told his own wife, "have a heart-to-heart talk to drive some sense into this fellow."

On his morning round on the hospital's third floor, Dr. Reddy was his jovial self. Utica's win the previous day thrilled the entire hospital staff; the news became the all-consuming topic in corridors and operating rooms. Dr. Reddy accepted all the congratulations with a smile and reciprocated the "high five" signs. All the while he masked the nagging pain in his back. He kept his spirits bright for the benefit of his staff and cancer patients who had enough problems of their own.

Many physicians stopped AR in the hospital corridors to congratulate him on his team's victory. They were very proud of their colleague and the performance of the Utica team. AR downplayed their expectations for successive games and predicted the series would likely be one-up, one-down. To Dr. Avi Singer, a personal friend, AK shared his sorrow that the big boys of Albany were taking their loss very deeply, both emotionally and physically.

Dr Singer said, "Oh! Snap out of it. You can send them my *raachmoanes* (sympathy)." The nurses told AR, "The Utica team is now in a league of its own. The win was no ordinary fifteen minutes of fame." AR enjoyed the greetings, kudos and the compliments and was glad he was back to work. Yet, judging from last night, he could have taken some personal down time.

On his rounds, AR observed a young patient being admitted to the oncology section from the over-flowing orthopedic floor. The teenager was in a body cast extending to his neck, with his lower limbs in traction. Dr. Reddy waved and gave the youngster a sympathetic smile. "Got it from playing ice hockey, Doc," the young man said, smiling back. That remark hit Dr. Reddy between the eyes with as much force as a flying puck!

Radiation Oncology is a sub-specialty field in medicine devoted to the treatment of cancer using radiation. Also referred to as Radiation Therapy, the X-ray beam that is used is similar to an ordinary light beam. Both beams travel as electromagnetic waves but with different wave-lengths. A radiation beam used in cancer treatment has an energy ranging from 6 to 20 MeV (million electron volts). The X-rays go through the body the way light goes through glass. Along its path, the X-ray causes ionization of the water (in and out of the cells) which starts a chemical chain-reaction leading to cell damage, DNA impairment and cell death. It is the inequity of cell damage, repair, death and recovery between the normal and cancer cells that are exploited in destroying the cancer cells and preserving the surrounding normal tissues.

Radiobiologists are usually laboratory researchers and non-physicians who study these basic biological aspects of radiation. The radiation oncologists (Rad Oncs) are physicians who use their knowledge of radiation, tumors and patients in the treatment of cancer. In addition to the standard medical training, they have knowledge of tumor behavior, interaction of radiation with tissues, and the blending of the role of radiation with other oncological (cancer-related) fields. Oncology nurses, radiation therapists, dosimetrists, physicists and the administration of the department work with the radiation oncologists. The technical staff comprises college graduates with at least two years of training. Everyone has a "may not be my job, but I can help" attitude and a smile.

Workday of a Radiation Oncologist

Rad Oncs use radiation for palliation and cancer obliteration,
Done with daily radiation treatment - five fractions a week.
That's what the radiobiologists find ...and that's just fine.
They go to the Med Oncs, because they are also the trialists.
They check on the operation or the Surgeon's dictation.
Looking for tumor elimination, yet organ preservation.

They talk with the Radiologist and the Pathologist -
our colleagues Alicia, Joyce, Frederick and Frist.
Rad Oncs hone in on the details found with patience,
to do what they consider is best for the patient.
Curing cancer! That's a team challenge with precision.
That enhances the Rad Onc's reputation with distinction.

Let's check the latest reference to know the cutting-edge text.
That's where Rad Oncs and Med Oncs go next.
Let's figure the radiation dosage that will do the tumor damage.
Cancers feel the trepidation with all the radiation knowledge.
Synchronization, syncopation follows electron oscillation.
Cells undergo degradation leading to cancer annihilation.

Before going into technicalities, it starts with a finger wave.
The patients tell the doc, that's what they don't crave.
The doctors try to smile and understand,
why the patients does not want to shake their hand.
Sure, many patients marvel at the mysterious things,
the Rad Onc may see in their many openings.

After they complete that complex consultation,
they get the patient's permission after the presentation.
Then appointments are made, called prior arrangements,
because, they can't do much without prior scheduling.
So after consultation, it is on to treatment planning,
Let's do the preparation to get the patient for simulation.

So where are Leann, Rosy, Marge, Vicki, and Sandra?
Please, let's go girls ... we want to treat Brenda.
They get the bone scan, CAT scan and PET scan.
Next they go for 2-D or 3-D or 4-D or IMRT mapping;
This leads to dosimetry and the physics planning.
So the radiation team gets lethal without getting fatal.

So, receptionist Bonnie is the patient's anticipation,
nurse Rosalyn is their subsequent expectation.
A bit of Monica is all that the Rad Oncs require,
a crumb from busy Cheryl is the best they can acquire.
They do with a trace of this and a morsel of that,
Becky is who Dr. Reddy taps with physicist Teng in the clasp.

Therapist Shaream keeps working the radiation beam,
with a chunk of Sheen on the treatment machine,
and there's tall Bill to check on the two Shreems.
Doc does with a tad of help from this one and from that one.
To Lisa and Cynthia, "here I am,
you have my undivided attention, take it while you can."

A point from Dr. Reddy makes the department glitter.
The entire staff, working together, makes Dr. Reddy flicker.
Treatment days a week is just five with TGIF to round.
Jump up and down and shake hands with all around.
The doc shakes his head to all who are sensible,
and puts his signatures on all that is reasonable.

Take one step left and two to the right.
Take one step to the right, two to the left.
Take one to the back and two to the front.
If it looks like a circle, then the Rad Onc has it right.
Because they can't run and they can't hide.
All that Radiation Oncologists try to do is "touch the sky."

The field of radiation oncology has seen a broad technological expansion with progress in bioengineering, computer science, cell and molecular targeting. The radiation therapy staff may be described as multi-tasked, both clinically and technologically. Advances have led to the development of high energy linear accelerators which produce higher energy and sharply-defined beams of radiation, better imaging techniques to visualize tumors and computers to assist in improved targeting of the beam on the cancer while sparing surrounding tissues.

These technologies help shape the radiation beam to the individual patient's tumor. No longer limited by 2-D (dimensional) and 3-D external beam radiation therapy (EBRT), Rad Oncs now use IMRT (intensity modulated radiation therapy); 4-D; IGRT (image guided radiation therapy), gamma knife; SRS (stereotactic radio surgery) for brain, head and neck tumors; and cyber-knife. Tumor imaging has also improved through image-fusion of CT scans (computer tomography), MR scans (magnetic resonance), and PET scans (positron emission tomography) and SPECT (single photon emission computed tomography) images. And the high-tech, high-touch world of tumor imaging is rapidly evolving from anatomical viewing to functional and molecular imaging. Then, through a dynamic process of adaptive radiation therapy, radiation beams are customized to the tumor in each patient and targeted to the cancer from outside the body (EBRT). As newer diagnostic and treatment modalities emerge, they also converge to target the tumor precisely. Technology is also moving from computer to digital radiography and from monochrome to color displays of anatomy and dose.

Another way Rad Oncs use radiation is from within the body by placing radioactive seeds into the tumor (brachytherapy) or injecting tumor-antibodies tagged with radio-isotopes to deliver targeted radiation only to the tumor cells. These cells are besieged both by the antibody as well as the piggy-backed radioactive isotope - RIT (radio-immuno-therapy). Tumors are also treated by using chemotherapy agents to sensitize tumor cells to radiation as well as to attack cancer cells outside the field of radiation. Regardless of whether radiation therapy or chemotherapy is used, the new goals of treatment are to target only the tumor or cancer cells. Today's technology permits that in most cases. Combined modality treatment has been shown to improve the cancer cure rates and reduce the side effects of treatment.

In simpler terms, after oncologists assess the tumor and its spread, the first step in radiation therapy is to simulate the planned treatment. As part of this planning of treatment, the tumor (target volume) is "sliced" a quarter-inch thick with the help of a CT. The imaged slices are then fed into a computer. Each slice viewed on the screen is analyzed with the outline of the tumor and surrounding normal tissues. The various slices are then merged to present a 3-dimensional view of the tumor and the normal organs. This "target volume" is then "treated" on the computer with the screen displaying the dose distribution in the target and nearby normal tissues. After the optimum dose distribution is determined, the computer designs shields to protect the normal tissue and shape the radiation beam to the contour of the tumor.

In a high-tech world, the situation can sometimes get out of hand. The often-quoted example involves a dosimetrist's spouse who said, "My wife truly lives, eats, and breathes computers. One day while I was rubbing her back she said, 'No! Not there...Scroll down'."

Cancer is a major healthcare problem and the second most common cause of death in the U.S. One in three Americans will be diagnosed with the disease, while three out of four families will be impacted by it. Some predictions indicate that in a few years cancer will become the number one killer of Americans. Advances in science have permitted the early diagnosis and successful treatment of breast and prostate cancers – the most common cancers in women and men, respectively. Tests are being developed to detect the early stages of lung and colo-rectal cancers, the first and second most frequently occurring cancers, when their incidences in both sexes are combined. These four cancers form 55 percent of all cancers in the U.S. and account for half of all cancer deaths. Lung cancer alone comprises 12 percent of all cancers, and accounts for a third of all cancer deaths. The total number of new cancers diagnosed every year in the U.S. is 1.5 million, with an additional one million cases of skin cancer.

So, even with all the expensive and technological advances in radiation therapy and other fields of medicine, these benefits are outweighed by simpler approaches. An ounce of cancer prevention (stop smoking and use sunscreen) early detection (screening) by regular tests such as a mammograms, DREs (for prostate cancer), colonoscopies, PAP smears and other blood tests to monitor good health are valuable.

Radiation Oncologists need a sense of humor. A sign in the doc's waiting room is a testament that it is possible to convey a serious message in a light-hearted manner. The message reads, "This is a Non-Smoking Area. If we see smoke, we will assume you're on fire."

Dr. Reddy, as do other doctors, met a wide range of people and patients in his practice. Some see the funny side of their life-threatening illness. For example, one with an "earthy" sense of humor insisted on warning his doctor about his FF (future farts). "I thought you should know this about me," the patient said gleefully.

Dr. Reddy's routine question, "How do you feel?" often receives the response, "With my hands!" from patients who obviously enjoy puns.

One easy-to-please patient had a unique response when his doctor asked him, "Any complaints?" "None so far, I've been in your waiting room for only five minutes," the patient answered.

When another patient was asked if he had any questions replied, "How long do I have to ignore your advice?"

Some patients try to educate the doctor with their own version of what constitutes good health. "It is healthy to move the bowels three times a day - cleans the system!" one self-educated patient asserted.

On another occasion, an elderly man described in great detail the different shades of color in his stools. After the patient had bent the doctor's ear long enough, his seasoned nurse stepped forward and rescued the doctor. After some eye contact with the doc developed over the years, she smiled and demanded, "OK! Fess up, young man! Have you been eating your grandchild's crayons?"

Other patients offer Dr. Reddy their pearls of wisdom: "You know you're getting old when everything either leaks or dries up," and "I'm over the hill without getting to the top."

Perhaps the most hilarious event arose when Dr. Reddy began examining an elderly woman who had a slight hearing impairment. He placed the stethoscope on her chest and said, "Big breaths." The patient replied regretfully, "Yes, they used to be!"

The most uncomfortable situation arises when the doctor is caught in the middle of a family feud. Once, to break the ice with a new patient, Dr. Reddy observed, "Aren't you wearing your wedding ring on the wrong finger?" The lady replied, "Yes, I am! 'Cause, I married the wrong man." In the experience of doctors, nothing beats the account of the woman who complained about her tasteless "Kentucky jelly." A quick investigation revealed that she was using KY jelly.

The work of the oncologists and their staff includes providing psychological and emotional support to cancer patients and their families. They are wrestling with a life-threatening illness and are learning to cope and fight back (at times with the wrong person). But whether it's a stoic patient or a very anxious one, most human beings in these trying times are like "a bicycle that can't stand alone because it is two-tired." The oncologist's challenge is to hear the patient correctly, in a pleasant but subdued manner and strive to make accurate decisions often based on less than accurate information to stay one step ahead of the disease process. It is expected and common for the patient and family to feel overwhelmed by a diagnosis of cancer. In fact, not to feel so would be abnormal.

The doctors and their staff empathize with their patients. "If I were you, I'd do the same thing," they'd say. Dr. Reddy would counsel his patients, "It really doesn't help to look back and think about what could have been done differently, when and by whom. You've got to look forward now, and that will help you think positively." At times, Dr. Reddy added, "Don't forget - your cancer also affects your family and people around you." So while patients may want to vent their anger and frustrations, which in some respects is good in the early stages of the illness, these outbursts may exacerbate the emotions of the very people who are trying to help. In such situations, a psychological counselor may be the best resource for anger management.

An important tool to help the patient navigate the emotional, physical, nutritional and spiritual aspects is the patient's own family, who often are also experiencing the same emotions. As Dr. Reddy would often tell his patients, "A supportive family is not a choice but a crucial requirement. And each family member has a role to play." Hence fighting cancer is a family affair as well as a medical management issue. Cancer affects every aspect of the patients' and their families' lives. And the challenge for the patient is to have family support as "something to rely on instead of having to worry about." Dr. Reddy would encourage this support and tell all involved to get connected, with weekend visits and trips to a relative's home.

Many cancer patients need special motivation and effort to tackle ordinary chores while undergoing treatment. The cancer team is trained to have empathy and to provide encouragement and support. These medical professionals realize that patients entrust their lives to their care. It is an uplifting yet humbling feeling.

AR never failed to genuinely thank and recognize staff members who went "above and beyond the call of duty." Dr. Reddy was, on occasion, rescued by members of his staff, including the "head honchos" who worked to set the course for a smooth sailing ship. Dr. Reddy often said he was fortunate to have "alpha females" who ran the department efficiently and as a well-oiled machine. In fact, because of them, the "alpha male" could immerse himself and be involved in so many activities both within and outside the hospital. The therapy staff was truly Dr. Reddy's pride and his staff felt the same about their doc.

Dr. Reddy learned to deal with the hospital staff. Being a fast learner, he picked up on "women-speak," which has entirely different meanings than the commonly used phrases: "Now work with me on this," (just do what I say); "I am so lucky to work here," (with you imbeciles); "You have to learn to communicate," (just agree with me); "It's your decision," (the correct decision should be obvious by now); "How much d'ya love me?" (I did somethin' that you're really not going to like); "Do what you want," (You'll pay for this later); and "I'm not upset," (Yes, I'm upset, you moron!); "Tell me again how lucky am I to work here," (chuckle). Similarly, Dr. Reddy decoded words like: Fine, Nothing, Go Ahead. Of course, all of these reflect the close working relationships (with humor) the oncologists have with their staffs.

In addition to treating patients in the radiation therapy department, AR was involved with the medical staff in its never-ending meetings, conferences and programs for the hospital and the community. Most were successful and gratifying, while some were eternal end-runs.

Dr. Reddy's work, like that of all radiation oncologists, was most gratifying. The profession pushed the limits of the sciences of medicine, technology, bio-engineering and computers. The work was rewarding partly because of the high cure rates in early-stage cancers, including head and neck, prostate, breast, uterine and rectal cancers, to name a few. Cancer management is always thought-provoking; but the high technology involved in radiation oncology makes it especially stimulating. AR particularly enjoyed his rapport with his patients and thanked them for their trust and for the privilege of taking care of them as their lives hung in the balance. He came to know them and their families personally and supported them with sensitivity and kindness through this difficult period in their lives. He urged them to be active and eat well; he stressed that good nutrition can be half the battle. Then, unlike the cardiologists, Dr. Reddy would add, "All that tastes good may also benefit you. Go for it!"

During the next few days, the athlete-turned-patient on the third floor whom AR saw daily was never far from his mind. In fact, AR was haunted by the youth. Images of his cast were a constant reminder of the risks accompanying ice hockey. The triumph of the last game was being over-taken by the mental picture of the patient in the cast.

Relax, Recoup and Re-evaluate in Upstate New York

&

Curling - A cool sport that's hot on ice

Driving Sense
> 7 <

Utica is a city found in a country setting. Less than a half-hour's drive from Utica are delightful towns and hamlets, and the Reddy family enjoyed short sightseeing trips on weekends. They traveled on Routes 5, 8 and 12 - north, south, east and west - to towns big and small. In the rural, Mennonite, and Amish countrysides, the Reddys would drive along the picturesque country roads and absorb the quiet ambience of the area dotted with farm houses, red barns and silos. Here, they explored the simple, unhurried way of life of people best described as "the salt of the earth." During one trip, the family noticed a horse and buggy carriage parked at a gas station. The sight seemed like an anomaly. They took turns guessing the purpose of the stop – certainly not for gas! They admired human ingenuity when they saw Amish teenagers on roller blades along the main road. The Reddys checked out a part of the country which still thrives on farming but once flourished with leather stocking, textile, paper and knitting mills; logging and related industries. AR valued the ethos of "work hard, live simply and respect the people, land and the animals that surround you." One resident told AR, "The soil can do wonders for the soul."

Those who work with the soil and with nature are as American as apple pie. In spite of motorized equipment, farming is backbreaking work, done as a labor of love. Farmers have a sacred trust with nature that they accept as a force to be reckoned with rather than to battle against. They live with plenty of common-sense and with information they can rely on to keep them ahead of the game. Theirs is a life full of action with a spark of creativity. While most farmers don't play golf, they fear no bunker. They have a clean sense of humor: "To a grower, a day without sunshine is like a night," one farmer is quoted as saying. And another one told the Reddys that his wife trades bread recipes on a "knead-to-know basis." Farmers have their own opinions of "them" city folks: "Those who get too big for their britches will be exposed in the end." Their opinion of politicians: "A lot of money is tainted. Yet, 'taint yours and 'taint mine." Folks in rural America enjoy their unhurried pace of life with quality time together in surroundings where comfort is the essential ingredient to their happy living. Some areas of the New York countryside are still untouched by human technology.

For an in-depth look at country life, the Reddys often coordinated these trips along with social visits to patients and friends to get better acquainted with their families, interests and hobbies. The Reddys visited Stormin' Norman. In his shop, Norm used unique tools to style alluring art objects from deer antlers. His creativity was fascinating!

On another evening, the Reddys accepted Fast Eddie's invitation to visit his converted garage. In it, he spent days planning, designing and executing intricate inlaid woodwork. What made Ed special was that a chronic muscle wasting disorder confined him to a wheelchair. Yet that did not limit his ability to maneuver among his carpentry tools and heaps of various kinds of woods.

At a stopover at Capt. Jack's, AR observed how Jack handmade wooden canoes as a hobby - completely from scratch. His was a tale of science, guts and luck. A social call on Faith Faye, a forty-something mother of two, was an eye-opener. Faith had a full-time job and also volunteered as a teacher to help physically challenged kids. Faith had to breathe through transplanted lungs. She is a living testimony to the benefits of organ donation.

There also was Alice the Wonder Woman whom AR visited on Mother's Day. A single mom, Alice worked hard and put her daughter through college, but that was only one part of her story. Alice was also legally blind and an amputee, complications from her diabetes. She and her co-workers assembled and packaged products used all over the state. None wanted handouts and earned their living by hard work.

As any visitor to the Adirondacks knows, in certain months, black flies cut short the perfect outing. Due to the dedication of volunteers such as Dawson Darlon and his darlin' wife, Dee, the insects in their neck of the woods are no problem. The couple spends their spring weekends killing black fly larvae, guaranteeing a fly-free summer.

Dawson explained, "We treat about twenty-five miles of fast-moving streams, the black fly larvae habitat. We wind up walking at least fifty miles in the process."

Dee added, "Since the larvae don't all mature at the same time, a stream may need to be treated several times during the hatching season." Treatment starts in early April, as soon as the ice-melt has run off into the streams. The snow pack is usually several feet deep at that time, forcing the Darlons to use snowshoes. After the applications, the couple constantly monitors the stream to ensure that the larvae have not progressed to the pupa stage. The battle continues until June. It starts all over again the following spring. The Darlons use the bio-pesticide Bti (*Bacillus thurengensis* var *isrealensis*), a bacterial agent that kills only larvae with alkaline stomachs.

"Since black fly larvae are the only insects in the water with alkaline stomachs, they are the only ones killed," said Dee, adding, "Unlike DDT, Bti bio-degrades 24 hours after being introduced in the stream, making this treatment extremely safe for the environment."

The aim is to kill slightly less than a hundred percent of the larvae, in the stream. A computerized formula is used to ascertain how much Bti to apply and at what intervals. Then, carrying fifty pounds of Bti, assorted measuring gear, lunch and drinking water on their backs, they trek up to the starting point through thick mountain brush, snow and slush. About 24 hours after treatment, the stream is tested to determine the percentage of kill. The "Double D's" reward for all this mental and physical labor is the satisfaction of having done well the volunteer work they were assigned, and the freedom to enjoy the Adirondacks *sans* those pesky flies.

On one trip into the countryside, the Reddy's SUV followed a horse owner who was truckin' and trailerin' and going for a show at a ranch up north. *Choto beta* (young son) asked, "What would happen if the horse trailer had to make a sudden stop." The older son responded, "That would give that colt a jolt." Clearly the son was imitating his father's sense of humor and mannerisms.

Meeting "decent, clean-living folks," some who lived way out in the "sticks" was an education for the Reddys. AR took the opportunity to point out a valuable lesson to his sons. "A great society cannot be built by the work of just a few people. Everyone - the powerful and the weak - has a sacred trust. These people are heroes without attending a 'What does it mean to be a hero?' class. If they saw a need, they took it upon themselves to volunteer their services to address that need. They were proud to help with their talents, energy, time and cold hard cash." For them, their hobbies worked better than therapy. Fast Eddie could have said it for the rest when he revealed to AR, "My creative activities served me well and kept me from knowing my doctor on a first name basis."

"I think our family should take a break from contact sports for a while and just watch others have fun in the snow," Ajit said one morning at breakfast. He had seen an announcement in the newspaper for what would be the perfect event - the annual Ice Harvesting Festival in Millers Mill, less than an hour's drive from Utica. The newspaper carried a photograph of men using handsaws to carve blocks of ice out of the frozen pond. Ajit scanned the road-map to locate the little town.

That cold Sunday morning, the Reddys bundled up and drove along the snow-covered rural roads. Large hand-made signs directed out-of-towners toward the site of the festival. If anyone doubted that Millers Mill was sparsely populated, they merely had to catch sight of an unimposing sign nailed to a post at the edge of the town. It read, "Downtown Millers Mill. Population: 28 plus."

As the Reddys pulled into the makeshift parking lot, they were fascinated by a snow-mobiler making large figure-of-eights in fields covered with fresh snow. His white, undulating canvas stretched over several acres, allowing the driver to make wide turns. During the few minutes the Reddys stood and watched this side-show, the driver had created an artistic crisscross of multiple intersecting arcs.

They chalked up that viewing experience as a bonus to the main purpose of the day's trip. A short walk from the parking lot brought them to a 150-foot wide, newly-ploughed circular clearing on the iced-over lake. Several spectators had already gathered along the bridge overlooking the area. Always gregarious, the Reddys struck up a conversation with a couple standing next to them. The couple was from nearby Ilion and was delighted to share what they knew about the event with the Reddys. "It's been an annual event for the past century, and became well-known after it was featured in the TV show 'On the Road with Charles Kuralt'. Originally, the ice was used to keep milk cold during the summer, before refrigeration was commonly available. Today, the ice is stored in a barn, covered with straw, and used at the ice cream social hosted by the residents in July," the woman told the Reddys. "It's a wonderful way for the community to have fun in the middle of our upstate winters and then again in the summer," she added while her husband busied himself with clicking his camera.

At ten, several men with five-foot long manual saws stepped out onto the ice. AR quipped, "All the testosterone of this town is on ice."

The incision around the first block was made - about two feet long and 18 inches wide and deep. The men, using a pair of metal tongs that stood as tall as they did, hoisted that initial block onto the ice. In a few minutes, eight more blocks lined the side of the widening hole.

By this time, some adventurous bystanders had made their way onto the ice, along with their children and dogs. Some men even volunteered to help saw the ice. It didn't appear physically taxing. Much like loggers do, the men moved the more recent floes to the spot closest to the waiting front-loader. A wooden sled drawn by two Clysdale horses took the ice to a nearby barn. There the ice was covered and stored to await the July ice cream social, which followed the Millers Mill Sundae Run and 5-K Road Race. Ice harvesting used to be big business in many towns bordering the lakes prior to the days of refrigeration.

The frigid temperatures made the Reddys glad that hot coffee and lunch were being served in the Grange Hall. The sounds of chatter and hearty laughter inside were in sharp contrast to the stillness and cold outside. The camaraderie between the hosts and diners was palpable.

The other quaint towns that the Reddys loved to visit several times a year included nearby Camden, Oneida and Rome (home of the Griffis Air Force Base). These towns had long, glorious histories and their Victorian homes lined the streets, giving these towns a fairy-tale appearance. Their graceful front porches and cupolas are remnants of an elegant era gone by. Situated between these towns are Verona and the Turning Stone Casino run by the Oneida Native Americans.

Dr. Patel, the Reddys' long-time friend, invited AR to the Turning Stone Casino for Sunday brunch. This is where locals and visitors go when looking for fun and excitement - golf, entertainment, fine dining and "a piece of the action." The interactive high-tech playground has everything for the serious and not-so-serious gaming enthusiasts – blackjack and baccarat tables, slot machines, round-the-clock poker, high-stakes bingo, Braille bingo, craps, keno, and more.

Being the VIP that he was, Dr. Patel was invited to special events at the casino. His standing was linked to his service to the community, his availability for emergency cases, and his care for important patrons of the casino rather than any of his gaming interests. Dr. Patel's patronage of the fine dining at the casino, and his attendance at medical conferences held there made him a frequent guest.

The Oneidas were the original inhabitants of MoVa. White colonists first settled along the eastern seaboard of the continent, in both the U.S. and Canada. The New Englanders later moved west along the

Mohawk River into Oneida territory and Utica. This pattern continued for three hundred years. The Oneidas were hospitable and helped the pioneers rid themselves of the colonial yoke during the Revolutionary Wars, particularly during the Battle of Oriskany with General Nicholas Herkimer in 1777, later at Saratoga, and at Valley Forge with General George Washington in 1778. After a period of benign neglect, Oneidas have made a comeback with economic, social and cultural advances.

While touring the Turning Stone Casino, the doctors' guide informed them that, "Through the casino and numerous other business enterprises, the Oneidas are now the biggest employers in the county, employing more that 4,000 workers, 95 percent of who are non-Native Americans. Through vendor contracts, the tribe contributes to the livelihood of tens of thousands more across the upstate region."

The Oneidas have not forgotten their roots and their culture. The community, in keeping with tradition, is run by a Men's Council and Clan Mothers. The Oneidas raise the second largest herd of Angus cattle in the Northeast, grow a number of traditional crops, and provide their members with healthcare, graduate and post-graduate education, as well as housing. They are also engaged in the revival of their native language as well as wildlife and swamp conservation. The history of the Oneidas and other Native Americans can be explored through local exhibits at the Shako: WI Cultural Center and the National Museum of the American Indian at the Smithsonian Institute in Washington, D.C. The most compelling exhibit is a bronze statue of Shenandoah - the Oneida chief, Polly Cooper - the Oneida woman, and General George Washington. The sculpture's caption, "Allies in War, Partners in Peace" echoes the spirit of the new country after the Revolutionary War.

The casino is geared to pampering its high-flying customers who stay at its resort seeking fun-filled leisure. Guests such as Drs. Patel and Reddy enjoy golfing on the three magnificent 18-hole courses and two nine-hole courses. The masterpiece courses (Shenandoah, Kaluyhat and Atunyote) were designed by golf champs Rick Smith, Robert Trent Jones, Jr. and Tom Fazio. The casino aficionado told the docs, "These courses have received accolades such as 'One of Ten Best' places to play; a Golf Masterpiece; America's Best; World Class; Championship Caliber Layout; a New York PGA Championship Course; and a Certified Signature Sanctuary Course."

The golfers who visit Turning Stone range from the high handicappers like Drs. Patel and Reddy to the most accomplished players and pros. The links are one of seventeen courses across the U.S. which have received the Audubon International Signature Sanctuary status for preserving and enhancing the environment. After a round, the guests can spend the evening at the 5,000-seat Event Center or at the 800-seat showroom enjoying a celebrity performance or a sporting event. Clearly, when it's time to play, the Turning Stone Casino at Oneida is a wonderful playground. (*The Casino's print and electronic brochures).*

After an enjoyable meal of authentic Mediterranean dishes and outstanding wines at one of the resort's gourmet restaurants, the two docs ordered coffee and an assortment of dessert delicacies. Then, they settled down at the Twin Waterfalls; the tropical atmosphere inside was in sharp contrast to the snow-covered scenery outside. Dr. Patel picked this site as the perfect spot for him and AR to talk about ice hockey and their mutual concerns, which were identical but below each other's radar. Before they could settle down to talk, the CEO of Turning Stone passed by and recognized his friend, Dr. Patel. After greeting the docs warmly, the CEO invited them for a helicopter ride from the casino's newly installed helipad. In an impulsive moment, the two took him up on his generous offer, and off they went for an aerial view of the western region, including Syracuse's historical Armory Square and Onondaga Lake. The friends recalled their trips to MoST (Museum of Science and Technology) and the IMAX Theater (the only one in upstate New York).

The flight then took them west over the Bristol Mountain winter resort where they checked out the downhill ski slopes from the air. The two avid skiers and their families had tried the slopes in years gone by. They relived the experiences of those enjoyable winters. The guide told them, "The Mountain has a summit elevation of 2,200 feet with several runs, including a long two-mile run. The vertical rise is 1,200 feet, making it the highest resort between the Adirondacks, Catskills and the Rockies. The 32 slopes and trails meet the needs of most visitors with varying skiing abilities. The Bristol Mountain drop is truly vertical with the entire right side of the mountain being very steep." (*The resort's electronic and print information).* The docs took a closer look at this great ski resort and imagined skiing down the slopes; Dr. Patel exclaimed, "That's pretty cool!" Clearly from up here, they had breathtaking views. Snowboarders describe Bristol as "extreme." Night illumination of the ski trails allows Bristol Mountain skiers to experience the thrill of skiing and riding under a star-lit sky. The docs wished they had their cameras with them since, they confessed, "our photographic memories never got developed."

The helicopter then turned north over Beaver Lake Nature Center which the docs had visited two summers ago. They recalled touring the wetlands, home to more than 200 species of native wildlife, tens of thousands of migratory birds, frogs and turtles, as well as a large variety of flowers and plants. The friends made plans to take their families on a snowshoe hike there later in the winter. As they returned to the casino, the doctors realized it was getting late - a lot later than they had told their wives to expect. They decided to head home. The task at hand had not been accomplished. Lunch and the helicopter ride left no time for the physicians to have their heart-to-heart chat.

The sight of the athlete-turned-patient on the hospital's fifth floor was now indelibly etched on the minds of both docs. Every day's meeting with that patient was a soul-searching experience for AR who still nursed dull aches and pains in his joints. The "high fives" of friends or peers congratulating him on his success at the ice hockey game were now met with less and less enthusiasm and passion. It did not help when a buddy commented, "Sure, there have been injuries and even some deaths in ice hockey, yet most injuries are not really that serious." AR was honest with himself. He realized he was having doubts about his involvement in the game. Yet, how would he tell his family, friends and those who had encouraged him all the way?

To help AR recover from his physical and mental bruises and to enjoy the upcoming weekend, the Reddy family decided to visit scenic Old Forge. The hamlet, located about 60 miles north of Utica is one of the southwest gateways to the Adirondack Park which stretches over nearly a third of New York State. The park comprises about 6 million acres (9,375 square miles) of pristine forest and is the largest nature preserve outside of Alaska. Though it is easily accessible, the park is miles from any noise, pollution and the clamor of civilization.

With their car on cruise control and Ravi Shankar's music on the CD, the Reddys traveled along charming Route 12. They laughed heartily when they spotted a mannequin's arm sticking out of the luggage carrier atop a minivan; the flopping arm looked as if it was waving to passing motorists. When they were together, the Reddys could appreciate humor even during stressful times.

Rest and Recuperation
> 8 <

As the Reddys drove north, they enjoyed the sights of the rolling hills that form the foothills of the Adirondack range, the snow-clad valleys and the small towns north of Utica. They took in the breathtaking scenery - the white snow-capped mountains in the distance - and talked about their next ski trip before the season ended. They joined Route 28 that took them to the park entrance; here the landscape changed to a more wooded one. As they did during all of their road trips, the family had a ball pointing out humorous sights and playing trivia games along the way. The Town of Webb is the largest township in New York State. It is named after Dr. William Seward Webb, son-in-law of William H. Vanderbilt and builder of the Mohawk & Malone Railroad (St. Lawrence and Adirondack Railway) in 1892. It was called M&M, especially by its employees. The project was completed in 18 months and the railroad still survives as the Adirondack Scenic Railroad. When the railroad was first built, the township was reminiscent of an old frontier town in the “Wild West.” Gradually, the railways brought multitudes of people who were either looking for employment as loggers or for fun and relaxation in this region of the Adirondack Mountains. The township's year-round residents now number 2,000; during the tourist season, that number increases to tens of thousands.

In the spring, the Reddy family often joined others from Utica and drove to Old Forge for a day of whitewater rafting or kayaking. Along the way they would catch sight of millions of wild flowers in full bloom and whitetail fawn gamboling in the first, fresh grass of the season while their parents grazed or strutted alongside.

Bill Green, whom the Reddys met on their last visit to Old Forge, informed them, “The cooling waters make fish more active; as a result, interest in fishing rises in the spring season. This, the heart of the Adirondacks, is a timeless natural world where ‘forever wild’ and ‘nature preserve’ are not wishful thinking, but the law. The Park is one of the most successful nature conservation projects in the country.”

Last summer, the Reddys had ridden the Adirondack Scenic Railroad from Utica to Old Forge. The tour guide, Richard Icicle, provided an informative commentary over the PA system. The region calls itself the "Year Round Adirondack Relaxation" and is famed for its hiking trails in the deep wilderness as well as its abundant locations for canoeing, fishing, boating, paddling, kayaking and wind surfing. The downhill and cross-country ski trails double as mountain bike paths in the summer when diamond biking replaces diamond skiing. Horseback riding, golfing and seaplane rides are the other attractions.

Old Forge was the Reddys' favorite haunt throughout the year because the spectacular change of seasons provides fertile fodder for lively conversation. For short ski trips, the McCauley Mountain is the "best hardcore little mountain" with an altitude of 23,000 feet, and a steep drop of 633 vertical feet. It has between 14 and 21 trails covering 3,000 to 5,000 feet in length. One can zip back to the top on double chair lifts, T-bar lifts or by a rope tow. The mountain offers challenges to the best of skiers. (*Resort's print and electronic brochures).*

AR gave his children a short lesson. "This ski slope is the most challenging little mountain in the upstate region. The average snowfall here is 200 inches. All levels of skiers find slopes and trails to meet and challenge their skills." Down in the hamlet, the pines were laden with snow and the homes were topped with icicled roofs. Its 500 miles of groomed, packed trails for snowmobiling has earned Old Forge the title of "Snowmobile Capital of the Northeast."

Snow-shoeing is a great family activity, simple enough for anyone who can walk. The sport is enjoyed in places not accessible to cross-country skis or snowmobiles. Snowshoes permit a casual hike or an alpine climb in the environs of Old Forge. The area also boasts facilities for tobogganing, snow-boarding, snow tubing, ice skating, ice fishing, sledding, and cross-country skiing for various skill levels. Some try the new sport of cross-country skate skiing and telemarking. The Ski Patrol Training Center for central New York is also located there. Understandably, the area has produced some internationally-ranked skiers. Two Olympic skiers have come from Old Forge, including the 1975 world professional Alpine ski champion, Hank Kashiwa.

In town, the Reddys met James, a historian who shared with others his knowledge of Old Forge. "The area has activities to please all kinds of sports enthusiasts. Attractions include sailing the Fulton Lakes which are named in honor of Robert Fulton, an early state surveyor. There are many lakes, eight of which are named in numerical order. The best known to whitewater rafters is the meandering Moose River, which is as diverse as it is spectacular and provides the perfect rafting trip. One can enjoy the jagged rock-faces towering over the rivers and lakes while floating away one's stress." The Reddys invited James to a hearty lunch, a genuine body booster. Along with many other visitors, they reveled in the delightful camaraderie and the isolated splendor of the region – perfect antidotes for tired bodies and drooping spirits.

Last year, the Reddy family had met Good-Time Charley, who told them, "The rafting levels span from easy to extremely challenging. The Middle Moose is ideal for leisurely paddles along the scenic river which is not intense or technical until you encounter the first rapid. The lower part of the river is very difficult to maneuver and recommended only for the experienced. Rafters are cautioned to have a high skill level of four or five before taking on this part of the river where the trip is truly an adrenaline-filled adventure of a lifetime. A rafting trip down the river is a combination of teamwork, fun and outdoor adventure. This world-class rafting is the ultimate in outdoor adventure thrills. Whether you're in the water or on the banks, you can appreciate the force of nature and have a memorable family outing."

The Adirondack Park is not a federal, but a New York State Park created in 1892 and covers an area more than double the size of Yellowstone and Yosemite National Parks combined. The Adirondack Park has awe-inspiring views of rugged ridges and heavily wooded valleys. Historian George Snow informed the Reddys, "A number of American presidents have visited the park. While he was being driven from Mt. Marcy to North Creek in the early morning hours of September 14, 1901, Vice-President Theodore Roosevelt learned that President William McKinley had died. He had been shot in Buffalo, New York, eight days earlier. At the North Creek station, TR was informally sworn in as the 26th president of the United States." At that time, the President's security detail consisted of perhaps one or two individuals. Today, security for the president involves five or six layers of agencies, including FATASS (Federal Air Transportation and Airport Security Service). George continued his history lesson. "Presidents Benjamin Harrison, Grover Cleveland, Warren Harding and Calvin Coolidge owned summer homes here. These are just four of the ten U.S. presidents who have visited the park. A visit to the Adirondacks is like reliving history."

As there was so much to learn about the region, the Reddy family decided to take a guided bus tour. Along the way, the park service ranger, Rolling Sherman, informed the group, "Famous visitors to the

Park included Robert Louis Stevenson, the author of 'Treasure Island', 'The Strange Case of Dr. Jekyll and Mr. Hyde,' and 'The Master of Ballentrae: A Winter's Tale'. Stevenson had a cottage at Saranac Lake. So did Sigmund Freud, and the families of Stephen Crane, Winslow Homer, WW Durant, the Vanderbilts and other 'robber barons' who were rail tycoons, financiers and captains of American Industry." This was the Gilded Age of America - between the Civil War and the First World War.

Sherman added, "Other visitors to the park included members of 'The Philosophers' Camp' which was built in 1858. Its most famous member was Ralph Waldo Emerson. The members tested theories of Transcendentalism and communing with nature; Emerson also wrote the poem 'The Adirondacks'. Esther Mountain is named after Esther Macomb, who made the first recorded ascent of the peak when she was just 15 years old. It is one of the 46 highest peaks in the Adirondacks and the only one named after a woman. The park has about 3,000 lakes and ponds and 36,000 miles of rivers, brooks and streams. Here serenity, beauty and history abound." *(The park's print and electronic brochures).*

Along with the various physical activities, tourists also engage in sedentary and solitary pastimes. The previous season, the Reddys had met the mountain man himself, Robert Hill, who told them, "The area is a delight for bird watchers – ducks, mallards, American blacks, blue-winged and green-winged teals, American widgeons, northern shovelers and wood ducks. Among the tens of thousands of migratory birds that pass through are the canvas backs, scup, redheads and common and hooded mergansers, great blue herons, green backed herons, American coots, common moochers, and bitterns."

The rugged man smoothed down his long beard and continued, "Fishermen angle for small-and large-mouth bass, bullheads, perch, northern pike, speckled, brook, brown, rainbow and lake trout, landlocked salmon and a variety of pan fish. The fisher, pine marten and spruce grouse are distinctive wildlife." The lakes make the perfect setting for loons which require almost a quarter-mile of water on which to run before becoming airborne. These creatures are long-lived and territorial, often returning annually to the same lake to breed. Bald eagles, peregrine falcons, ospreys, ravens, beaver and moose have all made a comeback.

For year-round residents, the lakes, rivers and streams become part of their life and psyche. City life holds little lure for them. Instead, they prefer to absorb all the beauty and magic that nature has to offer. As Jack Frost pointed out, "Neither time nor advancement will change the environment here. No other place is quite like it. The Adirondack Mountains present the perfect atmosphere for high energy athletes and quiet philosophers alike. Most are attracted to the variety of flora, fauna and the captivating sights of wildlife habitats. The peace and calming influence of water flowing down from the mountains is therapeutic. As the water-towers of the world, what happens on the mountain tops affects every thing that lies in the valleys and seas."

Each of the hamlets has its own year-round attractions - fairs, festivals, concerts, lectures, and art shows. Visitors can revel in the foliage and various ethnic festivals, including Oktoberfest. There are boat planes and boat cruises. The Reddys enjoyed the mountains - their majesty, stability and strength - and the spectacular granite peaks and forest slopes which took on a special beauty in the fall. It was the season when the Reddys could catch numerous sightings of wildlife: deer, otter, owl, as well as native and migratory birds such as the great blue heron, Canada geese, mallard ducks, and the common loon. Nothing beats the majestic tapestry created by brilliant red, yellow and orange leaves mixed with evergreen pines against a clear blue sky. The beech-birch-maple group reaches its crowning glory in the Adirondack forests. The Reddys visits to Old Forge and the Park were always hectic ones. Often, AR would say, "Ok guys, let's check this one out." And with that invitation they were off to explore another facet of the area.

Yet on this visit, it was quiet relaxation amid nature's beauty which Ajit and Anil welcomed. They still had to deal with their concerns about their father's safety as an ice hockey player. The strain of the practices and games was beginning to show on their father's face; he was experiencing increasingly pensive moments. The boys felt compelled to attend all their father's ice hockey practice and competitive games which meant they had less time to spend with their own friends. Though the sons were very supportive of their dad, their priorities often did not match. The issue of whether their father should continue his involvement in such a strenuous sport continued to surface and the boys decided to broach the issue with their mother to see where she stood on it.

Anita and her sons rehashed the pros and cons but could not come to any consensus on the final verdict. Should AR or shouldn't he continue to play? The family was at a crossroad. Anita was determined to once again raise the issue of the "old boy" playing ice hockey. However, there was a time and place for everything. During the nightly family time together there was plenty of affection and genuine concern for one another. Anita did not feel the family was unduly stressed, but tension was just under the surface. Soon, she would have to seize the opportunity to admit the family's concerns to AR.

Anita decided the family needed a long weekend break and decided on a trip north to Alexandria Bay, located in the heart of the 1000 Islands. The two-hour trip would take them to an area that the Native Americans named "The Garden of the Great Spirit" which is located on the banks of the St. Lawrence River and Lake Ontario. In 1687, the French cartographer, Jean Desbayes, christened the region between the U.S. and Canada "Les Milles Iles" – The Thousand Islands. There are more than 1,800 islands -1,864 to be exact. To be part of the official count, an island has to be above water year-round and support at least two trees. This region was the site of numerous encounters between the two neighboring countries during the battle of 1812. Since the late eighteenth century, the area has become a vacation destination. Wealthy residents of New York and Canada started building summer homes on private islands where the only access to each house was often by boat and the home's garage door would descend to just six inches above water. Among these exquisite homes is Singer Castle, a 100-year-old 'mysterious' landmark on Dark Island built for Frederick Bourne, president of Singer sewing machines.

On the trip up north on Interstate 81, the Reddy family had a lot of fun guessing the nicknames of various states. So they continued the game with nicknames of well-known cities in the U.S. Paterson, New Jersey, is referred to as Silk City; Toledo, Ohio, is labeled the Glass Capital; and Allentown, Pennsylvania, is dubbed Cement City. The enthusiasm for these mental games was so high that a break to "make one's bladder gladder" did not interrupt the competition; young Anil made sure of that. The game continued until the Reddys reached Alex Bay, making the trip yet another memorable outing for the family.

During their visit to the Thousand Islands, the Reddys met Bridget Steel of the Army Corps of Engineers, who told them, "Construction of the Thousand Islands International Bridge began on April 30, 1937; the official opening of the bridge was held in 1938. The structure is a series of bridges across the St. Lawrence River and is located at the western end of St. Lawrence River and the Thousand Islands. The bridge is a symbol of how two countries can live side by side, cooperate and allow their people to easily cross over to enjoy their neighbor's hospitality." (*1000-Islands print and electronic brochures).*

The bridge system extends from near the Alex Bay to nearby Gananoque, covering a distance of eight-and-a-half miles and providing a direct connection between America's Interstate 81 and Canada's Highway 401. The traffic on the bridge flows efficiently probably because it is run not by either government but by the Thousand Island Bridge Authority, an international agency which also oversees the Boldt Castle located on one of the islands. The multi-span bridge provides a convenient panoramic aerial view of the 1000 Islands and the cargo ships that sail from the Atlantic to the Great Lakes. The overpass is a 4,500-foot suspension bridge spanning the American channel from the mainland to Wellesley Island and then crosses the international border via a suspension bridge with an 800-foot main span, between Wellesley Island and Hill Island in Canada.

The Reddys enjoyed the Thousand Islands in the winter because the area provided solitude and serene scenes of nature, all covered in a white blanket of snow. The ambiance was one of *amour real* (real love). Between the walks and the hearty snacks, the family played a wacky word-wrapping game and came up with the following list:

Bull Moose on the loose;
See you in St. Louis, Louis;
Frank Lloyd Wright got it right;
Bloomin' thing is blooming again;
To take time you have to make time;
Regrip it and really rip it (the golf club);
For a great game of golf, hurtle to Myrtle;
Ladies can get a bikini for a ridiculous figure;
The women's movement is now broad based;
Can't un-relate to someone who is related to you;
The police raided the nudist colony and got busted.
Queen Mary (ship) is having her bottom scrapped;
You're always a wiener at the Las Olas restaurant!

During the summer, the Reddy family loved taking boat cruises on Alex Bay to enjoy the scenery or visit the area's museums, castles and well-preserved mansions. They had other choices, including wreck-diving, fishing, birding, whitewater rafting and go-kart racing but these held little interest for the Reddys. They preferred companionable family time together, long summer walks and time to unwind. A vacation here was relaxing and provided fun for the entire family. They especially enjoyed the beautiful sunsets when they dined out.

Tour director Florence Lawrence told the Reddys, "A major attraction in this area is the Boldt Castle built by George Boldt, the owner of the Waldorf-Astoria Hotel in New York City. The German-style castle which was built on Heart Island has six stories with 120 rooms and has its own yacht house on Wellesley Island with a drawbridge and Italian gardens. The castle has been compared to the Taj Mahal, which has been called 'the grandest Gilded Age Mansion – a testament to one man's tragic love story'." *(Boldt Castle's print and electronic brochures).*

On their return home after fun and fabulous food in the Thousand Islands, the Reddys laughed together and played the trivia game of matching coins with the famous faces on them. Since the family was focused on the topic of coins, Anita reminded the kids about the Susan B. Anthony dollar which honors the Rochester, New York, native. She led the Women's Suffrage Movement which resulted in women's voting rights and the 19th Amendment of the Constitution. Dad talked of the Sacagawea dollar portraying the Shoshone Indian lady and her son Jean Baptiste who led Lewis and Clark's "Corps of Discovery Expedition" through the Northwest Territory.

The issue of AR's safety as an ice hockey player was still unresolved. Anita evaluated the risks involved in the sport and her husband's enthusiasm for it. He'd spent a lot of time that year in practice sessions and had developed camaraderie with the team. She remembered how he'd taught their sons the sport in their own backyard ever since the boys were toddlers. Now her hubby was a valuable player on his team and would hate to let his fellow players down. On the other hand, her family was feeling the strain.

Anita's goal was to rescue AR before he suffered any serious injury. AR, too, had similar concerns of his own. There were times when he said to himself, "I am behaving like a 'Dad Adrift'." The kids asked themselves, "How much more can we take of this 'will he, won't he' predicament?" Anita decided her "perfect timing" strategy was becoming, "an escape to nowhere!" Anita realized that if she did not work to resolve the issue quickly, the family might be forced to deal with severe injuries to AR, perhaps during the very next game.

The thought was scary. She told herself, "He is one dear baby I can't throw out with the bathwater." Anita saw that she and AR were becoming stressed-out parents. Life for her was changing from "You take my breath away," to "I feel like I'm suffocating." Whenever she tried to approach the subject with her husband, she could not find the right words to express her fears for his safety and her own sense of insecurity. There was no loss of affection between them. Yet the laughter that soothed the mind and restored the body could not balance the tears and fears that she also felt. Perhaps a little good old-fashioned pillow-talk might have the desired effect and help solve the problem. When the lights went out so did the words she'd been practicing; and in the days that followed, the sequence of events repeated itself. Whichever way Anita looked at it, she could not bring herself to counsel her husband to give up the sport he enjoyed.

One evening when she was feeling especially helpless, Anita decided to talk to her mother-in-law and solicit her help in this delicate situation. It was to Anita's advantage that they shared a harmonious family relationship. Grandma Reddy, too, was having misgivings about her son playing such a physical sport. With ease and kindness, as she had done a million times in the past, she offered to have a chat with her *beta* (son) that evening. After dinner was done and the dishes put away, Grandma and AR lingered at the dinner table – he, from exhaustion; she, with a definite purpose in mind.

At an opportune moment, grandma Reddy began, "Son, *beta*, you're getting advice from people who don't know anything about ice hockey. Locals who have never held a hockey stick and *desis* who have never worn ice skates are cheering you on and giving you tips. And so, *bichara* (pitiful person), you are lost and confused."

Grandma Reddy had a calm, cool and confident manner. She went on to add bluntly, "Take your mother's advice. A contact sport such as ice hockey is not meant for a string-bean like you. I think you'd do much better in curling, just like our neighbor, Elmer, does. In all the years he has been a curler, he has never been injured. And that is the bottom line. Think about it."

Grandma Reddy added, "When we first came to Utica, Elmer invited us to watch his team play at the curling club in town. He referred to curling as 'a cool sport that's hot on ice!' After that, I loved following the curling competition at the 2002 Salt Lake City Winter Olympics. With your eye-hand coordination skill you, too, could be a good player. It is easy, extremely safe, and fun for the whole family – a wonderful way to spend the winter." She compared curling to shuffleboard, bocce ball, bowling and chess, all played on ice. Then she cleverly added, "But a lot more skill is demanded from a curler than from a bowler."

Grandma Reddy's recommendation and advice came at a very propitious moment. They cut through all the soul-searching that everyone in the Reddy family had been doing. The issue had been lurking on the surface, but her direct approach "lanced the boil." As the matriarch, she rarely spoke; when she did, it was always in a soft voice and with dignified confidence. Like most women of her age, she had wisdom gleaned from years of experience.

Grandma also had a delightful sense of humor. She loved telling and retelling the "older than dirt" stories. She had a "when I was your age" story for any situation. "We didn't have fast food when I was growing up. All the food was slow," she'd say. "My parents never drove us to games because we never had a car. I owned a bicycle that had only one speed – Slow. We didn't have a TV either, so we entertained each other with music, acting and stories." Anil told his grandma, "Your mother was lucky not to have a car." He explained, "My friend, Timmy, told us that his mom has been stopped so often for speeding that the police have given her a season ticket."

Curling is just one of the many highlights in Oneida County. The county is also known for its many colleges such as Hamilton College, chartered in 1793, past and present businesses including the Vernon Downs Horse Racing track, Oneida Arts, Oneida Glass, Oneida Pottery, Oneida Cutlery, Oneida Textiles and other fabric-related industries during the "loom to boom" era. Utica was an important rail junction; at its "rail peak" in the early 1900s about 100 trains stopped at the station daily. Now, Utica hosts The Boilermaker, the largest 15-K (9.3 miles) run which ranks among the "Top 100" endurance races in the country. Interest in the event is so great that the organizers have capped the number of participants to 11,000 runners and 3,500 walkers (8-K), with unlimited youth runners and wheel-chair division participants. The event is held on the first Sunday after July 4.

When Opportunity Knocks
> 9 <

It turns out AR's family was not the only one doing some soul-searching about ice hockey. While they were concerned about physical injuries, some other dads in the league were going through other stresses associated with the competition. More than a few dads reported that their families had shifted gears and gone from "go-dad-go"...and..."fab-dad" to "take it easy, dad"...and..."chill pop."

Facing Our Challenges

When life deals one a blow,
And events are not aglow.
If sailing is against the wind,
And the days are often descending.

When the illness one has to bear,
Sorrows with no one to care,
Living is like one continuous combating,
Emotions a continuous tear-drop pouring,

When the bank-balance is down to the dime,
And obligations are overwhelming all the time.
We yearn to beam with a smile mile-high
Yet we moan and groan with a deep sigh.

When care is pressing one down,
Relax one must...but not with a frown.
Failure is triumph with a curve and a twist.
One will still succeed if one continues to persist,

Make lemonade from lemons recovered,
the results of our talents when they are discovered.
One never can discern how close we really are,
Sweet triumph may be within reach instead of very far.

The sport of curling arrived in Utica along with émigrés from Great Britain who came to the U.S. in large numbers in the early 1800s to build the Erie Canal. The Utica Curling Club was formed in 1868, making it one of the older clubs in the U.S. The club is in Whitestown, a suburb of Utica, and is the largest, with six sheets of ice; it has hosted numerous national championships, international and Olympic Qualifier events.

Curling originated in the 1500s, when it was played on frozen lakes (lochs) in Northern Europe. Scotland is accredited with providing the world with curling, golf and Scotch. Some say curling, as it is now known, was preceded by a similar game called "*Eisschissen*" - ice-shooting involving the use of a *loofie* - played in parts of Europe. More than thirty countries now have curling clubs and the sport is monitored by the World Curling Federation. As a winter sporting event, curling shot to prominence after it was first included in the 1998 Olympic Games at Nagano, Japan. Since then, several national and international meets as well as extensive television coverage at the Utah Olympics have given this sport worldwide recognition.

Every October, the Utica Club hosts the annual international "I Love New York Curling Open." The club was randomly selected to host the 2005 North American Championship and the Continental Cup match-up between the North American and European champs.

Elmer Morrison was delighted to invite AR to the Utica Curling Club. The friendly club members made AR feel right at home at the club, where the room's temperature was kept at 42 degrees Fahrenheit and the temperature on the ice was 24.5 degrees Fahrenheit. After AR became familiar with the layout of the premises, he received his first lesson on the techniques of sliding the rocks. The sport, he soon found out, demanded great control of movement as well as finely-tuned hand-eye coordination. This was a new challenge that AR decided to tackle. His ingrained, top-notch sporting habits and techniques were an asset to him. Once he mastered the basic strategies, he learned the rules and then began picking up the subtle maneuvers. AR tapped into his analytical side, plotting the shape of things to come. The learning curve was short.

He could hardly wait to return home and tell his wife about the new sport. "I have found another outlet for my energy. Curling is an amazing sport!" he announced. He shared information on some of the finer points of the sport with his sons. "There's a fine line between too much and not enough energy when delivering the stone," he said. Then he added a dollop of his characteristic humor, "The hardest part of curling is the ice."

The players had to be adept at offense and defense. Atul's years of ice hockey had taught him that good judgment comes in good time. He would be patient and merely enjoy participating in this new sport at the beginner's level.

After the games, it was time for "Broom Stacking" - having drinks together. Before the teams went into the recreation area for their tall frosted ones, the players would stack the brooms they had just used in the game. Thus the term "broom stacking" was coined. The post game camaraderie is considered part of the game. Traditionally, winners pay for the first round of drinks. Every curling club has at least a bar for this important social aspect of the game. At smaller clubs, curlers trickle in with six-packs of beer in tow. Curling is believed to be the only sport where opposing teams socialize after the game and every player is "part of the gang." While they socialized, the players exchanged anecdotes and replayed deliveries. Curling is not a contact sport but a blend of competition, good sportsmanship and decorum. It has no referees or judges (except in competitive games) and relies on an honor system. Curlers as a group tend to believe laughter soothes the mind and restores the body. At special-event games, their celebrations are even grander.

The competition lane /sheet is 146 feet long and is covered with an ice sheet half an inch thick; the playing length is 130 feet by 15 feet wide. The game is played by two teams of four players each. The aim is to slide a 42-pound granite stone or rock down the lane and have it come to a halt closest to the "tee" at the other end. The ice has the texture of an orange peel and the stone rides on the raised pebbled layer of ice, without touching the ice's lower flat surface. The player holds the handle atop the stone, slides on one knee and the opposite foot and then releases (not pushes) the stone. The thrust is provided by the body's motion, aided by a flick of the wrist to curve or "curl" the stone in the desired direction. Slowly, the stone progresses with one or two spins as it glides along to reach the "tee" or knock the opponent's rocks out of play. The rocks are directed toward the bull's eye at the center of a circular target called the "house," which is 12 feet in diameter and situated at each end of the lane. Within this house there are two other circles four feet and eight feet in diameter, and the tee is located in the center. This allows the game to be played from both ends of the lane. Curling is usually a team sport but now individual competition is gaining ground.

A team called a "rink" is led by a captain or "skip" who is in charge of both providing strategy and reading the ice to determine how much the rock is curling. The first player of the team is called a "lead" and throws the first rocks. He is followed by the second player and then the "vice- skip". The skip plays last, after directing the other players on the best direction of their stones. The last stone played is called the "hammer." Each player throws two rocks, alternating with his opponent. This is usually done eight times during regular games and ten times in championship rounds. As the rocks travel down the lane, they tend to curve, which some believe explains how the sport got its name. Each "inning" involves throwing all sixteen rocks and measuring the points, with the rock closest to the center earning one point. Only one team can score points during any inning. To help the rock reach its intended spot, team members assist by "sweeping." The brooms were originally made of corncob; today a push broom made of synthetic shimmies is used. Two team members vigorously sweep or brush the ice in front of the rock. This friction polishes the ice and briefly heats the surface, melting the ice. The "hydroplane effect" encourages the rock to slide, curl less and travel as much as 10 to 15 feet farther than if no sweeping occurred. The skill is to have the tiny ice pebbles on the surface break in the same direction. Ironically, the lack of ice pebbles causes too much ice-friction and deprives the game of its grace.

Curling is played from October through mid-April in more than thirty countries, including the circumpolar region. In the U.S., there are about 125 active curling clubs with 15,000 members. However, that number is miniscule compared to Canada where the game is immensely popular, ranking second only to ice hockey. In the under-populated state of British Columbia alone, there are 107 active curling clubs. Of course, Canada is home to many immigrants from Great Britain where the game originated. This explains its popularity in Canada, where there are 1.2 million curlers (80 percent of the world's curlers).

The curlers keenly keep abreast of the North American Games, the National Championship Games (Brier Cup), the Continental Cup and Winter Olympics. The 2006 Winter Olympics will be held in Turin, Italy.

At the local club level, the game is a family sport and includes players of all ages. Children as young as four years old play, using a 20-pound stone. There is no mandatory retirement age.

While curling is similar to golf, with the player trying to get the ball close to the pin, the curling club more closely resembles a bowling alley on league night – the spectators watch from behind a glass screen in the upper gallery. Curling is a lot more difficult than it appears to be at first glance. It is a test of one's concentration and dexterity in maneuvering the stone through its trajectory, release and rotation. The game combines individual skill and teamwork. It takes about two weeks to learn the fundamentals of the game; like golf, it takes a lifetime to master it. Most experts agree that only in about the third year of playing does one understand how complicated the game is; it takes five years to actually become good at the sport. Curling is all about strategy and the reading of the ice, a thinking person's game in which the sense of touch and control make all the difference. Hence the game is often described as "chess on ice" with its own art-form.

The game is played by both men's and women's teams, and also by mixed teams. Because of their upper body strength, men usually perform better at heavy sliding for double and triple take-out shots and at sweeping techniques, while women are better at soft, precise shots. The sport is fairly strenuous; an average game involves about two miles of walking, and the sweeping motion can rapidly raise the heart rate. Pre-game stretching is a requisite for this demanding sport. The players undeniably need to employ dedication, good hand-eye coordination, balance, concentration, endurance with mental fortitude and good sportsmanship – skills that AR was rapidly developing.

The rocks used in curling are made of high density Blue Hone granite found on Alisa Craig, an island off Scotland's west coast. The granite is polished to a bright, smooth sheen, and a released stone resembles a swan gliding on water. There are two types of curling shots – the "draw" and the "takeout." Each of these two broad types has about a dozen variations, depending on the purpose of the play. The draw-shot is aimed at getting the rock to stop at the most advantageous spot at the other end of the lane. Take-out shots are designed to impact and take out rocks from play. To assist the stone in meeting its goal, the rock is released or delivered in a rotational curling motion, either clockwise or counter-clockwise.

To help the player direct the shot, the skip stands at the target end of the lane and uses hand signals to communicate the direction of the shot and the weight of the rock which have an impact on the trajectory and movement of the rock. The player provides the strategy, timing and talent to read the ice. This helps the player decide how hard to slide the rock, its direction and curl. The delivery is assisted by two team members who sweep in front of the rock. Knowing how much to sweep so that the stone arrives on target is a skill developed over time. For curlers there is no “stupid head” but rather a “we can do it” attitude. Well-seasoned players are wont to say, “Individuals and the team make the shots!”

AR became an accomplished curler at the club’s league games and was the hands-down favorite at the club’s bonspiels - a Scottish term for weekend curling tournaments. After a few practice deliveries, he developed a feel for the quality of the day’s ice which could be fast or slow, swingy (causing too much curling motion) or straight (does not permit curling easily). He found out that every sheet of ice is different as is every rock. He mastered the technique of placing a guard - aiming the stone to prevent the opposition from hitting a rock in the house - and throwing a take-out to remove another stone from play. AR also learned that when the ice is slow, one needs to deliver the rock harder; when the ice is fast, one should slide the rock easier. Some members began calling AR “The Prince of Curl.” The games last between two and three hours, and the team plays seven or eight games during a weekend of competition. AR joined Vinny Talerico’s rink (team) for the league tournament. He transferred his team spirit from ice hockey to curling.

The Talerico rink included McBride, Novak and Reddy - players with similar temperaments and great relationships on and off the ice. They came from different walks of life, yet they were all modern-day techies. When they played together they resembled the “fastest running piston.” Skip Vinny Talerico was a veteran of the sport; he knew there was more than one way to move. He was a wizard at determining a course of action and in planning an exit strategy. He claimed his mamma trained him to anticipate events each time she warned him, "Just wait until your dad gets home." Off the ice, he worked with head-spinning electronics.

Pat McBride was the Vice-Skip and a southpaw, a left-hander, with an Irish accent and a sense of humor. He had the knack of projecting confidence. He praised his mother for teaching him logic. "If you fall out of that swing and break your neck, you're not going to the store with me." He was wired and plugged and was your tech-savvy dad.

Teddy Novak was the team's manager and everybody's favorite. He was a straight-talking workaholic with a reputation for "flying" faster than a speeding bullet to his job at the Rome defense lab. He was detail-oriented and could see around the bend. He ascribed his keen perceptions to his Ma. When she scolded him she would say, "Answer me when I talk to you and don't you dare talk back to me!" He still laughed when he recalled his Sunday chore: "Polish the Polish furniture." As team manager, he made sure the team was a perfect fit.

AR was skilled at configuring the delivery and working on the path of getting the rock to where it should stop. He soon became the "prince of curl," giving lessons to other curlers on ergonomics and the slide of the rock on the pebbled ice. He attributed his knowledge about genetics to his mother. "You're just like your father," she would say.

Coach Max Mayer was thoughtful and masterful, having curled for eons. He learned the strategies and moves from playing and watching countless games. For every game, he could cook-up a special strategy. He praised his Mom for training him to think about the next move. "You are going to get it when we get home," she would threaten. Experience had taught him how to thwart the situation. He could make the game super-spectacular.

The Talerico team had great chemistry and knew that those who don't have a sense of humor don't have any sense at all. "Don't take life too seriously; no one gets out alive," they would remind one another. In Dad's Land (garage or Do-It-Yourself workshop in the basement), these Techie Zeitgeists had the latest electronic software and hardware.

At first the team practiced traditional approaches and made the effort to master the basics. After honing that skill, they concentrated on defining critical disaster and fine-tuning disaster recovery. Life off the ice was not always a serious matter - the team went for the big laughs, especially when their game went south. That helped them overcome the "fear factor" with innovative approaches. Soon the team had the goods to be a great squad with the insights on how games were won.

They were focused, determined and drilled in strategies to ensure their team's success. And when needed, they would rethink their strategy.

Due to their sportsmanship, camaraderie and knack for throwing great parties, the Talerico team became the favorite, one with which everyone wanted to play. There were no elitist snobs on the team and they were all eager to play with any average working-stiff group of curlers. This strategy allowed the team to tidy up their act, work on glitches and comebacks, know their strengths and weaknesses and cover all their bases. In a short time, the Talerico rink became the hottest team in Utica. Playing against Team Talerico meant competing with seasoned sportsmen who also knew how to have fun.

Party time was no longer pasta-fasta, top-crust-pizza on the go, or pizza delivered on ice. After practices or league games, it was time for bratwurst, kielbasa, tandoori chicken, papadums, andouille, pastafagiole, veggie lasagna, beer-sausage and chicken wings. For bonspiels, the menu included roasted beef tenderloin with red wine gravy and yogurt mint lamb kebabs. Of course, all of this food went down smoothly with plenty of beer.

Soon, playing the hottest team in town began to attract a wide circle of relatives and friends wanting to see the game as well as to partake of the grand cuisine. There was plenty of yapping, bickering, barking and wild parties to follow. These observers from behind the plate glass soon became "plate-glass skips" (captains) acting as Monday morning quarterbacks. They clamored for perfect shots with no misses. Some went over-board with loud and boisterous discussions on strategy. The veterans of the game watched the overnight gurus and smiled knowingly as these novices called for strategies that at first seemed to make sense. Then the "born-last-night" sages would see it all blow up in their faces a few shots later.

After competing against so many teams the Talerico team became "rink rats." They had the time of their lives! They traveled to other cities to play their teams. On the road their favorite song was, "In heaven there is no beer - that's why we drink it here." And they laughed at one-liners such as: "The trouble with bucket seats in cars is that not everybody has the same size bucket," and "An imported gadget claimed it was guaranteed to work throughout its useful life." Because of their roars of laughter at the bonspiels, the team was dubbed, "A mean lean laughing machine." Their travel stops to change drivers always set off a wee-wee chain reaction. Yet, they also remained disciplined enough to concentrate on the game and develop a team rapport and a cohesive spirit. They developed a lead, second, third and skip roster and could change the lineup, depending on their strategy. The skip, usually a jovial guy, learned and mastered the trick to a "poker-face demeanor."

The team adopted Fred Astair's axiom, "Great dancers are those who make their partners look good." The Talerico players enjoyed themselves as they walked, danced and curled on the "Wild Side."

At times it was difficult to know how eight regular guys from two teams could attract such a large crowd of friends and well-wishers. The most frequent team to play against the Talerico squad was the one led by Big Jim. One day, Jim remarked to his wife, "We have fun curling with the Talerico team and have become great friends."

His wife cut him short: "Jimmo, if you don't cut back on your eating and reduce your weight, you will have all those friends at your wake." But she was a caring wife, not one trying to dissuade her husband from taking curling too seriously. She wanted him to have an active life style and make smart food choices by cutting the trans-fat calories in his after- curling meals, which lately were going overboard. She wanted Big Jim to get the skinny on ways to replace simple-carbs and trans-fats with the right carbs and right fats. Off the ice, Big Jim was a home body, an indoor daddy. His wife warned him, "Unless you diet, your body and your fat will become really good friends."

Jimmy's teammate Samuel, nicknamed Safe Samo, also had a caring wife, who encouraged him to aim high even in his hobby. "Play the big-league boys of Utica rather than the boring teams that do not make curling the thinkin' person's game it is," she advised him.

Samo had eliminated the trans-fat-loaded cookies and chips and bid farewell to the bedtime snacks. He shared with his teammates the names of tasty snacks which didn't result in an increase in weight.

The other teammate was Heart-Throb Bob, who was being joshed about his recently changed marital status. He was the curling club's stud-muffin prototype male. At Bob's stag party, Samo, the longest married man present, offered his unique take on the pros and cons of marriage: "Marriage is an agreement in which a man loses his Bachelor's degree and his honey-bun gains her Master's." To which, Heart-Throb Bob replied, "Glad to lose my titular Night-hood."

The fourth member of the Big Jim team was Dan-the-Dapper-Man. He asked Heart-Throb Bob if he knew the difference between a boyfriend and a husband. Without waiting for a reply, Dan answered the question himself, "Forty-five pounds," he yelled. Dan assured the groom-to-be that he could be on an Only-See-Food diet for now.

The rest of the evening was spent in ramblin' on and good-natured teasing, along with liquid refreshments and put-meat-on-your-bones dishes. The best tip Bob got from his curling mates was: "The man who fights with his wife during the day will get no piece at night."

After spirited games, the curlers had a great time exchanging humorous stories. AR spouted his dose of medical wit: "Laughter is hazardous to what ails you."

Novak told the players, "One hundred percent of curling is half mental." McBride pondered the issue. "So if you succeed in curling mentally, have you half-won?"

Talerico chimed in, "Our team is great. It's as though we have ESPN." Samo corrected him, "You really mean ESP. Your slip isn't as bad as the one about the new immigrant who asked if a quarterback was a refund." Big Jim added, "He is probably the same one who thought that Taco Bell is the Mexican Telephone Company."

AR said, "As a favor, I offered to teach the FOB guy cross-country skiing. He turned me down saying, 'Cuz *Emrika* is a big country'."

Novak stated, "The trouble with being punctual at work is there's no one there to appreciate it."

Connie-the-Comet was a star player. She had her own curling story to tell. She confessed, "The first time I stepped onto the ice I was bowled over by Lazy Louis." Her friends thought that was very romantic. Connie-the-Comet quickly set the record straight. "There was no romance. It was the bloomin' 42-pound granite stone." Hoots of laughter erupted after that clarification.

Silly Steve was moaning that with the high price of fuel, he was planning to sell his car. "Then I'll have enough money to buy gas. I'm not crying about it, though, because that's what lassies do." According to him, "Tears are the hydraulic force by which masculine will-power is defeated by feminine water-power."

A senior citizen declared, "An 'all-nighter', means not getting up to pee!" His spouse added, "At our age, 'getting a little action' means, 'I don't need fiber today'."

Since it was the Christmas season, Steve asked AR, "Do you know why Jesus was born in a manger?" Steve then went on to answer the question himself. "That's because all Joseph had was a cheap HMO."

Anita Reddy also entertained the crowd with ethnic stories. "My friend, Vicky Rocha got all the roaches out of her apartment overnight by asking the Roaches for a commitment."

AR added, "In Mumbai, the mosquitoes went after the Misquitas." Soon the team members had learned a lot more about other ethnic groups, their type of humor, proverbs and maxims. The team practiced what they had learned as kids, "Keep humor out of religion, politics and family, and one can 'laf' about the rest." Occasionally, no matter what was said, someone took the humor seriously; but that did not prevent the curlers from exercising their "right to laugh." As a rule, curlers themselves are not worry warts.

Coach Mayer devised a set of hand and arm signals for the skip to use when he instructed the team on the strategy and line-of-attack to be employed. Weeks of practice paid off when the team participated in a series of bonspiels and round-robin league matches and scored even more victories.

The skip's modus operandi was: Plan our work and work our plan. The coach's catch-phrase was: Shoot to be consistent and predictable. Soon the Talerico rink was not only curling, but doing it with finesse.

In the lead–up to the Regional, the team visited towns and cities in the northeast for curling bonspiels. With a few losses and numerous wins, Team Utica rose through the point system to be one of the final four contenders for the USA championship title match. When the team returned from these out-of-town games, the members shared with their fellow curlers the techniques they had picked up and the local humor.

The Regional-final at Buffalo, New York, was attended by busloads of curlers from the Northeast and Midwest, as well as Canadians from just across the border. At the final, Team Utica won the U.S. Regional after banging knuckles and knocking off Team Boston in the Grand National Curling Club (GNCC) regional meet of clubs in the Northeast. The Uticans gave a stellar performance and received a two-thumbs-up from their opponents. The Boston paper described their home team as losing "kicking and screaming." The refreshments served for broom-stacking included chicken wings, beef tenderloins and charbroiled hot dogs with a selection of local signature beers.

The high-spirited Uticans sang, "We will, we will rock you!"

The next day, the hosts took the teams on a tour of Buffalo, Niagara Falls and the Seneca Niagara Casino. On their tour they learned about the Underground Railroad, as well as Buffalonians William Fargo (founder of American Express and Wells Fargo), Presidents Millard Fillmore and Grover Cleveland. The team was invited to stand on the spot where President Theodore Roosevelt took the oath of office after the assassination of President McKinley. They also drove down Millionaires' Row and relived the Gilded Age.

At first, Team Utica impressed the Uticans by outdoing home teams. Then they surprised even themselves with their prowess on the ice when they climbed up the ladder to the Regional. Team Utica was on a winning streak with decisive actions that resulted in sinking the rock against the out-of-town teams. The post-game celebrations always included feasts with dishes such as sesame-coated chicken stuffed with ricotta and spinach, lobster bouillabaisse, roasted salmon with citrus-caper relish, and a selection of cheese cakes.

The National Curling League competition for the U.S. title was held in Chicago, where Team Utica confronted the San Francisco club - the MOPAC (Mountain Pacific) regional champs. These Californians were escorted into the Windy City by a retinue of chic and elegant Hollywood rock stars led by their superstar governor.

The Uticans showed the rivals there was more than one way to move and to get the rock to the right spot. They ran smack into the Bay Club. The game took a downturn for the Californians at crucial points. This was not what Utica was expecting, yet they gladly accepted the excellent chance they had of winning, and played aggressively against their competition.

Team Utica became the United States Champions! The National Championship curling game was not carried by any TV news channel because curling is not a major spectator event in the U.S., unlike Canada. The Utica TV networks, though, reported the outcome with pride and joy, "This will make the Utica team a force to contend with." And curling became a byword in the lexicon of the average Utican.

The victory was followed by broom stacking and a bountiful celebration. The tables were laden with huge platters of Creole shrimp, grilled salmon and tropical salsa, pork ribs, sirloin steaks and tandoori chicken with mango, followed by heavenly chocolate desserts and a wide selection from the best micro-breweries of the Midwest. The feasting was accompanied by plenty of storytelling, lottsa laughter, backslapping, and a play-by-play analysis of the game. The general consensus was that the game was "pure brilliance." Utica's small guys had landed a big job as Team USA and their confidence soared.

The organizers gave the visiting teams a tour of the Windy City and its architectural landmarks including the Auditorium Building (built 1886-89) and a slide show presentation on the works of Chicago's most famous designer - Frank Lloyd Wright. They admired the recent gems - Marina City (twin towers of Chicago, 1964-67) and Lake Point Towers (1967-68).

On returning from Chicago the newly crowned Team USA had a big reception at the Utica Curling Club. The members were animated and energized about the success of their leading team. There was eating and drinking, talking and toasting. Team USA shared some of their experiences in the Windy City, including samples of the city's humor:

"See you later over-taker...I am the undertaker"

At the tire shop: "Invite us to your next blow-out"

On an electrician's truck: "We will take off your shorts"

At the propane filling station: "Thank heaven for grills"

"Cigarettes do the smoking. The smoker is the sucker"

At the beauty shop: "We need your head to run our business"

Most Uticans who had watched their heroes in the competition praised their techniques at peel (hard take-out that knocks off the guard) and steal (scoring the last point without the last stone advantage). Others thought their better skill was at "hit the broom" (stone thrown accurately to its exact desired spot). They were all in agreement on one fact: "AR could get the rock to spin."

At the curling club, the celebration continued into the wee hours of the morning. The next step for Team USA was to compete for the North American Championship title match in a mega event. Team USA was going to knock heads against the Canadians in hopes of being the best on this side of the Atlantic. The Canadian squad, skipped by Chirac and coached by Bill Redic, was considered a "dynasty" in Canada, and the team included Peters, Lucas and Martin. They were the three-time Brier Cup Champs, after beating their fierce rivals in sudden-death playoffs. Given the traditional strength of the Canadians, Team Utica knew that the neighbors to the north would be more formidable than the team they would face at the Continental Cup, if they made it that far. With all the recent wins, Team USA felt they were more powerful than a locomotive on a roll. There were big issues facing Utica's little guys. Team Moscow would play the Karlsborg Kurling Klub of Sweden for the European title. The countdown began on both sides of the pond!

The Decisive Games

Redemption or Repetition

&

Bright Days And Starry Nights Please, take me to heaven!

Attitude

> 10 <

Curling is a gracious but intensely competitive sport in which spirits can run quite high! Tension is palpable in do-or-die games against arch-rivals. In addition to the players, the excitement often extends to their devoted fans. Depending on how their team is faring, the shouts range from "Go, Go, Go" to "phooey."

The word was out locally and regionally that AR had made the switch from ice hockey to curling. His die-hard ice hockey fans and buddies moaned the change. Most friends of the Reddy family and his patients supported his decision. Some in the community - athletes and couch potatoes alike - were keenly aware that AR had become a whiz with his great curling prowess and his ability to "read the weight of the rock and its speed on ice." The games attracted a large audience and the stands were packed. Many of those who had witnessed their hero in practice sessions praised his techniques "at peel" (hard take-out that knocks off the guard) and "steal" (scoring the last point without the last stone advantage). Others thought his better skill was at "hit the broom" (stone thrown accurately to its exact desired spot). But they were all in agreement on one fact: AR was an artful spinner of the rocks.

The practice games were getting "hotter on ice" as the title match approached. At these practice games, AR's devoted fans included the *Manu chacha* and *Koki chachi* (generic names for grandfather and grandmother in Hindi) of Utica. Some developed a magnetic board to plot their own strategy for winning as the game evolved. Interest in curling across the eastern U.S. and especially in New York soared to new heights. Memberships in curling clubs doubled and scores of fans braved snowstorms to practice for their local league games.

The Utica team, now Team USA, was to play the Brier cup (Canadian) champions for the North American Men's Championship title. The Uticans practiced and perfected their techniques. They were going to play to win and were prepared to reconfigure at any time to achieve that goal. Their strategy was geared toward trouncing the Canadians. The players threw laser-beam shots. The skip and coach were competitive and demanding but displayed good humor and quick wit even under pressure. The skip was determined to stop the Canadians and derail their hopes of a win. Utica was excited! Adrenaline flowed and the town was spruced up to host this mega-event. The team was having a banner year with their games attracting the biggest crowds. The Utica Curling Club was now one of the hottest spots in town. The city was in a roll 'em in mode.

For the mega-event, seventy press passes were distributed and international satellite connections were all in place across North America and Europe for a live telecast of the match. The Canadian and U.S. bookies were on hand to take any wagers and to cater to the bets coming in from Canada, the U.S., France, and Britain. For the international competitions, Saranac ads urged the fans to, "Think global; Drink local." That's what most Uticans did. Fans eagerly anticipated next weekend's game at the Aud. The tension was so heavy, one could cut it with a knife.

Other members of the club were present for the practice sessions to cheer on their friends as well as to pick up some pointers. They helped decrease the tension by adding to the camaraderie. After watching the final practice before the big meet, the crowd dispersed into the chilly night, complaining about the unpredictable ice and missed opportunities during the practice games.

The fans eagerly anticipated next week's competition at the Utica Aud. Team USA spent the weekend watching televised accounts of the opponents' last few games and hoped they would serve a souped-up version of the same. Based on such thoughts, they developed their own game plan and strategies with plans B and C up their sleeves. The day before the games, the Utica newspaper predicted, "If history repeats itself, we can expect the same exceptional performances by both teams again! Uticans are all geared up for tomorrow."

The Ind-o-US community in Utica was in high gear. There were parties at various homes every night of the week to analyze, explore, scrutinize, evaluate and develop theoretical strategies on every aspect of the game. It would be difficult to know how much of the discussions got back to Team USA. Since curling is a family sport with no age limits, *dadas* and *chachas* (grandfathers) turned up for the strategy sessions. The *chachis* (grandmothers) stayed at home babysitting, praying and fasting. The routine was the same every night. The *biwis* brought their favorite *desi* dishes and the *babus* each had a Saranac

12-pack in tow. After some time it became difficult to know whether the upcoming game was the primary reason to meet or just an excuse to chomp on the tasty chicken *Kholapuri, paneer makhanwala*, vegetable biryani and the many appetizers. The Weight Watcher's diets went kaput. Everyone made pious resolutions to diet as soon as the games ended. Then the same groups would huddle together to continue the previous night's analysis of the game. Some described the rivalry as "a dog-eat-dog battle" and others figured "Team USA has the upper-hand going into the game."

An Ind-o-US whiz in quantum mechanics explained, "The curling delivery is a functional motion. Physics dictates the line of travel, the effective weight of the stone, friction, traction and rotation in addition to the consistency in delivery from the moment the stone is released."

These "experts" and on-paper players were thinking more freely and independently than the actual players.

Others listening to the MIT (Massachusetts Institute of Technology) and IIT (Indian Institute of Technology) *maharishis* said, "Hundred and cent per cent sure *maaaan*! *Pukka*!" (exactly and precisely).

Not all comments were on such a serious note. Some women wanted their husbands to learn to curl. Their reason: "If nothing else, it wouldn't hurt to get our *patis* (husbands) into the rhythm of sweeping."

Men with decades of experience in the "wedded bliss department" shared their opinions on the matter with bachelors looking for prospective mates. The elders counseled, "Every man wants a wife who is beautiful, understanding, frugal, and a good cook. But *beta* (son), the law allows only one wife."

An elderly gentleman revealed his theory, "Marriage teaches you patience, understanding, perseverance and loyalty and a lot of other virtues you wouldn't need if you had stayed single."

The wives did a bit of chit-chatting of their own. An older woman's assessment of married life: "Before marriage, a man will lie awake all night thinking of something you said. After marriage he will fall asleep before you can finish your thought." A newcomer to the U.S. inquired of her friends, "Why is the time of day when the traffic is slowest called the rush hour?" Another asked, "Why do we park in the driveway and drive on a parkway?" A seasoned resident brushed aside the questions with a curt remark, "Fire engines are not engines on fire."

Those focused on the game philosophized: "How does Atul-*bhai* attain that spin on the stone? Is it in the wrist movement?"

The doctors in attendance discussed various joint movements of the wrist and how they could be synchronized and sequenced to give that curl. Everybody and their mother-in-law had their own theories.

A novice to the sport inquired, "How does he get that rock to curl?"

A curling wannabe, using hand-movements, explained that curling is like "motion-on-the-ocean - forward, sideways, rotation and wobble, on ice and all at the same time."

The IIT, MIT and RIT (Rochester Institute of Technology) professors and graduates did have their priorities. All conversation stopped when dinner was served and it was time for "munch in a crunch." Indian meals are as varied as the states that make up the country. With Fusion cooking gaining in popularity, typical European dishes were becoming Indianized, while traditional Indian dishes were being tempered with western flavors a.k.a. "go slow on the spices." A dinner table may hold many different types of kebabs, lentils, curries, *masala* and *sadha dosas*, potatoes, rice and *rotis,* and a variety of relishes.

With the game on the line, countless Utica residents formed groups at work or at their clubs to study tapes of prior games, watch TiVos, dissect different tactics, look for weaknesses and plot offensive moves under different scenarios. Some were skillful and developed complex schemes to shut down the offensive moves of the challengers and confuse them. These strategists were confident that the U.S. team would retain its steely nerves and prowess even under the spotlight.

Before the game started, some TV stations aired a short video to educate the uninitiated viewers on curling's basic moves and the tactics used in the sport. The commentator explained, "To deliver the stone, the player assumes the crouch position with one foot in a foothold and one hand on the rock handle. Pushing off the foothold, the player forms an outstretched position with the rock in front, along the line of delivery."

Folks at the Senior Citizen Center also were excited about curling, a game some of them had played while growing up in Utica. They enjoyed the pre-game commentary and the analysis of the line of attack of the two teams. A few college students decided that the Senior Citizen Center would provide them the best view of the game since the center had a high-density big-screen plasma TV. The recreation room was crowded and some of the residents struck up conversations with the young visitors; the topics were not confined to curling!

"In the good old days, we were happy to play ball in the street or in the park – no fancy uniforms or gear," an old timer told one of the college students. "Now you youngsters want games organized, sponsored, and the winners announced in the next day's paper."

The collegian replied, "It is impossible for your generation to understand ours. You grew up in a different era. Today we have TV, jet planes, space travel, nuclear energy, computers, cell phones, space satellite tracking." Taking advantage of the pause in the student's litany, the Old Timer agreed, "You are right. We didn't have those things when we were young, so we invented them."

The Canadian players were respectful challengers, and the Utica team and club members were equally gracious hosts. After all, this was curling. After the rival team arrived in Utica, they were given a tour of the city and its various museums, the Munson-Williams-Proctor Arts Institute and the Turning Stone Casino.

Both teams were keenly aware that this was a marquee match-up which surpassed the Continental Cup! Team USA was not daunted by the high-stakes North American Championship. The team was prepared to knock heads and put the kibosh on the Canadians. Team USA comprised young whippersnappers with nothing to lose and everything to gain. They could smell victory and were ready to capture the trophy. The skip's drive and determination were unmatched. He hated losing, and the entire team had worked hard to compete in this event. Pat could be counted on to provide the enthusiasm and good humor. Under that smile, he also possessed tremendous shot-making abilities. Teddy was the team showman and could execute some of the most unimaginable shots. AR delivered the curve that confused even his friends. The key requirements for winning were in place. Team USA had a resolute attitude and went into the game with confidence.

Many Canadians wanted to watch the history-making game live and had made the long trip to Utica from Ontario, Quebec and other eastern provinces. Regardless of whether they were Quebecois, Anglos or in-between, the multi-cultural Canadians waved the Maple Leaf, draped the Maple Leaf flag as a cape or had their faces painted with the emblem. In some sections of the Utica Aud, the friendly banter was carried out in French: "*Je m'appleel Jacques* (My name is Jack)," followed by "B*onjour Messieurs-dames, Bonjour Mademoiselles, Bonsoir Monsieur-Madame* (Hello Sirs, Miss, Madams). "*Comment ca va?" "Tres bien et vous?"* (How are things? Very well, and you?). "*Parlez plus lentamente, s'il vous plai,t"* (speak more slowly, please) and "*Il fait beau,"* (It is good weather).

From the Anglos, there were also the customary, "Hi, mate! Going to be a great game, eh!" followed by beaucoup handshakes. Few dressed as Mounties, complete with the RCMP (Royal Canadian Mounted Police) paraphernalia and sang "The Maple Leaf Forever." Canadian fans who could not get tickets for the game, watched the game on TV in their local hotel bars. Their comments included, *"Je voudrais une bierre,"* (I would like a beer) and "*Il fait beau aujourd'hui,"* (It is nice today).

The American hotels had stocked up on the Canadians' favorite brands of beer - Labatt, Ales and Guinness. Instead, the Canadians chose to sample the various flavors in the Saranac 12-pack. They judged this brand "the best." The Canadians expressed their appreciation with plenty of "*Merci beaucoups,"* (Thanks a lot).

The bars were more than happy to respond with "*Nous parlons francais*," (we speak French) and "*Bienvenue!"* (You're welcome).

Some Scots flew in for this event. They wore their tartan kilts, a custom developed long before the U.S. became a nation. They lived up to Robert Louis Stevenson's description, "The happiest lot on earth to be born a Scotsman." Their chests were pumped out, their jaws clenched square and their mustaches curled up when the bagpipers played "Scotland the Brave" and the march accompanied the curlers.

Americans greeted each other with the usual, "Hi buddy!" which was accompanied by spirited high-fives and much back-slapping. In the viewing stands, the metro crowd mingled with the local hot shots, including the mayors of the city of Utica and the surrounding towns. As this was the North American Title match, the state's elected representatives and congressmen were in attendance. Also present were the senior senator from New York and the governor. The junior senator sent her good wishes. Compared to ice hockey spectators, this crowd at the Aud was more sedate. Most residents of Utica and the surrounding MoVa watched the game at home on TV, or on mega-plasma screens at their favorite bars, clubs and at the casino. Beer flowed freely, forcing brewery employees to work overtime.

Syracuse, the nearest major metropolis about forty-five miles west of Utica, took pride in its little sister city. For that day, big sister referred to Utica as "Almost Syracuse." Spectators warmed up with chants of "Leave no stone unturned," and "We'll rock with you, USA." Team USA was relaxed, knowing they had the hometown advantage.

Before the game Team USA's spokesperson commented: "With the USA title under its belt, the home team has all the experience and finesse that is needed. It is battle-tested for the championship games."

Team Canada's spokesperson expressed his confidence in the outcome. "The Canadian team's track record is strong, spanning several years. After all, it has won the Canadian Cup on several occasions. When we play against Team USA, history is on our side."

The TV analysts didn't take sides. The consensus was: "Neither one is a Johnny-come-lately kind of team. Both teams are weighing their options with no lack of possibilities."

The game started solemnly. As the teams stepped onto the ice, the bagpipers played the march, a tradition that came with the Mayflower. Then they played "Pomp and Circumstance" followed by the "Star Spangled Banner" and "O Canada." The announcer welcomed the viewers and recognized the VIPs in the stand. As the spectators settled down, TV and radio commentaries began: "Each match entails ten rounds. One inning is complete after all 16 rocks - eight stones per team - have been delivered. Only one team can score points at the end of a round. The point is scored by the team whose rock is closest to the middle of the house." Because curling is a genteel sport, the commentators praised the good shots of both teams.

Team USA decided to alternate between an aggressive and conservative game stratagem for the 10-inning event. Coach Mayer and skip Talerico possessed the insight on how games were won and also had a perfect plan for "disaster recovery" with a superb exit strategy. As the skip, Talerico had the responsibility of throwing the hammer (the last stone). The team carefully assessed the condition of the ice. The plan was to play Novak as lead - to place a guard or knock out a rock. Then Reddy would place the stone closest to the center to score the point, outmaneuvering one or two stones placed by the Canadians. AR had to uphold his reputation as the King-of-Curl. Southpaw McBride would add another block or play for a point if Reddy's stone was knocked out.

Once the game began, Novak and McBride earned respect for their strong performances and they were regarded as the games' best safeties. The game was just as much about shooting as making sense. The Americans played brilliantly, shot after shot, as the game marched inexorably forward. Each had the skills and chutzpah of great players.

The spectators in the stands were supercharged. Over and over again one could hear comments: Twist...Rotate...Turn...Knocked off... That's a curler...Nice rock...That curl was a pearl!

In bars and clubs, Team USA's fans contributed their own loud and raucous voices to the commentary: It's a beauty...Curl-baby-curl...Get the guard! Get the guard!...That's a zinger...One, two, three, rock...Slow-baby-slow...Easy does it...Yeah-baby-yeah...Go-go-go...Rollin'- rollin'- rollin' ... and Yippee! As the game progressed, Canadian back-seat drivers in the stands and in the bars called out: *Erreur* (mistake)...*Pire* (worst)...*Qu'avez-vous?* (what's the matter?)...*Tu stultus es* - You're an idiot! A few commented, "That wasn't the smartest thing to do!" Some Canadians had already imbibed one too many, but weren't about to quit their frothy drinks!

Team USA's performance defied all logic with the rock ending just where the skip wanted it, right on the button. The players were focused. When they were at an impasse, they went for the fast break to fix the flaws. Soon they would finish forward with a winning hand. These deliveries wrecked the Canadians' plan, forcing them to shift gears. AR consistently delivered the stone in an unorthodox manner and made impossible shots. Talerico thought his way through, working the angles and the possibilities. He was a battler and a scrapper; the entire team locked horns with its rivals. The Canadians couldn't outplay the Americans, who played a strong hitting game, forcing the visitors to respond with a draw-game tactic. The Utica Curl was born!

Team Canada displayed an intensely competitive spirit as it wanted to do its best at this ground-breaking game. The Canadians realized they had to juxtapose their deliveries if they were to win against Team USA and its dominant players. The Canadian game was tough. It was a see-saw battle all along up to the end of the eighth inning. Hard though the Canadians tried, the game did not go their way. Team USA out-smarted them and wrung them dry by making excellent shots even under pressure. The Americans set the pace and the opposition had no choice but to follow. There were a few scary moments, but things were kept under control by skip Talerico and coach extraordinaire,

Mayer, who plotted some consistently great strategies. The Utica players were outstanding shot-takers who made the big shots that out-curled the opposition. Team USA set the standard of achievement. After every Canadian move, Team USA upped the ante.

Curling fans in the Aud, elsewhere in Utica, throughout Canada as well as the U.S. had a blast watching the plotting and counter-plotting. The players displayed a seriousness and respect for the sport that befit thoroughbred pros and set the benchmark in originality, creativity and diversity of shots. They also laid the groundwork for new styles and techniques. Team USA hit the mark right from the start - and that was the shape of things to come. Team USA didn't wait for a lucky break and delivered the "right stuff" with a breakthrough performance.

Team USA derailed the Canadians by doing an all-around bang-up job and pushing the limits. There was terrific defense and offense, carried out with the enthusiasm they felt for the sport. After one-up and one-down pattern, the North American Championship game ended with a 10-7 score. Team USA was the North American Champion! The underdog USA team first surprised themselves by their success as the Talerico team, then their hometown of Utica as Team Utica. Now they astonished the U.S., Canada, and the world as Team USA!

After the "friendly" confrontation on the pebbled ice, the team members shook hands with each other, the aficionados and the VIPs in the stand. The players then proceeded to the lounge to unwind. In keeping with curling tradition, the winning team presented its opponents with consolation Saranacs. The visitors took their loss in stride. They knew a major celebration still awaited them at home, as they did exceptionally well during the season.

In North America, the event made the national news in radio and print. The game was the lead story on all the evening TV news channels. Curling became the featured sport. Discussions began on the next round against the Russians who were the European Curling champions. At the after-game dinner, the players were treated to Utica's culinary treats: Amore pizzas, prosciuto di Parma with fresh mozzarella and chicken Cordon Bleu, all washed down with Utica's Saranac and Canadian Labatt. There was also plenty of Blanc and Bordeaux (wine) to go around.

Even while the teams enjoyed the refreshments, they evaluated the game. The Canadian skip's verdict: "Team USA's shots were 'boutique delivery' and pulled off quite an all-round memorable event."

Talerico, the U.S. skip, responded, "*Merci*" *(*Thank you).

The Canadian skip replied, "*De rien; Il n'a ya pas de quoi*" (You are welcome). The Canadians had hoped for the big break, but the Americans refused to drop the ball. A win was just not in the cards for the Canadians, hard though they tried. Their vice-skip moaned, "Life just changed from croissant, cappuccino and latte, down three notches to toast and plain coffee." His lead added, "And now instead of being in the penthouse, we have been moved to the doghouse." Their coach added, "We have been transformed from heroes to villains."

Talerico tried to cheer his opponents, "Don't you be so hard on yourselves! You played a great game!"

Though the visiting team was disappointed, their Vice-Skip praised Team USA. "You guys deserve an A ++++ for your good attitude, determination, temperament and concentration."

Privately, the Canadians admitted that they were still surprised and *enneuyeux* (annoyed) that small town guys from Utica had walloped their giant opposition and that the curling leviathans from the north had to leave their pride south of the border. The Canadian first lead conceded, "Team USA had gutsy determination. They exemplified the non-quitter's slogan: When the going gets tough, the tough get going."

The Americans did not gloat. Instead, Coach Mayer praised the Canadians. "You guys were *Grande* (great) and *Gracieux* (gracious) and you had plenty of curling smarts."

The U.S. vice-skip McBride consoled them, "Your game was nothing to sneeze at; but sometimes, stuff happens."

Novak complimented the Canadians. "You guys were complete pros to the core. You had the razzle dazzle."

AR empathized, "Look to the future and the nicest thing about that - it always starts tomorrow."

The visiting team's lead returned the compliment. "Your team is in a league of its own - tough, talented, adept and accomplished."

Their second added, "You Americans are curling's best kept secret. Whatever move we made you guys kept raising the stakes."

Mayer said, "Wouldn't it be nice if when we messed up we could simply press 'Ctrl-Alt-Delete' and start all over?"

AR told the curlers, "Stress is when you wake up screaming; then you realize you haven't fallen asleep yet."

After a few drinks and feasting, the Canadians were relaxed. The mood and the conversation changed from curling to good humor. The

Canadian asked AR a question: "Since you are a doc in the U.S which has all the high tech know-how, let me ask you this: now that all the drug prescriptions are done on computers for drug-drug interaction, would that undermine my grandma's advice, 'Never, under any circumstances, take a sleeping pill and a laxative on the same night'?"

That night, the Canadians marveled at the dead-eye game of Team USA and its curling smarts. The Canadians realized they'd have to brace themselves for a transfusion of more knotty curling techniques, especially on nosing a peel and figuring out AR's recoil motion of his arm after delivery. For the next few days, they were content to have their quiet celebration in Utica as guests of the city and the mayor.

There was wild celebration in Utica after the match. The home fans were primed for this major title victory and their hometown heroes did not disappoint them. At the festivity on Main Street, Team USA was called, "The Wizards from Utica." Everywhere there was spontaneity with a six-pack of beer – the traditional curling drink - and fun-filled celebration. The city went wild and crazy with more kinetic energy than a nuclear reactor. With all the "frosties" downed as the evening progressed, some revelers became the funniest things on two feet; a few were determined to be slap-happy comedians. For its home town, Team USA had star appeal.

The songs of choice at the after-game parties included "Old Time Rock-n-Roll" and "Rock-a-bye-baby." The young and the old sang and danced along, doing the Hip-Hop and the Bee-Bop. With spirits buoyed, many fans did the "usual and customary" which was to go to their favorite fast-food place for a late lunch. Utica's eateries displayed their share of innovative window advertising. One poster admonished, "Don't stand there and be famished. Come on in and get nourished." A pizza restaurant's ad-man was obviously a pun lover. "Seven days without pizza makes one weak," a banner read. Before the spontaneous gathering downtown that evening, every deli, bodega, trattoria and pax food bar was swamped. After the three hours of carnival-like hoo-how and wild partying, the exuberant Uticans finally made it to their Belissima Gourmet Restaurants. For Utica, this was March Madness.

The scene was repeated all over New York. The next day's headlines in all of the upstate newspapers crowed: "Canadians Canned!" or some phrase to that effect. The lead story in one morning paper read, "Uticans just handed the top-ranked Canadian team its first defeat. Team USA proved it was not automatic for Canada to win. The U.S. team had aggressiveness, intimidation, determination, as well as quiet confidence with competitiveness and imagination." The local newspaper seemed to have run out of complimentary expressions. The hometown crowd raved, calling their team "A Curling Machine." Every Utican felt the city had earned its bragging rights. Team USA certainly did not have an image problem and made big news in curling circles.

Indian-Americans were ecstatic, each claiming that their own strategy for winning had been adopted by the team and that "the outcome was just as I had predicted." Everyone was in a festive mood at the victory party the following weekend at Dr. Mehta's home. The divas wore delicately-embroidered chiffon saris or *salvaar-khameez* speckled with crystals, which they had purchased in the "Little India" section of New Jersey. The mini-divas sported their favorite designer's figure-hugging dresses and jeans. The *sahibs* showed off their trendy cashmere cardigans and sweaters, while the *Nanas and Chachas* (grandparents) donned traditional attire especially brought out for the occasion. The Ind-o-US had every reason to be impeccably dressed and to display their pride at this once-in-a-lifetime event. College students, nicknamed "*Jassbiyar*" because they habitually call for "just beer" even before they introduce themselves, were present in full force. The meal represented a spread of epicurean delights from India - north, south, east and west.

Utica was in the national spotlight, on the map, and not to be mistaken for Ithaca or Attica any longer. The city and the country both were being primed for the Continental Cup Championship game. The next day, the players and the city received congratulatory messages, including kudos from the White House. Utica officials invited the players to a performance of Gianni DeCristo's rendition of "Expect the Unexpected," at the Stanley Performing Arts Center which is on the National Historical Preservation list. The Center's ornate marquis makes it an eye-catching structure on Genesee Street in Utica.

Before the performance, the guests were given a guided tour of the theater. The docent, Luca, proudly explained, "The 2,945-seat movie palace theater opened on September 10, 1928, and was designed by Thomas Lamb, a prolific theater architect of the time. The Center was part of the Mast Baum chain of theaters, and was named after Stanley, one of the Mast Baum brothers." Luca reminisced about paying a quarter to watch a movie at the Stanley when he was a lad.

"The Stanley was the premier entertainment center for anybody growing up in Utica and its surroundings," Luca continued. "With time and the arrival of designated movie houses, the old-fashioned gilded theaters saw hard times. In 1974, the Stanley was purchased by the Central New York Community Arts Council which spent more than $4.5 million on the theater's renovation. All the mechanical, electrical, and safety systems were upgraded. Most of the interior, including the seating, was restored to its original design and the new carpet matched the original pattern." *(Theatre's print & electronic brochures).*

As the group made its way around the building, the opera aficionado pointed out that the theater is an example of "Mexican baroque" architecture because of its unique blend of styles. She went on, "The terra cotta and tiled mosaic exterior shows the Mexican influence. The Hapsburg lions, Indian faces and a multitude of angels and cherubs which grace the lavish baroque 'gold leaf' interior of the theater, reflect the style of the 1920s. The Moorish influence is apparent in the star-splashed ceiling and the twisted columns on both sides of the stage. Some of the drapery treatments in the organ lofts have an art-deco look." Luca added, "These represent American arts and culture on the eve of the Great Depression. Currently, the elegant lobbies are used for receptions and meetings. It is a local tradition for bridal groups to have their photographs taken on the grand staircases in the lobby. Legend has it that one staircase was designed to resemble the grand staircase on the Titanic. In addition to presentations by national and international troupes, four major local groups -: the Broadway Theatre League, Munson-Williams-Proctor Institute, the Utica Symphony Orchestra and the Mohawk Valley Ballet - host events at the Stanley."

Utica also showed the visitors the city's famous golf courses, several colleges, and two great healthcare facilities - St. Elizabeth's Medical Center and Faxton-St. Luke's. Because of the city's strong support and patronage of the arts, The Munson-Williams-Proctor Arts Institute, the Stanley Performing Arts Center, the Symphony Orchestra and the Mohawk Valley Ballet thrive. The Canadians were also given tours of the Utica Zoo, Marsh Wildlife Reserve, Memorial Auditorium,

Children's Museum, Oneida County Historical Society Museum and the National Distance Running Hall of Fame.

Two days after the Awards Night, the Canadians boarded their bus for the ride home and bid their hosts farewell. The guests waved and yelled, *"Au revoir"* (see you again) and *"A bientot"* (see you soon) as the bus pulled away. The teammates knew a big celebration awaited them on their return to Canada.

With the *babu* in the game, curling became an interesting sport for many Asian immigrants on both sides of the border. Many Uticans were separated from their relatives by a border as well as by team loyalty. After the game, next of kin of the Ind-o-US and other émigrés who were residing in Canada had to tone down their smugness. Some offered lame excuses such as, "How naive could I have been?" Others expressed their apologies for their unwavering confidence in Canada's victory. They had claimed, "A win for the Americans is impossible!"

The next weekend, the City of Utica held lavish parties, music and celebrations in honor of their curling stars. As the North American champions, Team USA was feted with a victory parade followed by wild street parties. The disc jockey from the local rock radio station picked songs which had the word "rock" in their titles: "Your Mamma Don't Dance And Your Daddy Don't Rock 'n Roll" and "Rock Around the Clock." The crowd spontaneously danced the East Coast and West Coast Swing, the Jitterbug, Lindy-Hop, Rock and Roll and Shim-Sham. The disc jockey's final number was a tribute to all New Yorkers - "I love New York." With so many parties, there was a sharp rise in interest in ballroom dancing. And many Uticans went from plain pedestrian to fancy dancin'. The recent win and the upcoming cup match resulted in an escalation of collective excitement among Uticans. A black-tie dinner was held at the Hotel Utica with music by the Annie Trio to honor Team USA, the North American Curling Champions. The music set the stage for a variety of dance styles – Latin, Country-Western and Classic American. Nothing stopped the crowd and the curlers from demonstrating their Swing, Quick-Step, Lindy-Hop, the Bop, the Carolina Shag and other Latin dance moves.

On to the Continental Cup Championship! Team USA would play Team Russia from Moscow, the European Curling Champions! In addition to the North American and European media, journalists from TV-Asia and the Indian print media would cover the game. Utica was on the world map and getting ready for an international event again!

Utica – Small City with a Big Heart

> 11 <

Utica is a small city with a population of about 60,000. The city and the surrounding region make up the Mohawk Valley, MoVa for short, with a combined population of around 100,000. Utica, like other towns in Oneida County, is an old town which was first occupied by native-Americans and later, by white settlers as they "migrated west" along the Mohawk River. The region enjoys a long and prosperous history. The main streets are lined with stately homes and buildings, some built more than a hundred years ago. MoVa has a rich cultural history and its residents reflect the immigration patterns of the U.S. Utica's Refugee Center is one of a few centers in the U.S. that welcomes refugees and assists them learn the culture, language, and economic system of their adopted country. As a result, cultural diversity and unique experiences await the newcomers. The city is famous for more great pizzerias per capita than anywhere in the U.S. It is said, only half-jokingly, that in Utica, the Friday fish-fry is almost a religion.

Among the numerous institutions and corporations located in Utica are the Masonic Care Community of New York and the internationally recognized Masonic Medical Research Laboratory (MMRL) which was founded in 1958 by the Grand Lodge of Free and Accepted Masons of New York. This is a cutting-edge medical research center which addresses today's major healthcare issues. It has made its mark in experimental cardiology and molecular biology, including the study of abnormal heart rhythms, the discovery of the 'M cells' in the heart muscles and their role in sudden deaths, a well as the development of pacemakers. More recently, MMRL established an immunology program. Funding for this research comes from the Grand Lodge and other extramural grants. The Masonic Care Community offers an all-inclusive array of residential and healthcare services, along with independent retirement living. It's the only such Mason facility in the entire state and naturally the pride and joy of New York's Masons. *(MMRL's print and electronic brochures)*

While much is changing in Utica, much stays the same. One such example is the F.X. Matt Brewing Company, which makes the region's famed Saranac line of specialty beers, lager, ale, Twelve Beers of Winter and Summer, as well as non-alcoholic drinks. The company has the distinction of being the first to introduce a beer – the Utica Club - exactly one hour after the 21st amendment was signed and prohibition repealed. The brewery was established in 1888 by F. X. Matt (Francis Xavier), an immigrant who learned the art of brewing in the Black Forest region of Germany. The brewery is now run by the family's third and fourth generations. This seven-storey brew house is the oldest family-run brewery in New York State, and the second oldest in the country.

After a week of celebration, Team USA began to knuckle down and prepare to challenge Team Russia, whom they were scheduled to face in three weeks. Coach Mayer got busy cooking up another set of his innovative game plans. Team Russia was known for its aggressive style. In anticipation of their maneuvers, Team USA prepared for turnovers and tactics to counter their opponent's explosive moves. During a pre-game interview with the press one week before the showdown, Talerico stated, "It is important to be ready for pressure and to be well-prepared. My job is to make sure the team is confident and composed going into the game."

"We're confident of our success," McBride insisted. "There are a few moves Team USA has to hone in order to strengthen our strategy."

Novak added, "I don't think we are at a disadvantage. We'll have to prove it when the time comes."

AR predicted: "The game will be a magical moment, a sequel to the 1980 'Miracle on Ice'. Our game will inspire yet another generation."

The players had been on a roll with nine consecutive major wins. Team USA was the bookie's favorite. Skip Talerico had an air of calmness, confidence and defiant unwillingness to accept less than total victory. He was gunning for gold.

The Ind-o-US members found themselves back to their game plans. At the first meeting, they presented their hero *Atul-bhai* (brother Atul) with fresh flower garlands, hugs and a rousing rendition of "He's a Jolly Good Fellow" followed by "Hip, Hip Hurray." The mommies and the *devis, bablis, tinis, mas, kaurs, biwis, bibis, bharyas and srees* (Indian women) were clad in *jari* (gold embroidered) saris and richly-decorated *salvaar-khameez*. Many proclaimed AR as the team's MVP. After many toasts and speeches, the group made a dash for a fragrant culinary spread - *ragda petis, chicken mulligatawny, and Bumbai aloo,* among other dishes. Atul and Anita had to leave early to attend a reception across town.

After they had gone, the guests analyzed the team's SWOT – strengths, weaknesses, opportunities and threats - to formulate a plan for success. The consensus was: "Atul has this curl on the rock that ensures victory."

One postulated, "It is the flick of his finger that permits him to curl the stone as he releases it." Another compared the curling motion to a *googly* – an Indian term used in cricket to curl and roll the ball as it is bowled to the batter. Dr. Mehta weighed in with his opinion. "It was the *googly-ungli* (finger) that was the secret weapon." He considered himself the sage, the unofficial medical guru of Team USA, and he fielded inquiries from the Indian TV and print reporters, giving them a crash course on understanding the game.

Dr. Reddy's radiation therapy staff also expressed their opinions on the game and the players during the lunch hour. Some staff members felt they were the doc's best counselors because they had his undivided attention for more than eight hours a day. This was also an opportunity to pass on to their "champ" and Team Utica as a whole, the pointers, tips and advice that the patients offered.

Break times were rife with suggestions on some aspect of curling. One nurse observed, "I don't think doc sleeps, and yet he never looks tired." The staff also agreed that Dr. Reddy's fingers had a special kind of deftness that did the trick and got the job done. Marge predicted, "That finger of his will take him places," and the others nodded in assent. One technician who watched the practice game said, "Curling is distinctly different from throwing darts."

On TGIF (Thank God It's Friday) dress-down Friday evenings, most staff members assembled for their usual after-work social hour at the nearby bar. After downing a few drinks, they were in a jovial mood and let their hair down. They talked about protecting the doctor's fingers, at least until the games. This led Margie to remark, "I know how and where that finger can be shielded", as she pointed to her cleavage.

Vickie chuckled, "A few martinis can work miracles!"

"A few more of them and I'll have to be your DD - designated driver tonight," chimed in Rosy, the only sober one in the group.

They went on to talk about a prospective employee. "She is so boring, she should be an anesthetist," one woman complained. Later that evening, they recalled the week's funny incidents at work. For a few, it was ROTFLMAO (rolling on the floor laughing my anatomy off).

The staff glowed with a lively sense of humor which matched Dr. Reddy's. As care givers to cancer patients, their lightheartedness was vital both for the patients and themselves.

A popular meeting place in East Utica was the Sons of Italy Club on Bleecker Street. Italian-Americans met at the club seven days a week. In the late nineteenth century, Utica had become home to more Italian immigrants per capita than any other city in the country. Vinny was a regular patron at the club and many members knew Dr. Reddy professionally. Team USA's success was naturally discussed in great detail at the club. Gesticulating for emphasis, Mrs. Guido voiced her opinion, "Dr. Reddy is the best. He is *sempre* (always) smiling. When he sees my Angelo, he has a surprised look and a smile. That tells me my Angelo is a miracle. The doctor is happy to see him alive, *cinq ano* (five years) after his cancer that had already spread was diagnosed."

Paisano Graziano added, "The doc always told me, 'Ralph, bad stuff happens. You often can't control it. But you gotta have hope'."

Kumpar Napoli added, "At my last check-up, the doc advised me to enjoy the summer and see him in one year. That's a great relief!"

Signore DeSantis explained how the game of curling is a lot like bocce ball, and that the secret to the curl lay in the elbow movement. Flexion-extension, pronation-supination of the forearm was demonstrated carefully. The Italian-Americans were impressed.

"Vinny can be relied on to work any ice," concluded DeSantis, and the group agreed. Some members of the club knew more about Vinny than what he knew about himself. All the *Signori* (Sirs and Ladies) were proud to continue the traditions of the Sons of Italy – a hundred-year-old organization which represents the second largest ethnic group in the U.S. After a *"Benvenuti a Tutti"* (welcome to all), everyone at the club raised a toast to Vinny Talerico, one of their own and skip of Team USA. *"La Banda Rosa"* played renditions of Dean Martin's "That's Amore" and other classics, as well as *"L'Italiano", "Serenata", "Bambina Baciani"* and *"La Lontananza."* The evening ended with the singing of the "Star Spangled Banner" and "*Himmo Nacional de Italia.*"

At the Irish-American club, Patrick McBride, vice-skip of Team USA, was the main topic of conversation. His dad regaled the crowd with a little history lesson on curling and his family's involvement in the sport.

Curling was his ancestors' sport of choice all the way back to the Green Isle. The members also remembered the day young Pat was inducted into the Ancient Order of the Hibernian. Several men knew Dr. Reddy, too. Bob was one with a complaint about Dr. Reddy. He explained, "The doc spends too much time talking and being nice to me wife. And I have to pay him for that? No siree!"

His wife, Mary, quickly came to the doc's defense. "Robert, YOU are not paying him for his kindness. Medicare pays him for his work." Bob was not mollified. "Blimey, that's OK! Yet, you are still ME wife."

Mr. Murphy, who wore a kilt, weighed in for the doc, "The doc takes good care of me. He said to me, 'You've got cancer but you should still be yourself - meet your friends and keep your social engagements. If the boyz call you for a Guinness, just go with the flow'."

A ten-year cancer survivor, Mary-Jane, added, "Dr. Reddy and his staff encouraged me to return to my true self. They gave me the power of 'Yum' right on my taste buds. Now I've got a second chance."

Peggy, wearing her green hat, chimed in, "Cancer patients are so freakin' lonesome. The folks at the Cancer Center taught me the power of positive thinking and encouraged me to believe in ME."

Interruptions aside, the group mainly talked about the Gaelic sport of curling and its origins in the lochs of Ireland and Scotland. The sport was brought to the upstate region by Irish and Scots when they arrived in large numbers to build the Erie Canal. The first section linking Utica and Rome was opened in 1817. The Irish were in Utica long before the Great Potato Famine of 1845–1850 which in turn led to the Great Hunger – *An Gorta Mor*. St. John's Church in Utica, built by the Irish in 1819, was the first Catholic Church in the state, west of Albany.

As the festivities at the Shamrock Club continued that evening, McBride remarked, "As close as we are right now to winning the world title, we can almost taste it."

Rev. Fr. Gaffney then gave the Benediction and the Irish prayed for Team USA's success. Fr. Gaffney told his listeners, "God responds especially to knee messages."

Paddy and the other Irish club members danced the jig to "Green Alligator" "Danny Boy," "Peg 'O My Heart," and "When Irish Eyes are Smiling," while a trio played their fiddles.

Tadeusz (Teddy) Novak was a lifelong member of the Polish-American Club on Columbia Avenue. Most Polish-Americans in MoVa are descendants of immigrants who arrived between 1900 and 1920 from West Prussia and Austrian-occupied Galicia. They settled in West Utica and the adjoining suburbs of Yorkville and New York Mills where, as the name suggests, abundant woolen and textile mills were located, making Utica and MoVa the leather stocking region of New York State. The Poles built the Holy Trinity Church in West Utica and a few years later, St. Mary's of Our Lady of Czestochowa in New York Mills. These immigrants also set up local lodges or "nests of Polish Falcons," which became the forerunners of the Polish-American Clubs and the Roselawn Hall.

At the Sunday's polka dance, 65-year-old Maria quoted Dr. Reddy's words to her at her last visit: "I don't know what you did when you were young, Maria. Looks like you did something really good. There is Someone up there looking after you, so you'd better give Him credit."

Several club members recalled that Dr. Reddy and the oncology nurses and therapists would encourage them to have a positive attitude in spite of what had been dealt to them.

One related the caring nod she received from Dr. Reddy when she blurted, "Cancer stinks!" Then she added, "Now on my annual check-up, he says, 'See you in a year when your social calendar permits'."

Ciotka (aunt) Helga who made it her duty to keep track of all the happenings in the community said, "I have heard good things about Dr. Reddy, especially that he's a skillful physician."

Rev. Fr. Bezak offered prayers for Team USA's future success at the Continental Cup - the World Championship game.

Tadeusz Novak was honored at a gala black-tie dinner at the Roselawn, where the crowd danced the traditional and hop-polkas and waltzes performed by The Pulaski Trio. The band played foot-stomping renditions of the Beer Barrel Polka, Pennsylvania Hills and *Maryska polkas, kolomejca and Krakowiak*; and the Tennessee Waltz.

At the Maennerchor Klub (founded in 1865 as one of the Gesangvereine - choral musical societies), German-Americans sat before the fireplace discussing the game's strategy. Coach Mayer was a longstanding member of the club. Many members reminisced about Mayer's prowess at yodeling as well as his skill at dancing the polka, waltz, schuhplattler and other German folk dances. Max had traveled with the Klub to countless Oktoberfests in and around New York State, home to many German-Americans - the largest ethnic group in the

U.S. Some Klub members were Dr. Reddy's patients and knew him well. Mrs. Fritz said of Dr. Reddy, "The guy is a sweetheart; I could cuddle him in my bosom." Her pal, Gerda, advised her, "Make sure you don't suffocate the little guy."

Rudolph was not a member of the doctor's fan club. "The first time I went to him for a consultation, he asked me if I had a wife. I informed him I was his patient and asked him why he was interested in my wife."

Gerda defended Dr. Reddy, saying, "Maybe he wanted to know if you had someone to fix bratwurst, liverwurst and sauerkraut for you."

Rudy was not moved. "Will he cook for me if I don't have a wife?"

The *fraulines* (wives) just rolled their eyes.

Then 60-year-old *schwager* (brother-in-law) Heinz added, "Now when I go for my yearly cancer check-up, Dr. Reddy says to me, 'Heinz, I want you to attend all the Oktoberfests in New York. A little *prosit* (to your health) won't hurt you'."

Soon the conversation refocused on curling and the Continental Cup. Herr Fritz, being the demonstrative type, showed the others how the curl in the rock was produced by the movement of the wrist at the moment the stone is released. Everyone agreed that Max was the master craftsman of the game who "did not overlook even a minute detail." The German-Americans knew Team USA was in good hands with detail-oriented Mayer as coach. He was the recipient of *prosit* (toasts) over and over again. At the Klub's dinner-dance, the button-box band honored Max and the team with renditions of Blue Skirt Waltz, *Schutzliesel*, *Solang er Alte Peter, Die Lustigen Holzhackerbaum, Watsch 'n Platter,* Waltzing through Texas and *In Muchen Steht Ein.* There was plenty of yodeling.

At Tariq Aziz's home, the Pakistanis met for the March Moharam religious celebration. Several were dressed in traditional *Kurta or Khameez* (shirt) and *Shalwar* (a baggy style of *pajama* tapered at the ankle). Some *mem-sahibs* (ladies) were in their *Peshwaz* (a long high-waisted gown) or *Shervani* (a formal knee-length coat fitted to the waist). Other divas displayed their *Shatoosh* (fleece of the Tibetan chiru antelope which is spun and woven into fine shawls). The women's clothing had delicate embroidery around the neck and hemline. Some had their soft and warm pashmina shawls around their shoulders. After the customary salutations: *Marhaba* (hello), *ke falke?*

(how are you?), the talk and earnest deliberations centered on curling, Atul Reddy's performance, and his famous trademark curl.

Zia pontificated, "Well, Atul used to play cricket. So, he's got the moves from cricket! Pakistan's Ali Khan was famous for this bowling technique. With the rotation of the shoulder-cuff muscles he could curve the ball and thus googly the batsman."

All the listeners nodded in union. "Well said...*ustad* (professor)."

"We agree with you cent-per-cent," said his cousin.

Other listeners joined in the affirmation: "He knows! He knows!"

In another corner of the house, the conversation was more family-oriented. They talked about what's hot and what's not. Khan explained that his *habibi* (sweetheart) Mumtaz wanted to exchange car insurance information after she had backed into a telephone pole.

A better-half complained that the first thing her hubby said when he woke up on Sunday was, "Where am I, Shalini?"

"Why did that upset you?" a listener wanted to know.

"Because my name is Sultana," was the answer.

Parvez talked about his vacation in the Islands. "Everything was fine until we went to a local coffee shop and ordered tea," he recalled.

"Make sure my glass is clean," his wife warned the waiter.

Ten minutes later the waiter returned and said, "Two teas for y'all. Which of you asked for the clean glass?"

As the evening drew to a close, families regrouped to calls of *"Yalla* (let's go)." The devout prayed together for the team's success and concluded the prayer with the customary, "*Inshallha* (God Willing)."

At the Russian club there was much excitement, too. After downing a few vodkas, the crowd discussed curling and the team, as well as past games and the upcoming decisive one. Seventy-year-old Michael, a former patient of Dr. Reddy, said, "He's inquiring whether I'm married. I'm the patient. What's my married life got to do with him? I don't ask him about his personal life."

Ileana defended the doctor. "He wants to know if you're getting enough borsch, goulash and emotional support while receiving your cancer treatment. He hopes you're not living on canned soup and baloney sandwiches."

Viktor was a Dr. Reddy admirer. "He's always tells me to hang in there. He is a good doctor. He knows we Russian people are very persevering." Ludmilla added, "He always encouraged my Ivanovich to look forward to life and live in the present rather than look back."

Katrina and Ivan who had never met Dr. Reddy, had a personal matter to iron out between themselves. "You dented my car when I lent it to you," she accused him.

Ivan defended himself. "It wasn't my fault...them Utica cops were chasing me...So what if I was speeding?"

At their get-togethers, Utica's chiropractors also analyzed the release and curl in AR's delivery. A member who had analyzed the body movement involved in the movement summed it up by saying, "The trick is in the rotation of the spine and the glide of the vertebrae." As men and women dedicated to matters of the spine, the chiropractors insisted, "We are the ones in the know. "

A member recounted his experience while standing in line at the local bank. He noticed the spine of the man ahead of him was way out of alignment. Unable to control himself, the chiropractor grabbed the man and right there on the spot manipulated his spine to perfect alignment. The unwitting patient was not appreciative. "What are you trying to do?" he demanded.

"I'm a chiropractor and I just couldn't bear to see your spine out of line!" the chiropractor replied. To which the "patient" retorted, "Why don't you keep your hands to yourself? I'm a lawyer! You don't see me 'lawyering' people ahead of me!"

At their monthly meeting, the orthopedic surgeons reported that they had closely studied the TiVo digital images of AR's delivery. They discerned that the rotation of the rock and its curl were due to hip movements as the player slid forward on one knee to deliver the stone. One surgeon remarked, "Hips are our bread and butter. We know them up-and-down, inside-out and back-to-front. We've studied skeletons and have seen the flexion and rotation of the pelvis on the femur."

During the Happy Hour that followed, one doctor amused the others with his usual supply of lawyer jokes. An attorney had asked him, "How do you handle "those" medical questions from women at social functions?" The orthopedist replied, "I just tell them to strip – and then I send their husbands the bill."

"Ah!" said the attorney, "Now I recall. I paid your bill."

In the Ind-o-US homes, the twice-a-week get-togethers were rife with analysis, re-analysis and counter-analysis of curling. The mood was building to a fever-pitch as the crucial game approached. Tactical advice and tips kept arriving from across the country and even from India where news about AR's prowess on ice spread like wildfire. The main TV stations in India began covering the game of curling and explaining the rules of the game. TV Asia was planning to broadcast the contest live. With long-distance telephone call rates between India and the U.S. less than nine cents a minute, a lot of conference calls were being made between India, England, the U.S. and other parts of the world where Asian-Indians live. Dr. Mehta, gesticulating wildly, expressed his concern, "The Utica team is a consistent winner. The 64-thousand dollar question is whether they have found the secret to staying on top." Many retirees with lots of free time to ponder such issues suddenly were experts on curling, at least on paper.

One aging *pundit* (wise man) confessed, "Certain line-of-attack moves keep going through my head - the plays which I think must work - at least in theory."

Arun was the local quantum mechanics whiz with the most in-depth study of curling under his belt. He worked out all the permutations and combinations of the game on his "super-computer" and claimed, "We try to position every possible stone after reviewing the films, team notes and computer-reconstructed 3-dimensional models. We've got the formula for the stone-stone interaction down to a science." The problem lay in whether he and the other physicists and mathematicians could explain the formula to the curlers who didn't have the foggiest idea about the science of quantum mechanics.

One *babu* claimed he'd figured out how Atul got that rock to twirl, curve and move forward all at the same time just like the planets in the solar system. The *babu* said, "It's like Einstein's Theory of Relativity. It's motion in the fourth dimension. That's up and down, sideways and forward and in a rotating movement, all at the same time."

His listeners gravely nodded in agreement. "This *desi* knows his stuff. His analysis is *pukka* (accurate). This chappy is not a banana man." The *babu* continued, "As I was saying, this is like the Renaldo soccer technique that makes the Brazilian players so deadly. Some of those Brazilian soccer players haven't even finished high school."

A guest, *Choto Maya* (Short Maya) pleaded with the host, "It's so *garam* (hot)! Please on the fan, no!"

Most of the dinner conversation was a combination of chatter and cross-talk, colloquially referred to as "I-talk-she-talk-and-all-talk-*beech-beech* (middle) and *jib-jab*. "

Some guests liked to tell Indian jokes. Rakesh's favorite one was about Americans who thought their co-worker, Tush Push, was a member of the KKK. The confusion arose because his wife, Sunita, had secretly told them, "Tush Push is a wizard under the white sheets."

Samir told about a *desi* who went for a job interview and was asked to fill out an employment form. He had no problem filling in his name, age, and address. He hesitated when he came to "Salary Expected." After much thought he wrote: "Yes!"

Some *bacche-lok* (kids) just dropped by with their boos (boyfriends or girlfriends) to say, "Heelll-llo y'all" and chow down on some Indian cooking. They shared some wacky words of wisdom: "Artificial intellect is no match for natural stupidity," one said. Another, with financial woes added, "By the time you make ends meet, they move the ends!"

This young crowd preferred Curry-in-a-Hurry to Curry-with-a-Flavor. This was clearly a crunch-n-munch bunch. After they finished their meals and offered a few *Namastees* (respectful greetings) to all the aunties and uncles, the hip pack left as quickly as they had appeared. "Ciao bambino; u take care; ok i think i stop or else u mite; make sure u do ur homework 2nite!; Ciao bella lulu petite," they yelled as they left.

The mothers admonished the kids to make sure their homework was completed, "before daddy-mummy get home."

One *desi* teenager, *Chotu Jaya* (young Jaya), was in a recalcitrant mood. Her mother tried to cajole her. "Why don't you wanna do your homework, Jaya-baby? You wanna your teacher to detain you?"

As it often happens at Indian social events, the *devis* (women) flocked to one area, away from the *sahibs* (men). One woman asked Neena Nair, a psychologist, "Any interesting problems in your work?"

Ms. Nair recalled a client who complained, "When we were newlyweds, my wife brought me the newspaper and my slippers, and my dog went around the house barking with excitement as soon as I came home from work. Now, when I get home, it's my dog that brings me the newspaper and slippers, and my wife who barks with agitation."

Before counselor Nair could continue, she was interrupted by a lady with a round red *bindi* on her forehead. "So! Whaaat's the problem? He is still getting the same service, no?"

Other *biwis* (wives) doled out advice to the single women in the room. One said, "Many girls like to marry a military man. He is disciplined and can cook, sew, make beds, is in good health, has annual physicals and he's already used to taking orders."

Other biwis itemized all the health benefits of Indian spices.

Some retired *babus* lingered at the parties well into the wee hours of the morning. Most mothers were home by nine o'clock to make sure their teenagers were home on time, ready for bed, their homework done, and that they had said their nighttime prayers. Before mummy arrived home, the cell phone chats and text messaging were ended, written in shorthand only teenagers understand: i msg being recd; try try as 4 me i nvr, u give up 2; u mite chnge places; take care 2day; u take care now; more 4 2morrow; Y U R mad?; and I'm FAAK (falling asleep at keyboard).

Excitement in Utica continued to build up to a fevered pitch, fueled by daily doses of local TV and print news. Young and old, athletes and couch-potatoes alike, all felt part of the team. Their philosophy: "They also serve who only stand, wait and cheer."

This game represented more than just Team USA competing against Team Russia for the Continental Cup and to become the men's international curling champions. Uticans hoped it would be the curling version of the Miracle on Ice. Such a win would be a reprieve from the professional ice hockey season that never was in 2004-2005. The fans were getting restless. A few bought digital video camcorders with super-zoom capabilities, rewind technology, and slow motion digital reconstruction. Others invested in TiVo and the more complex TiVoToGo to digitally record the game for posterity and to replay the event, frame by frame. The level of adrenaline was sky high! The fans knew they'd have to pace themselves for the raucous post-game bash. A white stretch limousine had already been hired for the Team's Victory Parade. At the rally, the musical entertainment would range from rock and roll to rap.

Team USA players participated in the sport as an after-work hobby. The impression among the Uticans was that Team Russia spent the morning practicing, the afternoon reviewing game plans, and the evening reviewing films of the past games - never breaking a curfew or bending a rule. It was the old, disciplined regime still at work.

Coach Mayer counseled his players, "You must be yourselves! Let your traits and personality show. Have fun." He did not want his team to run the risk of putting in more energy in practicing for the game than in the game itself. In short, he didn't want his team to peak too early and be burned out before the championship game even started.

The press, radio and TV commentators collected their own data to help them compare the statistics, performances, safety and offensive records of the teams. Each team had delivered countless exceptional and breathtaking feats. Several foreign news service organizations hoped to hire local commentators and assistants rather than send their own staffs to cover the event. Curling was going to receive mega-exposure both in the U.S. and across the globe. Many clubs were sending players to watch the game and learn key strategies.

At the Utica Help-Desk, there were a lot of inquiries about the upcoming World Curling Extravaganza. One recorded message was: "My name is Sam; How can I help you? Oh! You don't get my American pronunciation? You want me to spell it in Indian? It's S for Sundaram, A for Andhra, M for Mysore. SAM." Another recorded chat: "Hi! My name is Amy. You don't get my American accent? Is it my New York accent? It's A for Alaska, M for Montana, and Y for Y-oming."

A caller from the Russian News Agency got this response from a Utica volunteer: "How can I help you? My name is Anil...That's ANIL...Not ANAL. Oh! You're Russian and you don't get my American accent? Let me spell it...It's A for Andropov, N for Nikita, I for Illych and L for Lenin. No problem!" The Russians were confused!

1st Russian: ANIL? That's not an American name. These darn Americans. They are trying to confuse us again. Why don't they realize that the Cold War is over? And now their best curler is Indian.

2nd Russian: What is the guy's name again? Give me the paper where you've written his name. Well, let's give this American bloke some credit. He knows our great Russian history.

1st Russian: OK. They say this American star curler actually grew up in Bombay in the 1960s. I wonder if our KGB agents met him there. You know, that was the time of the Cold War and the whole city of Bombay was swarming with KGB agents. They had millions of contacts in the local Communist party and the labor unions.

2nd Russian: In the 1960s, this Indian player must have been between five and seven years old. Our archives might show that some retired KGB agent gave this young fella some American chewing gum. Then we can get our comrade to 'suggest' that this fella just throw that rock instead of spinning it the way he does.

3rd Russian: Yea, Yea ... that's a distinct possibility. Yet, as you said, the Cold War is over.

2nd Russian: Darn it. Those days were full of fun. We were everywhere, except in Mother Russia. Now President Putin has us all Put-In.

The (INS) India News Service assigned the husband-and-wife team of Raju and Virginia Kumar to cover the Continental Cup. The Kumars were journalists who worked for TV and radio. They decided to fly to Miami and then board one of the famed great trains and journey up the eastern coast of the U.S. to Utica. They figured the trip would provide them with rich material to comment on and write about on their return.

When they arrived in Utica, the Kumars met the local Ind-o-US crowd who introduced them to the Reddys, the game of curling, and all that the upstate region has to offer. At one of the Ind-o-US get-togethers, Raju recounted an interesting experience on their Great Train Ride. He claimed he found the trip, "surprisingly rather restrictive, given the freedoms and liberties Americans are known to enjoy. "

Dr. Mehta: Hey, Raju, how waassaah the long-distance flight from Mumbai and the rail trip from Miami?

Raju: All was perfect except for the train ride up here.

Dr. Mehta: Whaddayah mean, Raju?

Raju: Well, we boarded the train in Florida. My better half, Virginia, packed a big basket of extra-special Indian and *mui-bien* (very good) snacks. She brought along the special bottle of the best *feni* (Goan alcohol) which we had carried all the way from India. We also packed Cuban cigars that we picked up during our stopover at Heathrow Airport. We were looking forward to enjoying the relaxing trip across this great land. Everything was honky-dory on the train until we got hungry and opened our snack basket.

The conductor came by, wagged his finger at us and said, "No eatin' this car. Y'all use the banquet car." So, my beautiful Virginia and I went to the dinin' car. We ate a really big dinner and started to open our bottle of the finest *feni* to enjoy on the best "great train ride" in the USA. The conductor walked by again. Once again, waggin' his finger he said, "No drinkin' in this car. Y'all uses the saloon car with the bar."

Off we go to the saloon. While sipping the *feni* and taking in the wide-open spaces of this great land, I started lighting up my big cigar. The conductor showed up again, wagged his finger and said, "No smokin' in this car. Y'all go to the lounge car in the caboose."

So we go to the lounge car and sit on the luxury leather swivel sofa. I relax and smoke a couple of my big Cubans, puffing to my heart's content while enjoying the sight of the charming Carolinas pass by in the evening sun. After an hour or so, my gorgeous Virginia and I, we go to the sleeper car and go to bed. We were just about to get comfortable and snuggle up.

The conductor again walked through the hall and shouted at the top of his voice, 'Norfolk, Virginia! Norfolk, Virginia!'"

Several in Raju's audience did not understand the humor. The few who did "get it," admired the Indian journalist. He represented the new genre of suave Indian writers with an impressive command of English.

Some Ind-o-US get-togethers across the U.S. were specifically organized for *Pujas, Bhajans, Aartis, Kirtans* and other religious services to pray for the success of Team USA at the Continental Cup. After *prasad* (offerings), it was time for social interactions and revitalization of the culture with *desi* cuisine including *tikka* chicken, *idli sambar* and *samoosas*. In the senior citizen section of one get-together, a four-year-old wandered in to see his *nana* (grandma).

Sheila (a guest) inquired: Whose kiddo is he?

Nana: He's John and Usha's *beta* (son) - *desi-masala.*

Sheila: Is that a dish–*masala*?

Nana: No! It's a mixture of Indian spices - Heinz-57, *desi* style.

Before the Ind-o-US in Utica dispersed, they acted like cheerleaders at a school game. There was one more round of energizing cheers: "just win baby, repeat the blast from the past;" "go for a head-to-head;" "give us a gigantic showdown." The parting thoughts on everyone's mind were: "Will this be a huge win with dynamic action? Will the game pin us to our seats? How will Team USA and Team Russia minimize their risks of defeat?"

The Russians arrived in Utica to a warm and affable welcome. To help them recover from jet lag and the time-zone changes, they came ten days before the event and stayed at the posh Radisson Hotel, in the heart of Utica. It was close to every location the team needed to get to and had the ambience of luxurious living. The chef was familiar with Russian cooking as the hotel often catered for the large local Russian-American community's events. The advanced planners had carefully coordinated the visit down to the minutest detail to help Team Russia stay stress-free. Their country's prestige was on the line.

All Eyes On
> 12 <

The host committee had prepared a delightful program to welcome the Russians and help them enjoy a slice of Americana before and after the big game. The team, their coaches and the accompanying fans were first bussed to various sites in the Adirondack Forest. Later in the week, they were driven to the Catskill forests, which are the only constitutionally protected forests in the U.S. The Russians spent some evenings visiting the Turning Stone Casino, the local museums and the art centers. The committee also arranged for the visitors to tour the Thousand Islands.

The Russian Orthodox Monastery and Holy Trinity Cathedral in nearby Jordanville were naturally on the list of places the Russian team visited. A young seminarian named Igor escorted them around the grounds and informed the group, "The Cathedral has just commemorated the conversion of Russia to Christianity in the year 988." The Jordanville institution, renowned throughout the Russian Orthodox world, serves as the Church's only seminary in North America. Holy Trinity's most revered leader is the Archbishop, who is also the First Hierarch of the entire Russia Orthodox Church Abroad.

Igor added, "The church was originally built in 1935 after many monks fled to the U.S. from Russia, following the Bolshevik revolution of 1917. The present church was built in 1950."

For their weekend excursion, Team Russia visited the world-famous Niagara Falls. En route, the bus passed through small villages and towns in western New York, including the quaint town of Elba. Here, down–to-earth folks raise farm stock, potatoes, onions, corn and dairy cattle. The village clerk, Melba, who welcomed the bus group, said, "Elba has the distinction of being The Onion Capital of the World because its 'black gold' soil produces a special variety of onion. Also, by an act of Congress in 1896, the village was the first in the country to have the mail rural delivery system." The tiny village with no traffic lights calls itself, "A little town with a big heart!"

At Niagara Falls, the Russians enjoyed the spectacular sights and cold mists that awaited them at Prospect Point and again at Luna

Island, situated between the U.S. and Bridal Veil Falls. They were awe-struck as their guide, Cass, informed them, "Between 60,000 and 75,000 gallons of water flow over the falls every second."

Parts of the falls were covered with snow and ice, waiting for the arrival of the spring thaw. Cass took them on a brisk walk to Terrapin Point on Goat Island to enjoy the Horseshoe Falls, which is in the Canadian section of the falls. The Russians were so impressed that some resolved to return in the summer so that they could walk to the Cave of the Winds adjoining the falls. The warm weather would surely be a better time in which to sail in the Maid of the Mist, which travels almost to the point where the falls drop 190 feet (58 meters). From these vantage points the Russians were certain they would be thrilled with the sights, sounds and cool air of the falls.

After seeing the falls, the visitors toured the Niagara Aquarium and the Aerospace Museum. Later, the Russians tried their luck at the Seneca Niagara Casino which has more than 100,000 square feet of gaming tables. The play areas, decorated with neon lights and flashing panoramas, contain slot machines, table games and promises of big jackpots. (*Niagara Falls & Casino's print and electronic brochures).*

On the return trip, Cass informed the group, "About 20 percent of the earth's fresh water, which is captured from the Great Lakes and the surrounding areas, flows off Niagara Falls. This puts them in the same category as Victoria Falls in Zimbabwe and Falls de Iguaçu in Brazil. The immediate source of water over the falls is the Niagara River which really is not a river but a 'strait' connecting Lake Erie to Lake Ontario. Through this river 200,000 cubic feet of water flow every second. For those more familiar with the metric system, that is 5,720 cubic meters per second. Between 50 and 75 percent of the water is diverted to produce energy before the water reaches the falls."

The residents of New York State were excited by the attention and pride little Utica brought to the region. Most New Yorkers had faithfully followed the Utica team's progress. They would pass the information on to their relatives and friends across the country and across the globe. And so Utica became: "Almost Albany," "Almost Rochester," "Almost Binghamton" and "Almost Buffalo." Even the Big Apple noticed what was going on in the small city in the upstate region. Team USA's success had an energizing effect on the entire state. Two weeks before the meet, all the conversations in New York State were focused on one topic: The Game! The Game! The Game!

For Team USA, this was "center stage" time and the players were determined to do it right, the first time around and for the last time in this curling season. Talerico observed, "We are here at last! It is a banner day for us and for our country."

McBride saw the finality in the event. "This is the closing chapter. The game is the last in a parade of big event games we've played over the last few months."

Novak, the emotional one, added, "It is another segment in our lives soon to be over, another experience shared. At this junction you've got to feel good."

The team could feel the rush of adrenaline. They knew they were in the hot seat both as a team and individually, and through it all, they felt positive. The one redeeming grace was that they were all in it together. This was the final destination they had dared to dream about reaching.

AR asked everyone present, "How do you measure desire?"

The unequivocal answer: "You can't!"

They all knew the outcome that would be most exhilarating and would make them want to shout with passion.

The day before the game, the team met to review the mind boggling and heart warming moments of their many victories as a team. The successes had led to this chance to become curling's top dog, its big kahuna, the big cheese. The team analyzed the strategies and signals.

Vice-Skip McBride made his prediction: "We're going to have to deliver a true performance which will become the gold standard. But we'll do it by keeping to the simple plan, with no fancy acrobatics in the arena. If things don't go according to plan, we'll get back with Plan B."

They knew their moment had arrived and that the game could be the best show in town, in the whole country - nay, the whole world! The team left early to get their much needed sleep. As they were leaving, the fans called out, "See y'a later, Hot Shots! Let's go for the Gold." The enthusiastic crowd partied into the wee hours of the morning.

The Russian President sent his team the country's best wishes and added, "The country's eyes are upon you."

The American President sent his wishes to Team USA: "We are very proud of you guys."

Team Russia had the advantage of being more experienced at playing at international events. This time, they were pumped up on all six cylinders to stay ahead throughout the game. They were prepared to respond to the pressure with brass-knuckle tactics and bludgeons.

The home team had one up on their opponents – it had recently beaten the Canadian National Champions! The American doomsayers refocused their cloudy crystal balls. Team USA planned to play both offensively and defensively, as the opportunity presented itself. The team would outplay the Russians when the stakes were the highest. The U.S. was ready for a near-perfect game that would make the Muscovites blink.

The burning questions were: Who'd turn every stone, and which captain would be the best engine, even though he was playing the position of the caboose on the team's train? Definitely, this was a match between two superb teams with a lot of wins behind them. The team with the consistency and the secret to staying on top would win.

The American commentators resurrected the events of the "Miracle on Ice" that occurred on Lake Placid on Februay 22, 1980, a quarter of a century ago. That date, when the U.S. beat the Soviet team 4-2 to win the ice hockey Gold Medal, continues to be the single most indelible moment in U.S. Olympic winter sports history. The Soviet Union received the Silver Medal, and Sweden captured the Bronze. And, as in 1980, the current U.S. team of curlers was made up of amateurs who had won against all odds. The comparison between the matches was strong and on everybody's minds - the Americans versus the Russians! Again!

One commentator asked, "While this is certainly a resurrection, will this end up being a redemption or a repetition of history twenty-five years later? The pressure is on! Will the dream come true? Which team will have its nose to the grindstone? The answers all hinge on whether or not the teammates can deliver the rock! Both teams have insisted they are going for the gold and don't plan on losing."

Another U.S. sports reporter added, "Team Utica has the reputation for upsetting the apple cart. When Team Utica beat Team Boston in the GNCC (Grand National Curling Club) regional, the Uticans stopped the Bean Town boys from playing the boys from the City by the Bay. These guys, the MOPAC (Mountain Pacific) regional champions from San Fran had a bigger fan club than their Forty-Niners or their movie star governor." Another analyst said, "The GNCC has not been a power-house in men's curling. The MOPAC clubs have quite a few

Canadians, who have migrated south of the border and settled in the region. Now with Team USA doing so well, curling is likely to become popular in the east. Team Utica's success will boost curling in the Northeast - the GNCC region."

For the benefit of his Asian, especially Indian viewers, commentator Raju Kumar explained that the skill and enjoyment of curling comes from delivering the stone consistently well. "The stone must be released before the near hog line. The delivery demands sharp mental skills and involves four technical areas: alignment, timing, balance and release, along with a delicate feel for the weight of the stone."

Virginia added, "There are two different shots in curling, namely the draw-shots and take-out shots. A screen on her teleprompter displayed the five possible draw-shots: Guard – a stone delivered to rest short of the house and used as protection.

Corner Guard – a guard position off to the side.

Come-Around - shot that curls around another stone.

Raise – tapping a front guard into the house.

Freeze – a draw shot that comes to rest while touching a stone.

Raju proceeded to explain the purpose of take-out shots (hit and stick or hit and roll) and the hand-signals used by the skip. "Take-out shots are generally released earlier than draw shots to give the stone more time to curl. A more rapidly rotating rock will travel a straighter line. A slow-turning rock will tend to curl more. The longer it takes for the stone to reach its destination, 'the faster' the ice and less weight is needed. If the ice is 'heavy', the stone will have to be thrown harder." Then Virginia described the role of the sweepers and the types of sweeping calls – hurry, whoa, yes, light and heavy.

Virginia put the game in historical perspective. "Playing in Utica is a good omen for the Americans. When the U.S. last won the Gold in 1978 to become the Men's World Curling Champions, they competed in Utica, New York." She slyly added, "That was before I was born."

The game was being broadcast live to the more than one billion people of the Asian subcontinent who, thanks to AR's involvement, were glued to their TVs. Most viewers were watching the sport of curling for the first time. The Asian-Americans and other novices of the game paid attention to the Virginia-and-Raju team as they explained the basics of curling and added Asian humor to their commentary.

Virginia, who was the wittier of the two added, "By winning this year's U.S. championship title, Team Utica left behind a trail of meteoric curling clubs - Minnesota, Wisconsin and Washington State – states which traditionally produced America's best men's curling teams. Not a single New York team made it this far in more than forty years. Isn't that just before you were born, Raju? "

They both concurred that the two teams displayed stunning style.

Ilean, the Russian commentator told his audience, "Predictions are risky and the opposition is tough at this mega-sized event."

Most Russians had rooted for Team USA against the Canadians in their quest for the North American title. The same commentator at that game had told his audience, "A bet that Team USA wins isn't a bad bet." Yet this time around, he was not going to give his listeners the odds. "In this game, every split second, every centimeter and every tap counts. The game's outcome depends on which team seizes the day with precise shots and functions effectively."

His partner Nadia advised Team Russia, "Team USA has the staying power, so, don't leave your best for last. Go for the first deployment, and be back on track fast when needed. Do not cave in even when they put the heat on you. The secret will be figuring out what makes them tick."

The two analysts agreed that these were tall orders.

Nadia added, "We are just skips in front of the mike and not on the ice." The Russians then ended the pre-game commentary, "This is the real thing, and the bravest deserve the best. We consider the outcome of the match a tossup."

The Utica Aud, the venue of the World Championship game, was all spruced up. The traffic was redirected for function and security. Even though Utica was a small city, this was a clash of the world's titans and the security committee realized that any crazed person would love to grab the headlines. Everywhere, Men and Women in Blue, and Brown, and Black were visible all over town maintaining law and order. Sharp-shooters were stationed on the tops of some buildings.

The teams were escorted to the Aud by a motorcade of police cars blaring their sirens and led by a dozen police on motorcycles. It was like royalty arriving in town! With dignitaries flying in and out of the local airport, FATASS (Federal Air Transportation and Airport Security Service) was out in full force. The Washington, D.C. and Albany dignitaries flew into Utica on charter jets, and had special police escorts to zip them to the Aud. Special diesel-powered generators were hauled in to provide more than enough electric juice for the Aud, the hundreds of radio and TV stations, as well as satellite communication equipment.

Though the Continental Cup game was scheduled to begin at 10:00, the crowd started filing in at 8:00. The tension in the air was palpable. In the stands were the New York governor and the junior senator in addition to a few other senators. The senior senator was out of the country and apologized for his absence! The retinue of state, regional and local politicos had received invitations from the mayor's office. The Russian, Indian and Canadian ambassadors were present as were several other VIPs. There were a few pop culture icons, other sportsmen and women as well as a group of Winter Olympic gold medalists. The Aud's parking lot became the site of the coolest wheels to come out of Detroit, with the latest models of the "hot rods." Utica's and the entire country's bars, sports and ethnic clubs were packed to standing-room-only capacity. The Turning Stone Casino had several giant screens strategically placed and the gamblers placed their bets in a wild frenzy.

The crowd clapped and cheered wildly as a dozen bagpipers played and Team USA marched onto the ice. Coach Max Mayer led the line, followed by skip Talerico, McBride, Novak and Reddy. The spectators applauded just as enthusiastically when the Russia team - Coach Boris Molotov, with skip Zhukov, Federov, Krakov and Pavlov – were piped onto the ice. The bagpipers played the "Star Spangled Banner" followed by "*Gimn Rossiyskoy Federatsii*" (Hymn of the Russian Federation). The TV camera crew and the press all buzzed with excitement. Finally, the pre-game ceremony began with a few short speeches of welcome. The crowd then settled down in hushed silence.

As soon as the game began, the commentators started describing the action with phrases such as: "It's a beaut...stone-throw...he's a curler...rotate...Atul used his secret tool...that's a curler...twist!...that curl was a pearl...knocked off!...nice rock...Hollis Mathis!"

Team Russia was off to a quick start. It started out aggressively and soon had a four-point lead. Their hometown commentator called it "the Russian blitz." The team had won their National Championship and the European Continental titles. Even with their titles and the quick start, they did not derail Team USA, though the point spread was too close for the Americans' comfort. For some hometown fans, "things looked bad" and a few called it "worrisome." Just then the Russians missed the cut and had three unplanned swipes.

During the game, one commentator pointed out that competing on ice which changes from week to week is all part of the sport. His co-host added, "That calls for a heightened level of strategy and skill."

Another station's newscaster said, "Good players read the ice when they throw the first couple of shots and then they tailor their actions accordingly. The ice changes just a bit with every single throw."

A Canadian straight-laced pundit, working for CBC (Canadian Broadcasting Corporation) TV opined, "No one ever said curling is only a game when their team wins. The Russians are not going to give team USA the game. Team USA is going to have to work to take it. Neither rink (team) is invincible." The curling commentator added, "This is a continuation of the battle among the top echelon of curling teams and both rinks are on a winning streak. The two teams will be doing their best to figure out each other's potential flash points."

Team USA began by scouting and reading the ice. After that, they went to Disaster Recovery with ease. Part of the Team USA's plan was to put an end to the Russian blitz and then to shift into overdrive to make the Russians fumble. Soon Team USA was energized and began making their comeback with some revitalized deliveries. Team USA identified their strategies before they escalated their tactics and put the big squeeze. That was a difficult thing for the Russians to recognize due to skip Talerico's poker face. He was a mastermind in determining a course of action and he proved there was more than one way to move the rock. By knowing the ice and keeping a cool head, his teammates knew the path to getting the rock to hit the exact spot. McBride's southpaw movements and AR's recoil arm action especially confuzzeled the opposition. Novak had a wicked sidespin. In short, each member of the team had his secret innovative stealth strategy within the battle plan.

The Utica reporter added, "No team has more drive and ambition than this team, which wants a repeat of the miracle of 1980."

Raju remarked, "If history repeats itself, I should think we can expect to see a repeat of the glory of twenty-five years ago."

The fans closely watched the action live at the Aud and at various locations including big screen movie theaters, bars and clubs.

Regardless of where they were, the spectators voiced their own opinions, advice and instructions to the players: "Easy-easy-easy...steady as she goes...Atul, use that tool!...Steady-steady-curl-curl-curl...that's a cliff hanger...stay cool and collected...curve-baby-curve!...it's a kisser...rock 'em baby...curl, baby, curl...yeah, baby, yeah...get the guard! Get the guard!...That's a zinger...slow-baby-slow...easy-does-it...real cool now... Gotcha! Gotcha!"

To get audience reaction, a commentator thrust a microphone before an obviously jubilant fan and asked for her opinion of the game so far. "I'm getting really good vibes about Team USA.," she gushed.

The Hip-Hop crowd watched the game with the rap artists. The curlers' moves were closely studied.

Cool Dude: Watcha he doing maan?

Rapper: Yo' Mamma!... Check out the Brown Boy!

Cool Dude: A Brown Boy did those moves?

Rapper: Maan!... I've never seen that move before.

Some spectators considered themselves skips and barked out instructions over the airwaves: "A little to the right...now go straight...keep going...OK! Just up, ahead curl...curl...slow...good ...good...right there!...Stop! Sweet and smooth...Mmwwaahh!"

Team USA recovered from the point spread, a feat they pulled off several times in the game which was going back and forth. The skip wannabes zoomed in on every move of the rock and players.

The fans' favorite chants were: "Deliver it, Doc...Roll that Rock... Rock it, Baby...Atta Boy!...Keeping on rocking...Rock Solid...Rock the World...The Doc Rocks...Over the Top...Bee-yoo-tiful...Rock is on and Roll is on...You can run, but you can't hide." The control freaks rejoiced over the special deliveries - special Ds, as they called them. Some transmitted these tantalizing plays and perfect deliveries over their "Get-it-now! Enabled phones." The messages they sent were on the quarter-hour account of the game that traveled faster and to more places that sunlight. The phones buzzed with descriptives: "finally got one...brilliant...lucky break...hit the mark...an instant success!"

Raju commented, "AR's rocks were both on the attack and on the defense. *Do second pehle nikal liya hota to kitna acha hota* (two seconds make all the difference). The tension keeps you enthralled even when the action is merely a positioning strategy. The teams are outstanding in the field and are staying the course."

Virginia joked, "With this doctor's delivery there is none of the 'push-push'; his delivery is smooth." She added, "You know the world is going crazy when in the U.S. the best rapper is white, top golfer is black, tallest guy in the NBA is Chinese and curling's MVP is Indian."

With inexpensive long distance call rates, some local Ind-o-US gave their many relatives in India a live commentary on the game - every turn and every curl played by the world's best curlers.

The teams were in a dead heat at the end of the sixth round. Then, without interrupting the game, Team USA switched to fourth gear and went on to stay on the offensive and garner points. Every release of the stone was a boutique delivery, tailored to the skip's instructions. Their plan was get ahead on the score board and run. They had a great sweeping tandem which made for unbelievable and seamless shots. The team displayed superb talent. Every time they played, they hit the bull's eye and took a big bite out of their opponents' efforts. There were no lucky breaks for the Russians. They had no strategy to confront Team USA and curling is no automated alley.

By the end of the eighth inning, the Utica players were taking their adversaries to the cleaners with some wonderful made-to-order shots. The strategic planning by the coach and skip was paying off. The members demonstrated teamwork and tenacity along with some crafty deliveries by everyone on the team. The men were at their best! AR continued to confuse his opponents with the recoil motion of his arm after the delivery. The point lead paved the way for innovation and unrestricted ideas. Every time a Russian screwed-up on his delivery, the other players threw their hands up in frustration. It did not help when their assistant coach screamed, "Bro' what are you thinking?"

By the end of the tenth round, Team USA had mowed down the opposition and outscored Team Russia 14-8. Team USA seemed to have the monopoly on knowing how to use the ice to the team's advantage. The players were proving to be wizards at the game! They won the Continental Cup and were World Champions! For them and for America it was a banner day, a day to be etched in the memory of each fan, one for the history books. For Utica and the U.S., the victory promised a celebration on a "March Madness" level and a time to let the good times roll!

At the end of the game, the Canadian analyst said, "Any way one slices it, the U.S. was a team with a mission, fueled up and on the move. They had nothing but charm, function and style. Each member of Team USA delivered nothing but a polished performance. The players had classy deliveries which would impress the most discriminating curlers." He went on to add, "They had versatility and their deliveries were comparable to fluid-motion consistency. They will be Olympic hopefuls for next year both as a team and as individuals."

With the fans still cheering wildly in the background, Raju added, "The only thing I remember about the game was how quickly it went - '*hava nikal gaya from the cykill*' (took the wind out of the sails).

The eagerly anticipated awards ceremony followed. Both teams walked in style down the red carpet. The president of the World Curling Federation met the teams and praised the players for a job well done. He said, "The play doesn't get any better that what you displayed today right before our eyes." The players were showered with floral bouquets. Fans positioned themselves next to their favorite players and smiled for the cameras. After the photo-ops, both teams enjoyed the customary celebration with their coaches, the support staff and the VIPs. The Utica Curling Club provided a delectable feast - Hungarian beef stew, chicken breast with an almond crust, salmon and spinach bake, grilled shrimp and tropical salsa, quesadillas and enchiladas. The drinks of choice, as usual, were Labatt and Saranac beers. There were plenty of New York and California wines to please the palate.

The team members complimented one another: "Playing this match was lots of fun; it will be something to tell our grandchildren about."

Team USA's skip Talerico complimented the rivals. "When the game started, you guys were off and running."

McBride empathized with the Russians' out-of-town status. "You are all a long way from home," he told them.

The Russian skip returned the accolades. "Hats off to you! This was quite an eye-opening experience for us. When we get back it will be back to the drawing board as you guys put us through the wringer. We thought we were invincible and then you dazzled us with your non-stop upgrades and pizazz to spare."

The lead continued, "Playing the game with Team USA has earned us a wealth of experience; we have learned a lot from you – your skills and your style." And another teammate directed his praise directly to AR. "You should be critically acclaimed as a great defender." Then he moaned, "We were hard-pressed to understand your 'nutso moves' and your unbelievable ability to curl that stone. That was no accident."

AR responded, "I'm just a rookie trying to make a good impression."

The Russian persisted, "Then you're the top rookie and deserve a Rookie Award. The way you deliver a curved rock is awesome!"

AR returned the compliment. "You guys are still big shots in our view. Now you have an opportunity to benefit from this game."

Novak assured them, "As sportsmen who have reached the pinnacle of the sport, you know how to walk comfortably past the obstacles in your path." He cheered them, "Don't let the perfectionist in you take your dreams away. You players are pro to the core!"

The good-natured Russian skip wisecracked, "At home we've likely gone from 'chanting and noble' before the game to Chernobyl now!."

The vice-skip kidded the Americans. "Now that you've got the gold and become even more popular, you've likely advanced from precision to perfection. You fellas more than lived up to your fans' expectations."

With a wink and a smile, Vinny replied, "Our life will move from a 'downer to ecstasy'." And the Russian lead said, "And ours will move from 'thrill to shrill'."

The Russian skip said, "You fellas were great 'mix masters' and you made us live through the shifts; and you did it with glitz and glamour."

Talerico replied, "Y'all had versatility and started out with great hits."

Boris, the Russian coach added, "You guys were the best and the brightest." Then turning to his team he added, "Our team needs some Viagra so that our delivery can be straight."

His lead player retorted, "We were doing everything to block them. But they were a generation ahead of us in their curling techniques and they've just raised the bar with their marvelously executed shots."

Boris told Team USA, "The diversity of your play made the game so interesting and fun to watch; all four of you showed the power of partnerships. Each of you is Mr. Consistent."

Coach Mayer responded, "You were innovative and were high-excitement players yourselves, especially the way you got out of the starting gate."

Boris countered, "In that case, with the passion you guys exuded, you had the steal of the millennium." And the two teams ended the evening by shaking hands as curlers are supposed to do.

They all agreed that they would relive the experience several times over for the rest of their lives. Wherever Team USA members went, they were mobbed. In their hearts, the players realized that, as predicted, this match was a repetition of the event at Lake Placid twenty-five years earlier. Team USA was prepared and psyched to receive good wishes from all across the country.

The crowd dispersed from the Aud in bright daylight which made the day fabulous and perfect. They soon reassembled in downtown Utica's main road - Genesee Street - to celebrate their Continental Cup and World Championship title. There was just enough time for most of the fans to grab a bite to eat. There were long lines for riggies, pasta fasta, submarine sandwiches and pizza wraps. Those who were hoping for a nice cold beer headed to the stores for a case of beer. In spite of producing three million cases of beer a year (case = 24 bottles) there was an "acute shortage" for Saranac fans.

The residents of the outlying towns were faced with long lines for stuffed-pizza at Cosmo's Deli, regular pizza-to-go at Fat Nancy's or Tex-Mex pork chops at High-on-the-hog. Countless had to settle for a quick snack at the Gas 'n Grub. Afterward, everyone made it to Genesee Street for some Go-Wild parties and the "buzz." Nothing in U.S. causes more excitement than a victory celebration and today was no exception; the day's events felt like the high point and the summit all rolled into one. Utica was all gussied up and it wowed the crowds with fireworks, great food, plenty of beer, unending politeness, a big bash after the game - the whole nine yards. This was definitely an escape from the ordinary. The city basked in both the limelight and the publicity. For the crowds, it resembled a "Super Bowl Win" and "Saturday Night Fever" in one evening. Many who needed a jump-start in their interest in curling a month earlier were now turbocharged about the sport. They kept saying, "Look no further. It's all here, right before our eyes." An old timer said, "You can't get moments like these with a MasterCard." For Utica and its residents, this was possibly the biggest event of the last century. Team USA members were superheroes!

Uticans and other fans cheered by chanting "U-S-A! U-S-A!" and "You soar like eagles!" Team USA's win was the third in a series of mega victories - the National, the North American championship and the Continental Cup. Curling was the talk of the town for the next three months and everyone in the upstate region went hog-wild with celebrations. The sense of ecstasy some fans experienced could be kindly described as "absolute madness." Many called the win, "A Class Act" and predicted that this would be "a once-in-a-lifetime event," which made them even more euphoric. They jeered those who made the mistake of claiming a few months earlier that Utica could never win the international title. The local buzz was, "So, who lost the bet?"

In congested downtown Utica, the friendly and easygoing crew of policemen and city workers kept the traffic flowing and the crowds safe and orderly without dampening their spirits. The same scene was repeated in all the major cities and small towns in New York State, which was now one with Utica – "The Small City with the Big Heart." The top priority on everyone's mind was to have an all round good time. Team USA was cheered all across the state, nay, the country. The stars and stripes were flying a mile high.

The headlines in the next day's newspapers across New York blared: "ENCORE: It's déjà vu - all over again." In portraying the game, the reporter wrote that Team USA's attitude appeared to be: "Why settle for standard when we can be spectacular? The team immediately went from simple to the sensational." The writer went on, "The game started 'nice and easy' and then the home team shifted to a one-two-punch and ended with a class act having paved the way with originality and application of unrestricted ideas. The whole game was just peachy. The opposition was flummoxed in the second half of the game. When the Russians were faced with the wizardry of the U.S. play, they went from 'this is what we do and how we do it,' to nowhere. They collapsed during the latter half under relentless pressure from the U.S. team. Team Russia redeemed itself by playing a very challenging game during the first half, thereby making sure a win for the Americans would not exactly be a knock-out result." The other papers across the country described Team USA's performance as "solid, focused and delivered perfect shots."

The next day, Utica organized a grand parade for the world champs. This was to be a great shindig. All MoVa residents were in attendance, or so it seemed. The folks from the upstate region swelled the crowd, and Utica's population tripled that day. Music and dancing filled the streets. There were live bands and the crowds on the cordoned-off Genesee Street danced the shim-sham, Lindy hop, jitterbug-stroll, the Madison and samba with salsa. The Puerto-Ricans did the panchanga and bachata. Guys and dolls, young and old alike, even ones with stiff knees were now movin' 'n groovin'. Restaurants offered a wide assortment of super-sweet treats. Later that evening, fireworks lit up the sky. Utica and its residents were living their dream of being crowned athletes with an international standing!

There was a tickertape parade in New York City the following weekend. After the parade, all the popular restaurants in the Big Apple went into overdrive. New York divas and the Beautiful People showed up in style to hug and smooch the country's new heroes. The fashion-conscious fans dressed in an array of dizzying fashions to accentuate their curves and make them look thinner. The "pretty dudettes" sported the spring's hottest hair styles and wore stylish accessories; they sported purses made of chiffon, crepe and faux fur.

The sight of all these sharply-clad New Yorkers prompted some tourists to describe the Big Apple as a "Walking Fashion City with a Cool Look." New York City, the visitors decided, had a fairy-tale uptown, and a gorgeous downtown. The city's bars were packed with patrons who generated more fusion energy than a chain-reaction in a nuclear power plant. Some revelers were the hilarious, amusing and even comical types.

After the parade and a tribute to America's best, the crowds went to the trendy restaurants and hit the hot spots for fast-paced night-life. The fun-filled celebration continued! The city's theme song, "New York, New York" blared from loud speakers at every corner. Some of the elite restaurants invited Team Utica's players to attend special dinner-and-a-show performances. Later the players were entertained with show stoppers at the "chic spots," which either had funky décor, were elegant or could only be described as "beyond the ordinary."

The curlers from upstate New York felt they had just stepped into a world of fantasy and make-believe. Opulence and grandeur were evident everywhere they looked. Store windows displayed an array of futuristic, high-tech gadgets. Skyscrapers gleamed, traffic crawled and huge billboards screamed for the passerby's attention.

The next day, the curlers were back to earth. Their feel-good mood continued as they enjoyed an elaborate Champaign brunch at the stunning Giovanni Palmieri (Jack Palmer) Restaurant which served a gastronomic splurge - lobster, teriyaki steak, vegetarian entrees and high calorie desserts. After a visit to the Bowery, the team was honored at receptions and posed for photo-ops with their admirers.

Members of Team USA were national heroes and the country's interest in curling peaked. The press had glowing words of praise for the team. "In the end, one is measured by how much one has accomplished and these players have delivered a lot."

Visits to the Capitals
> 13 <

Soon after the playoff, Team USA arrived in Washington, D.C. for an honor ceremony at the nation's Capitol. From the moment they got off the plane they were mobbed by the press and paparazzi. Some of the press and TV crews bought plane tickets so that they could get past airport security, hoping to get a leg-up on the competition in getting candid shots of the teams, while they were still "glam" and fresh. A few public relations personnel, wanting a five-minute sound byte, were pleasantly surprised to find out that Team USA also had a genius for drama; and that "these curlers didn't just curl up into their shells." The players answered questions graciously and humorously, even hammed it up for the photographers. Once the players passed the security gate, the flash-bulbs popped, momentarily blinding the players. And the scene was repeated at every airport across the country, wherever the team went. The "wow" factor was high, and that infused a major "power surge" into the Team USA players.

For the next month it was the same routine - euphoria combined with humility, and meeting the adoring fans with grit and a smile. Off-camera, it was bonhomie, laughter and autographs that broke up the serious routine. The team became a media darling because the press loved the players' candor and feisty spirits. It became apparent that each player knew how to be the trendiest guy in the group. One tabloid blared, "The Dream Team also wins the Mr. Popularity contest. The team is running on all four cylinders both on and off the ice."

The teams were invited to the White House and the Capitol. They received a grand reception in the Halls of Congress and elsewhere in Washington, D.C. At the White House the players and their families walked down the red carpet, comfortably and confidently. They were ushered into the West Wing and then to the Oval Office. At the "Rewarding Excellence" ceremony, the President praised them for their convincing win and for doing a bang-up job that made their country proud. He added, "You're committed to great curling and it shows."

They also received a history lesson on the White House from tour-guide Leroy White. He noted, "The office of the president in the White House is the Oval Office which was first inaugurated in October 1909 by President W.H Taft, the 27th President. Prior to this, the office was a rectangular room in the West Wing which was built in 1902 by President Theodore Roosevelt. The Oval Office is similar in shape to the Blue Room in the White House. The Oval Office is located in the center of the West Wing to make it more convenient for the President to be involved in the operations of his presidency." For the Uticans' benefit, the guide added this piece of information: "In 1909, President Taft's Vice-President was James S. Sherman from Utica."

The White House staff showered the curlers with souvenirs and autographed photographs of the president. Then it was on to the Capitol, which was originally built in 1793. Since that time, it had been burned, rebuilt, extended and restored. Daryl Washington, the team's escort, said, "This building houses the meeting chambers and offices of the U.S. Senate and the House of Representatives. It's a monument to the American people." Daryl went on to add, "Before 1791, the federal government had no permanent site. The early Congresses met in eight different cities: Philadelphia, Baltimore, Lancaster, York, Princeton, Annapolis, Trenton and New York."

Daryl continued, "In 1788, Maryland donated ten square miles for a permanent site. The following year, Virginia presented a similar gift. The French engineer, Pierre Charles L'Enfant, planned the new city. L'Enfant arranged the streets and avenues in a grid overlaid with baroque diagonals similar to the Versailles gardens. The Capitol building was located at the elevated east end." The site was, in L'Enfant's words, "a pedestal waiting for a monument."

The U.S. Capitol Complex includes the Capitol, (the House and Senate office buildings), the Library of Congress buildings, the Supreme Court building, the U.S. Botanical Garden, the Capitol grounds and various support facilities. A Capitol Visitor Center is under construction. Team USA and their family members received a royal tour and were able to sightsee in style. Mayer said, "This personally escorted visit is the coolest and easiest way to enjoy the city,"

From afar, the famous tourists were able to identify the cast-iron dome, the most visible symbol of the Capitol. Before entering the Capitol, they passed the parking lot reserved for senators, congressmen and - women and other VIPs with passes. The team admired the hot rods parked there, including the Cadis, BMWs, Lexus, Roll-Royces, Pajeros, Studebakers and other assorted styles of wheels, including a Jag and Ferrari. Utica's congressman was their proud escort to the Capitol and he met them at the steps of the building. Beaming from ear to ear, he said, "The dome was constructed between 1855 and 1866, and is the most distinguishing landmark of the building. Its design and construction came along as the architecture evolved. Only the west front terraces (1884 to 1892) and the east front extension (1958 to 1962) are more recent additions to the Capitol." (*Govt. print and electronic brochures)*

Wherever they went, the team got bear hugs from the exhilarated onlookers. The team was referred to as "The Wizards from Utica," and judging by the reaction of the crowd, they could have been the Wizards from Oz. The players had gone from being just the "talk of the town," to the "talk of the nation," and then "talk of the curling world!"

In the Rotunda, they came upon a large group that screamed, "Go, Go, Go," and "Y'a Rock, Y'a Rock, Y'a Rock!" That was just a hint of the shape of things to come...it was an impromptu rendition of "One o'clock, two o'clock, three o'clock, Rock!" The lady senator from New York planted a warm "Welcome to the Capitol" kiss on the cheek on each player. In her welcoming speech she said, "Challenges can bring out the worst or the best in us. In your case, it brought out the best and the finest. Your unsurpassed success makes all New Yorkers and all Americans proud."

The Capitol is dominated by the Rotunda - a large, domed, circular room in the center of the second floor. Its walls hold historic paintings depicting major events in U.S. history, including a giant fresco painting of the first President in all his and the country's grandeur.

From the well of the Senate chamber, the senior New York senator read his prepared text praising the American curling team and World Champions. His speech was punctuated with phrases such as "the right stuff," "the enthusiasm you have," and "you make us proud." From the well of that esteemed institution, other Congressional representatives also made flattering remarks about the upstate New Yorkers. The team listened to the speeches and then toured the Capitol like royal visitors. The elected representatives joined Team USA's entourage for a scrumptious meal of roasted salmon with citrus-caper relish, roasted beef tenderloin with red wine gravy, and Creole shrimp followed by orange-berry smoothies. After second helpings, several politicos were overheard confessing, "Over-indulged at lunch," and "Uh-oh, I ate too much!" and "We'll do it again at tonight's White House dinner for these guys." At the night's black-tie function the curlers were lionized by the Washington establishment. Music for dancing was performed by Irving's Big Band and the New Yorkers showed off their slick classical ballroom dance steps as they did the meringue, the tango and the salsa with the Cuban motion.

When New York's governor came for the Continental Cup game, he had invited both teams to the State's capital. The week following the match, the two teams were to be guests of the government for an awards event in Albany in the morning and later in the day the teams would take a trip to nearby Hunter Mountain for some skiing. So the Muscovites were treated to a bus ride down the entire length of the MoVa. Along the way, the players chatted and related personal and family stories. Vinny observed, "Prior to this game, the only Russian city I had heard of was Bloody-Bostok (Vladivostok). Now, I know about Majestic Moscow."

The Russian player responded humorously, "On our return home, we go to a quiet resort on the Volga River, a special place for our national athletes. It's called Volgology, where we study Errorology."

AR said, "That's where you guys pick up and go over your errors?"

Pat added, "We do the same thing here in the U.S. every Monday morning, while we are at work. And we get paid to do it."

Teddy admitted, "Some curling mistakes are too much fun to make them just once."

The talk got around to kids. AR offered his response to complaints about today's irresponsible kids. "If raising children was going to be easy, it never would have started with something called 'labor'!"

Then the conversation shifted gears and focused on the great camaraderie curlers have and the resultant weight gain. Novak said, "Brain cells come and brain cells go, yet fat cells live forever."

The Russian coach joked, "When I was young I went 'skinny dipping' in the Volga, now I just 'chunky dunk'."

As the bus drove along the foothills of the Adirondacks, the visitors were shown several glass houses. Mrs. Zhukov joked, "These homes surely have a basement. A woman who lives in a glass house should have a place to change her clothes."

Pat told the group, "My wife is an angel." The Russian skip replied, "I am so sorry to hear that. Yet, you are lucky. Mine is still alive."

Mrs. Federov told the crowd that she and her husband have disagreements: "He thinks he is god and I don't."

Mrs. Pavlov said, "The man who stands on the toilet is high on pot."

All the curlers had a good laugh and enjoyed the witty play on words. As a rule, the cerebral curlers do not go for potty humor as that leads to poopy jokes.

As the teams and organizers drove along Interstate 90, (New York Thruway), they passed Amsterdam, once considered the "Carpet City." The passengers viewed a documentary on the important towns and cities they didn't have time to visit to learn a bit of the state's history.

The town of Saratoga Springs was the most fascinating for the curlers. This town is a nineteenth century spa town which members of the Gilded Age visited to enjoy the mineral springs and attend the horse races to bet on their favorite thoroughbreds. The oldest racetrack in the country has flourished, especially during the summer, with activity peaking in August. The city's downtown streets are lined with cafes, bistros, bars and other boutiques. Downtown sidewalks are decorated with flower beds, period lighting and equine statues. The racetrack opened in 1864, and as expected, there is also the National Museum of Racing, as well as the Saratoga Performing Arts Center, and the Saratoga National Historic Site, which recounts the Battle of 1777 when the British General John Burgoyne, surrendered. The victory encouraged the colonial patriots and the French to join forces which led to their final victory at York Town in 1781. Other on-site memorabilia includes General Phillip Schuyler's house, where George Washington, Benjamin Franklin and the Marquis de Lafayette were entertained. The history buffs among the Russians made a resolution to revisit the area for a more extended period of study and fun. (*City's print and electronic brochures*)

Saratoga Springs and nearby Lake George are favorite summer destinations for Uticans, including the Reddys. The ambiance of the area was just what they needed to erase the stress of a hectic work schedule and the strains of life. Anita and Atul considered Saratoga Springs the best environment for a summer weekend getaway and often came here. AR recalled his many experiences in the area. "While walking downtown, my wife and I enjoyed admiring the latest summer fashions, wonderful window boxes, and bright statues. People-watching is also fun here. We see bosom buddies, some in trendy outfits and others in retro wear, strolling along or hanging around as singles or dynamic duos." He then praised the city's unique atmosphere. "There are bistros, cafes, gourmet restaurants, brasseries and confectionaries all serving their sinfully delicious delicacies and extensive wine selections. The boutiques carry the latest fashions and the art galleries display their timeless paintings and sculptures."

AR then described a typical day at the races. "We were fascinated by women who seemed to be well aware of their glamorous looks and haute-couture designs. There was no cheap chic in this crowd. Some walked with the distinct air of 'somebody-has-to-look-beautiful-so-it-might-as-well-be-me.' Last summer was a truly hot one and skin was 'in'. After the races, race goers spent their time wining, dining, reclining and whining. A few moaned about their favorite horse and talked about the tough course as well as the jockey who, in their opinion, was not all together there." Then AR added the tip he received from a bookie, "One way to stop a runaway horse is to bet on him." All this humor stopped at crunch time when the race highlighted the purpose of their being there. After that, the race goers were back to fun and frippery.

Downtown, the Reddys noticed a dramatic change in the crowd. The people were either older folks or families with small children in tow. The Reddys couldn't help overhearing an especially loud and jovial woman who regaled her listeners with one-liners. "I always look after a husband; I don't care whose"..."My own husband is an accountant, yet he can't figure me out"..."He's smart, he thinks twice before saying nothing." A listener said, "Is your husband hard to please?" She replied, "I don't know, I never tried," then joked, "Hubby and I are divorced. He thought he was divine and I told him what to do with his belief." The Reddys' visits to Saratoga Springs included trips to the museums and other must-see spots. All this walking made them hungry and they usually made their way to their favorite restaurant where they ordered sautéed red snapper with mango salsa, and strawberry sundaes. The chef once gave them an insider's look into his culinary castle - his *bella cucina* (beautiful kitchen).

Later on, they took in a stand-up comedy show. The female comedian obviously wanted to take a jab at lawyers. "Talk is cheap unless it's done by a lawyer, an individual who helps you get what is coming to him." She would add, "Lawyers are professionals who spend YOUR last dollar to prove THEY are right. Theirs is the only occupation that can write 5,000 or more words and call it a brief." Her parting shot: "Lawyers are people who can legally go from bar to bar - bar hopping - for your sake." This was one of the Reddy family's favorite Saratoga Springs' Sunday-night-special-dinner-out routines.

As the bus reached Albany, the curlers learned the city is the oldest in New York and one of the older cities in the country. Albany is located on the navigable portion of the Hudson River. The river itself is named after Henry Hudson, who arrived in 1609. The Hudson River is often described as "the arms of the Atlantic Ocean," with its tides coming up into the river. Albany began as a Dutch settlement in 1630 and because of its location it became a major transportation hub even before the Erie Canal was built. In 1825, when the canal, which connected the Great lakes to the Atlantic, was completed, the importance and the population of the city mushroomed. Later, the railroads arrived and Albany became the major link between east and west for everything from trade to cattle-shipping and human migration.

While in Albany, the curlers visited the Empire State Plaza - a vast complex of buildings which includes the state capital and other New York state and city government buildings, State Museum, the Plaza Art Collection, Visitors' Center, Corning Tower and the Empire Center at the Egg. Here they learned a few facts about the Empire State: state bird – red-breasted blue bird; flower – rose; fruit – apple; gem – garnet; tree – sugar maple; fish – brook trout; animal – beaver; insect – lady bug; fossil – Eurypterids Remipes (sea scorpion); beverage – milk; motto – "Excelsior (Ever Upward)"; muffin – apple. *(The Capital and City's print and electronic brochures).*

Their tour guide, Rose Kittle, explained, "The capital has been the seat of government since the 1800s. It is a marvelous culmination of three decades of craftsmanship and the visions of five architects." Built by hand of solid masonry, it houses the beautiful legislative chambers of the Senate and assembly. The curlers were amazed by the opulence of the Senate chambers and the hand-carved oak ceiling. The major portions of two walls are covered with gold leaf. The marble is Italian, the granite is Scottish, the onyx is Mexican, and the leather is from Spain. The sightseers could only imagine the kind of deals that politicians have struck around the two identical fireplaces, aptly called the "whispering fireplaces." The team was even more astounded by the Great Western Staircase, which took 14 years to construct. Rose noted, "It was completed in 1896, and nicknamed the 'Million Dollar Staircase'." Portraits of prominent New Yorkers were carved in stone along the upper edges of the walls. The skills of the stone carvers are evident on every pillar and wall. The most intriguing is the face of a gargoyle, about the width of a quarter, tucked obtrusively inside a larger carving. Pointing to it, Rose added, "The masons traditionally carved one of these in a church to keep evil spirits away." Rose also pointed out the governor's residence - a McMansion.

The curlers spotted their local politicians who were flushed with excitement and displayed their jovial and self-congratulatory mood. Though it was late-winter, not a single official was pale. Some had a hint of a tan, while others were quite "golden brown." Several talked about fairways and fishing holes and the hook-up and shoot-out. The tone of their conversations regarding their vacations made it obvious that they were control freaks. These were men and women who make a difference in the lives of New Yorkers and they were proud of their work. They and the curlers got plenty of airtime.

The players were introduced to the powerful who were snappy looking. No one was cantankerous, abrasive or overbearing, at least to these esteemed guests. The politicos enjoyed meeting the curlers and told them how the political system works. One seasoned politician said, "*Quando omni flunkus moritati* - when all else fails, play dead." A curler quipped, "That's the strategy often used in curling." Knowing the curlers were a humorous bunch, one senator remarked, "Sometimes a majority only means that all the fools are on the same side."

The award ceremony and the reception that followed were short. The governor told Team USA, "You have brought pride to our country and to our state. The reward for a thing well done comes from knowing you have done it admirably." The governor told the Russians, "You were top-shelf guys." Utica's assemblywoman said to the two teams, "There are no shortcuts to any place worth going and y'all have proved it in such an exemplary way." The senator added, "I watched your two teams play with so much grace. To use a stealth angler's terminology, all of you had 'smooth casting motion'."

The U.S. skip thanked the governor and the politicos for the event and their presence at the two games in Utica. The skip injected his typical brand of humor in his response: "What we anticipate seldom occurs; what we least expect generally happens." He then went on to explain what the politicians knew well, "Teamwork is essential - it allows us to blame someone else." At the press interview, Team USA shared its secrets: "When we need a laugh to relieve stress, we play a DVD of our bloopers and we laugh at our errors - everybody else does! When we poke fun at ourselves we exercise our inalienable and 'our own constitutionally' protected 'Right to Laugh'."

After completing the formalities, the teams continued on their city tour. At their next stop, the tour guide informed the players, "The Hudson Valley is called the Napa Valley of the East." The team visited the malls for quick shopping and browsing. Again, they were mobbed by throngs who yelled, "Go, go, go," and "Y'a rock, y'a rock, y'a rock!"

The stores carried the latest spring styles. The shopaholics were out in force. Judging from their possessions it appeared as if they had one goal - "Gotta see it, gotta get it." Window-shoppers and those suffering from cabin-fever also enjoyed the dazzling sights in the store fronts. Wherever the teams went, the crowds took a break from shopping to go absolutely gaga over the world's best curlers.

The curlers were amazed and amused by the number of people with tattoos. Teddy exclaimed, "Do you realize that in forty years, we'll have thousands of old ladies and men running around with tattoos?"

A group of Aussies who were also visiting the capital city spotted the players and yelled, "Owyergoin!...Y'a true Blue!...Awesome!" The Australians invited the curlers for shrimp-on-the-barbie, if ever either team traveled Down Under.

After some Pinot Noir and A Taste of Albany wine sampling at a nearby vineyard, the curlers boarded the bus and headed for the ski slopes. They were keenly anticipating getting onto the slopes of the famous Hunter Mountain Ski Resort. After welcoming them, a guide told the group, "Hunter Mountain is called the snow-making capital of the world." The ski season here lasts for about 160 days. Hunter Mountain is known as the closest big mountain to New York City. The mountain has 240 acres for skiers to enjoy, including forty-seven slopes and trails for all levels of skill and stamina for both downhill and cross-country skiing. (*Resort's print and electronic brochures).*

The curlers chose to ski in style far away from the maddening crowds and had a great time on the slopes. After the initial instant exhilaration and adrenaline rush, they enjoyed the smooth sailing down the slopes as they tried their various moves. Like other skiers, they tried gliding, snow-plowing and side-slipping. This was the last hurrah of the ski season and the holiday's grand finale. A group of Down Under skiers spotted the Team USA's players and shouted their accolades: "You rule; Ace; all right, buddy; all right, mate!"

Some curlers preferred snowshoeing and the network of trails at the summit of Hunter Mountain provided them with views of the pristine wilderness of the northern Catskills, far from the bustle and activity of the base lodge and ski slopes. Modern snowshoes are made of aircraft-grade aluminum and rugged neoprene. They strap on to any boot, allowing maneuverability in deep snow, crusty surfaces and on ice. The high-tech snowshoes are lightweight and not bulky in contrast to those made with wood and leather. With high-tech materials and clever engineering, new snowshoes allow the walkers to navigate through the deep snow as well as narrow, wooded trails.

As AR informed the others, winter is not the only time when Hunter Mountain comes alive. "For New Yorkers, Hunter Mountain plays host to all who enjoy the outdoors." The Reddys especially enjoyed the summer weekend festivals, including the German Alps Festival, Celtic Festival, Microbrewery and Wine fest and the two weekends of Oktoberfests. Whether these were ethnic festivals or not, the Reddys, like other revelers, dressed in casual and comfortable clothing to enjoy great family fun at Hunter Mountain. Most of these ethnic events were accompanied by arts and crafts fairs. In the summer, the Reddys would ride the cable car to the peak for a relaxing stroll amid nature, where all sense of time and pressures faded away. They inhaled the refreshing air, walked away from their worries and enjoyed the beautiful sunsets - a wow sensation!

After skiing, the curlers and their families regrouped for dinner at the ski resort's cafe. The Russians sampled scrumptious salmon as well as other delectable entrees. For dessert, many chose the all-American banana split with toppings. Friendships were made while breaking bread together. In keeping with that spirit, the players promised to keep in touch and perhaps visit one another again, soon.

Ingrid said, "Friendship is like wine, it gets better as it grows older." Anita had a different comparison: "Friendship is like good health; you don't know you have it until you lose it." Mrs. Krakov knew every woman would get her simile: "A friend is like a good bra - hard to find, supportive, comfortable, and always close to your heart!" Then she added, "Sometimes going bra-less pulls out wrinkles from your face."

Everyone looked forward to returning home and their routines. Being in the spotlight was initially fun and exhilarating yet the glamour soon wore thin. The players looked forward to "spring flings" with their families – a time to be themselves again, away from flashbulbs and autograph books. Before the Russian curlers returned home, they stopped at the Utica malls to do their major shopping for themselves, their families and friends back home. They had come to the U.S.

armed with their shopping lists filled with requests for American fashions, perfumes and jewelry. The players accomplished their task with gusto. When in doubt, they went for the lingerie and the sporting goods departments. The men had a mission: when they stepped off the plane in Moscow, they were going to do it in style as the European Curling Champions.

For Team USA, it continued to be a whirlwind of celebrations. At times, they felt they were living in a fantasy world. They were praised for their versatility, dexterity and tenacity. Yet the players did not consider themselves "big shots." They returned home the same regular guys they were before the big win; their families made sure of that. Their wives kept reminding the players that they now walked on terra firma not on (frozen) water. They still had to cart the weekly garbage to the curb. The kids made sure dad periodically got "reality checks." The players returned to their jobs; their bosses wanted productivity along with all the publicity.

The team members and their wives sometimes talked about the pitfalls of being in the limelight. Anita used curling humor to remind Team USA, "You guys can develop your appetites out of the house; but you gotta be at home for the main course." She was acting as spokeswoman for the spouse-sisterhood of Team USA. The ladies had female intuitions. They could detect changes in their "perfect mates." The spouses took turns to regularly remind the men of their priorities.

Angela, the skip's wife, said to the team, "Publicity is like poison."

Colleen added, "So, it won't hurt you if you don't swallow or inhale."

Ingrid gave it straight. "Remember, curling's not a contact sport - and let's keep it that way." Olga jibed, "Behind every successful man, there's a woman; and behind every failed man, there are two."

Anita added, "We'll let you chase girls but won't let you catch them."

This was all said in jest, and kept inside the winner's circle, but the message was clear. Team USA was getting to be a fatally attractive collection of stud muffins. There were curling champion wannabes asking the curlers to divulge some of their secret curling strategies.

AR reassured the spouses that the curlers' slogan was, "Beauty is in the eye of the beer holder." Teddy quoted a Polish proverb. "Our wives are being like *'Rodzynek – stroskane winogrono"* (raisin - a worried grape). Talerico added, "There are two theories to winning an argument with women. Neither one works." Mayer chuckled and reassured the team, "Take it easy! Just think if it wasn't for marriage, men would go through life thinking they had no faults at all."

While they enjoyed meeting people across the U.S., the curlers also took the time to visit the National Parks in the states they visited. Having lived in the shadows of and enjoyed the Adirondack National Park, the curlers and their families appreciated the natural splendor of this great country. At the parks, they enjoyed the solitude and breath-taking beauty. Their visits to the Western States (Colorado, Arizona and Utah) took them to different sections of the Stone Canyons of the Colorado plateau, where they enjoyed smorgasbords of Sculptured Stone at its best, especially the grand dame of them all - the Grand Canyon. Their visit to Washington State permitted them to visit the North Cascades, Mount Rainier and Olympic National Parks.

The highlight of the team's tour was undoubtedly their visit to the Golden State for fun-in-the-sun and tours of the cities in super-cars which invariably were the coolest models to come out of Detroit. Even their opponents at the National Curling finals played host to Team USA in northern California. Its world championship status was a consolation to the Bay Area curlers who lost to the New Yorkers in the nationals.

Team USA enjoyed the best the Bay Area had to offer in food, wine and song, followed by breath-taking sunsets across the Pacific Ocean as nightfall enveloped the waters. This was an enchanting atmosphere the upstate New York curlers rarely experienced - perfect nights out which ended with desserts beyond the ordinary. In San Fran, Team USA took time out to visit Angel Island which was "the Ellis Island of the West." From 1910 to 1940, the island was the gateway for Oriental immigrants, mainly the Chinese, who numbered 175,000.

Tributes to America's best curlers continued to flow in from all over the country and the curling world. The team was being inundated with tons of mail, all with requests for an autograph, which the fans promised to save "for the next generation." The team's families had started a new chapter in their lives. They were looking forward to relaxing holidays where they could regain their privacy and make up for the long, tedious hours they had spent on the ice before the game and on the road during the post-victory hoopla. For the moment, the team enjoyed the sensational adventure. Besides, they were an inspiration to the countless individuals who expressed their joy at seeing these working-stiff American curlers in the flesh.

Acclaim across the Country
> 14 <

Team USA players were the chief guests at numerous events across the country. At formal dinners, they were feted with fine wine and champagne; later, they were entertained with both American and Latin music. The dress codes at these packed-to-the-cheek parties ranged from "black-tie" to the "glam-rock" and "punk-rock looks" to "pompadour outfits" with retro jewelry and a spritz of expensive perfume. Some flaunted trendy designers' creations such as sexy cigarette pants. "Les Femmes" exuded drama with all the bling, including gold and diamond bracelets. High fashion statements galore! These were obvious the moment the guests stepped out of the wheels that brought them to the events - El Dorados, Cougars, Corvettes, Thunderbirds, Caddies, Porsches and Ferraris.

Like a group of seasoned politicians, members of Team USA loved to press the flesh at these appearances. The crowds admired these superheroes because they were professionals both on and off the ice, whom every young boy and girl could emulate. The crowds were even more inspired by seeing Team USA players in person. Their admirers found them to be really down-to-earth. Team USA was proud that they could inspire and be role models for the next generation, a feat which would make the curlers even more legendary.

Curlers in the audience praised the team for its exhilarating close-up deliveries; the rookies inquired about the team's offensive and defensive attacks as well as its strong hitting game. Team USA reaffirmed what every curler knows: "The skill lies in achieving consistency." For Team USA, this was turning out to be an enchanting April! Life was full of action and fantasies had become reality!

The team deliberately made these events a fun experience for everyone by going for the big laughs. Their lines included: "On the way here we discovered there is no egg in eggplant, nor ham in hamburger; English muffins weren't invented in England or French fries in France." The curlers told the youngsters, "Santa's helpers are subordinate clauses." At the close of the get-togethers, the team always thanked their well-wishers and told them that this whole experience was the upside of their downtime. "We are glad to be part of a sport which includes both the young and the old. Besides, it teaches so many valuable lessons. We want to share with you the fruits of our labor."

The curlers knew how to sing and dance to rock-n-roll music, especially the state's theme song – "I love New York." These tunes would also lead the audience to dance the swing, jitterbug, Lindy-Hop, Breakaway, Black Bottom, Carolina Shag and the Charleston - all classical American dances. Some did the Puerto-Rican charanga; a few also danced the salsa with the Cuban motion and the salsa suelta, in which it's not the moves but how you move that "turns a gaze." With all that bogeying going on, Team U.SA and their wives were developing some pretty hip moves on the dance floor. The wives became "Les Belles of the Ball" and their hubbies were called "the Mambo kings."

The team invited the audiences to learn to curl and said it would be well worth their time. They promised that curling would allow even the novices to, "lead off and show your moxie in style." The team always had a parting message for the crowds, "We love you all," which was spontaneously reciprocated by a thunderous standing ovation. Team USA loved this remarkable scene which occurred at every event. It appeared as if the players' plea was: "Please, take me to heaven!"

Physicians were prominent among the guests at every stop; the most energized participants in this crowd were the members of ASTRO (American Society of Therapeutic Radiation Oncologists) of which Dr. Reddy was a longstanding member. ASTRO members could be found in every city and formed their own little groupies at these events. They praised AR for his successes. Each Team USA member enjoyed the warm welcome, the enthusiastic bear hugs from the devoted fans and never-ending photo-ops.

Vinny Talerico and his wife, Angela, were congratulated across America by The Sons and Daughters of Italy clubs, Saints Cosmos and Damian Societies, and Orders of IL Romano. There was plenty of *congratulazioni* (congrats), music and singing of traditional Italian songs - both with accompaniment and a cappella. Vinny was already the hottest ticket for next year's Winter Olympics. In anticipation of their visit to Vinny's ancestral town, the Talericos brushed up on their Naples traditions, fluency with Italian and Tarantella dance steps. Vinny practiced the most important phrase: "*Ti amo* - We love you all."

Colleen and Patrick McBride were toasted with Guinness by Green Clubs, Shamrock Associations and Brigadoon get-togethers as they traveled across the U.S. and the Green Isle. Patrick and Colleen were entertained by Irish dancers and in turn, the McBrides danced the jig to "Kesch Jig" and the slide to "Chase me Charlie." Paddy picked up Gaelic words like: *Buakas Edia* (Thanks be to God), *Gurama Agus* (Thank you), *Nor harbarae* (Don't mention it / Same to you), *Sloan La* (Welcome) and *Sloan Awalia* (Safe trip home). He readily said to the crowds, "*Taim i' ngra leat* - I love y'all." He was ready to be the grand-marshal at the next St. Patrick's Day parade.

Olga and Teddy Novak were congratulated at Falcon Clubs in the U.S. as well as in Poland. The Novaks were getting good at hop polka. He revised his knowledge of Polish history and the contributions of famous Poles like Copernicus, Chopin and Pope John-Paul II. His *bratowa* (sister-in-law) Janet Lecki coached him and Olga on basic Polish customs which included singing traditional songs and dancing the *Goralski, Lubelski, Kujawiak-Oberek* (polka-waltz). The Novaks would proudly say, "*Mowimy po Polsku*" (We speak Polish) ending their speeches with "*Kocham ciebie* - We love you all."

Ingrid and Max Mayer were fêted with *Kleine Kappelle* (quartets) and dancing by the Deutsch-Amerikanischer Klubs across America. At the Klubs, the star was invited to join the choral group as he was an old hand at yodeling. It felt like Christmas and the Bavarian fest rolled into one event in April. Beer and *Wassail* flowed to warm the spirit and heart, followed by German entrées such as *Rouladen* and "the best of the *wurst*." Then Black Forest cake and other delicacies were served. It was all *wunderba*! Max and *frau* (wife) Ingrid were very much at ease saying, "*Wir sprechen Deutsch* (we speak German)." His closing words to the crowds were, "*Ich liebe dich* - I love you all." Before the Mayers visited *Alemannia* (Germany), they perfected their Rhinelander and Schuhplattlers dance routines which they had learned at the Maennerchor (German-American) club, many moons ago.

Team USA and their families traveled across the country at the invitation of the local curling clubs. All the invitations had to go through Novak who was the "Manager of the Boyz." He made the executive decisions and took the trouble to coordinate the schedule with their hosts. At various stops, the players were lionized by the local media and were feted with Country, Western, Jazz, Cajun, Rock, Bluegrass and Techno pop music as well as Square Dancing, the Two Step and folk dances. The driver made sure he stopped before the passengers complained that their "back-teeth were floating," which in his experience invariably led to a wee-wee chain reaction. Invariably, one of the kids would hold up the bus with the request: "Gotta drain me dragon." And the driver definitely preferred to stop than to mop. The traveling media circus had a field day.

At the after-dinner speeches, the curlers regaled the crowd with their one-liners: "For us, a weekend wasted isn't a wasted weekend" and "We don't let yesterday take up too much of today." One curler would invariable recount the story of a Utica derelict who had seen more than his share of hard times. He approached the Team USA player on the street and said, "Hey, Buddy, can you spare two bucks?"

The curler asked, "Are ya going to gamble it on a crap game?"

"No way, I don't gamble," answered the derelict.

"You wouldn't waste it on curling, would you?" asked the curler.

"Never," said the derelict, "I'm not into curling."

So, the curler asked the chap if he would like to come home with him for a home-cooked meal. The offer was eagerly accepted. As they were heading for the house, the derelict's curiosity peaked. "Won't the lady be angry when she sees a guy like me at your table?"

"Probably," wisecracked the curler. "Yet, it will be worth it. I want my wife to see what happens to a guy who doesn't gamble or curl."

Members of Team USA felt proud of themselves that they could inspire a new generation of Americans just as the U.S. ice hockey team had done twenty-five years earlier. The women, both young and not-so-young, had thoughts of their own on seeing this bunch of smiling faces. Each curler was a guy's guy – one with whom the tough-macho-superheroes and the suave-sophisticated-artistic types could identify. At the whistle stops in different states across the U.S., the events invariably ended with the singing of "God Bless America," or "America the Beautiful." The crowds and the beauty of America inspired the players to make these weekend trips and be back to work on Monday morning – bright and fresh.

The only task left for Team USA, the grand-daddies of curling, was to make reservations for the 2006 Winter Olympics in Turin, Italy. The team was positive that by then, they could charm the Italians with, "*Parliamo Italiano* (We speak Italian)." In turn, they would be ready to respond when the Italians said, "*Ciao Bambinos.*"

Asian-American communities throughout the U.S. also invited Dr. Atul and Anita Reddy - their new celebrities – to visit their towns. AR was awarded even more engraved plaques. The events were a "who's-who" of the local and regional Ind-o-US and Asian-Americans. Invitations came from the local Indian-American associations and chapters of AAPI (American Association of Physicians of Indian origin), of which Dr. Reddy was a lifetime member. Within this crowd, the overnight BUMA (Bombay University Medical Alumni) members strutted with pride.

Many BUMA doctors knew AR from undergraduate and medical school. Some flew in especially for the occasion and to get AR's autograph. In typical Bombay style, these avant-garde docs and their mates warmly kissed the cheeks of the chief guest and his wife. The BUMA grads from the big city of Bombay had a lot going for them. As students, they were either the studious types or Calamity Jane-like party animals. Like most individuals who settle down, they were now married, older, wiser and with kids a.k.a. *sudraod* (mellowed).

At each standing-room only community event, there was an area set aside for photographs. Mothers could be heard hurrying their broods to come for this prestigious photo-op. "Come, Come! Soon, Soon! Papa is taking the family photograph with the new Indian hero."

At the other end, the raucous crowd chowed down on delicious Indian finger foods while pop and classical Indian music played in the background. In big cites, the *desi-devis* (Indian-goddesses) displayed their avant-garde Indian and American fashion sense. They wore trendy outfits - *libaas* (ensemble), exquisite saris, *lehngas* (skirts) or *mashru* - wrap of satin, silk or cotton. Some of the garments were embellished with *zardozi embroidery* (metal-wrapped yarn) around precious or semi-precious stones. *Devis, bibis*, *pretties* and *petites* (glam gals wedded to Indian studs) coordinated their *vastra* (clothes) with stylish accessories as well as color coordinated *bindis*, *mang tikka* and *moti* (bead or pearl on the forehead). A few also wore the *sindhur* (red powder on the parting in their hair). Some displayed their *jhumka* (bell-shaped) or *mina kari* (colored) jewelry. Their outfits reflected the individuality, grace and fashion sense of *Bharati* (Indian) women. It was a scene from a hypothetical movie, "Lakshmi and Padma Devis meet Madonna Diva."

Few *babus* (Indian men) coordinated their traditional outfits with elaborately embroidered *jutis* (slip-on shoes with upturned toes). The

Reddys were *gazzaled* (serenaded) with songs of *Tum Mile Dil Khile, Pehla Pehla Pyar Hai, Ek Ladki Ko Dekha and Dilber Dil Jaani.* There were a zillion *namastes* - hellos and goodbyes. It was another occasion when the next generation of Ind-o-US and Asian-Americans could learn the traditional dances, chants and culture. Covering all the activities were the local TV stations, newspapers and the paparazzi.

These *tamashas* (festivities) always provided a place to share news, advice and humor among acquaintances and friends. Others developed new contacts and reconnected old bonds. The Reddys became the alter-egos of the two million Indian men and women in America who had sacrificed long and hard to build successful careers in a new land. They were steeped in traditional ways which included high-intensity parenting. The attendees were committed dads and "soccer moms." At these festive occasions, the socialites arrived in their fancy hot rods and classic cars, and then proceeded to compliment one another on how sharp they all looked – a mutual admiration society.

The younger female crowd of *sweetu, sweetie, babli, beti, tini* was in their slinky satin evening dresses. Each trendy style had a buzz of its own. The teens strutted some of the hottest American, European and Indian designer outfits. The crowds of pretty dudettes were a cross between (Indian) Jasmine and Jennifer (Lopez) with their chandelier earrings and haute couture outfits. The beautiful, confident, smiling first generation Indian-American gals could have been contestants at the U.S. version of "Lakme India Fashion Week" contest.

The crowd arrived in their sizzling hot-rods with daddy at the wheel - chauffeurs are rare in America. Garlands of marigolds or sandalwood (especially flown in from India) were presented to the honored guests and bonhomie speeches were made. The night could best be described as Lights, Dazzle, Diamonds and Show-time. Indian music rocked the house with old favorites and new songs for the listening and dancing pleasure of the guests. Excitement was in the air as were the aromas of spicy Indian food. At the end of the parties there was the usual rush by the inebriated to find their DD (designated driver). Old Timers were proud to see *apna beta* (our son) on top of the world!

At most Indian functions, there were toasts, acknowledgments and orations, little of which interested the crowd. The mood changed the minute Dr. Reddy stood up to speak. Then the crowd paid close attention. In his speech, Dr. Reddy thanked the organizers and the guests for their good wishes. He encouraged the audience to maintain their cultural values and then shared with them a humorous story:

A 70-year-old *chacha* (grandpa) who lived in Mumbai called his son in Chicago just before Christmas. "Your mother and I are sad to inform you that after fifty years of marriage we've decided to get a divorce."

The shocking news stunned the son, leaving him speechless. When he collected his wits he said, "Papa, let me talk to my sister in Washington, D.C. One of us will get back to you, very *jaldi* (soon) - within the next half hour." Fifteen minutes later, the daughter called her father. "I just talked to *bhai* (brother) in Chicago and heard the news. Do nothing for the next few days. Wait till we get there. *Samaj gya?* Understand?"

"Ok! *Accha* (yes)! Ok! No Problem!" said the grandpa and hung up the phone. Then turning to his *patni* (wife), he said, "OK! It worked! The kids will be here to bring in the New Year!"

While AR found the account funny, he empathized with the predicament of aging parents. AR understood how the elderly yearned to spend their last few important holidays with their children and grandchildren. From his own experience as a physician, he knew that as his patients aged, every year became a priceless New Year. This story reemphasized to AR that life is too short and unpredictable. He wished that children understood these facts and were not left with the regret, "I wish I had spent more time with my parents."

Then he gave his parting advice to the youth and shared with them truths he had gleaned through experience. "The road to success is always under construction...Someday is not a day of the week...Always and never are two words you should always remember never to use...and Smile - it makes people wonder what you're up to." AR ended with, "*Hum tumhe pyar karte hae* (Hindi) and *Nenu ninnu premistunnanu* (Telugu and Malayalam) - I love you all."

A big event awaited the Reddys in Los Angeles. In addition to the large local community and Hollywood celebs, the Silicon Valley and Bay area Ind-o-US crowd of Northern California drove or flew down en-masse. The buddies-since-childhood began crack-a-lacking and the Fo' sizzlers recounted details of their last trip to their chateaus. Twenty percent of Indians in the U.S. live in the Silicon Valley – Bay Area and they account for a third of Silicon Valley's High Tech start-up company employees. Naturally, there was the usual behind-the-scene horse-trading, handy-is-dandy, one-upmanship and deal-sweeteners, especially among start-up bigwigs and those planning an IPO (Initial Public Offering). All this wheeling and dealing went smoothly, with the Don Chandon and Don Perignon flowing as freely as water.

Several guests used their camera cell-phones to send digital pictures of themselves with their new hero to their relatives and friends. In true Hollywood and Bollywood style, the rich and powerful sat at corner tables discussing the staying power of big companies, their mergers and takeovers. There was a lot of croon and swoon among folks displaying high voltage zest, technologies and pizazz. The crowd was pumped-up. The elderly philosophized about nirvana; the younger set was in a spouse grouse mode. After the buffet meal, the crowd settled down for an entertaining evening of the latest Bollywood and *Bhangra* dance recitals. Later, the old timers and retirees regaled one another with riddles:

Q: In India what do you call a *babu* who holds a briefcase and sits under a tree? Answer: Branch Manager.

Q: A *barthav* asked his *bharya* (wife), "How did you get the car in the living room?" Answer: The *sree* (lady from Kerala) said, "I don't know! For a split second, I thought I was at a drive-in."

On the east coast, the Floridians were determined to throw an equally lavish bash for the Reddys. The celebration was held at the posh Miami Spice restaurant which was decorated with exquisite seascapes and served the latest in Indian cuisine. The crowd arrived in fashion fiesta styles - hot Indian and Latin outfits - and came close to being sartorial-perfectionists. Indian outfits with the *zardozi* (gold thread embroidery) were complimented by a matching *bindi* on the forehead. For this special occasion, some brought out the *mang tikka* (head jewelry). Others wore *ghaghras, kurtis and kanchlis* with *odhinis* (a veil) covering their heads and right shoulders. Some women had faux fur chappals while others wore laser-cut thigh-high lycra boots. The outfits were guaranteed to make the wearer look sexy. The men with discerning tastes preferred to make a fashion statement with their footwear made of exotic leather. There were performances of *Bharata Natyam, Desavatharam, Gawwali* and other classical Indian dances.

On the way to the party, the Reddys stopped at a gas station and met some Harley Davidson bikers who recognized the curler. AR admired the free spirit of the bikers, their leather pants and jackets.

At the party, the favored drinks were Cuban-rum cocktails and red wine. After the speeches and toasts were over, the guests feasted on the sumptuous dinner. The menu included *Shammi Kebab, Rogan Josh (Kashmiri* lamb*), Vindaloo* (Portuguese pork), Moghul-style chicken and *Jingha Gucci Biryani.* After the crowd ate their fill of spicy food, the men sipped their brandy and smoked their cigars.

An "ol' fella" (Generation Viagra) jokingly recounted his experience in a No-Name Isle café:

"Waiter, watch out! Your thumb is in my soup!" he said.

"Don't worry, sir. It's not that hot!" the unflustered waiter responded.

That anecdote led to a few restaurant stories like the one about the waiter who had his thumb over the steak as he came to the patron.

Patron: "Are you crazy? Your thumb's on my steak!"

Waiter: "I don't want it to fall on the floor again, sir."

Customers should have realized "the sticky situation" when they read the following sign on the maitre d's desk: "OPEN SEVEN DAYS A WEEK AND ON WEEKENDS."

The Ind-o-US in the Windy City, too, showed their pride in AR and Team USA and organized an evening of song and dance. Several older women were clad in *ghaghra* (an ankle length gathered skirt, usually flared) or *baluchar* (brocaded silk sari). Others wore *bandgala achkan* and close-necked *shervani* with *churidar paijama* (tight-fitting paijama). Women in the embroidered *salwar kameez* (paijama and tunic) displayed their matching *dupatta* (long scarf). A few draped *pashmina* shawls to keep themselves warm.

The men talked about their latest high-tech gadget acquisitions and their cardiac stress-test results. The young crowd was poised in their well-heeled attire and Hello Bello fashions.

The local Indian dance troupe performed the lively *Bhangra,* the graceful *Kathak*, *Kuchipudi* and *Odissi*, in addition to other classical dances, all of which attested to the dazzling diversity of South Asian dances. Very visible were the Indian and American sanctioned paparazzi hoping for posed and candid shots, sound bites and interviews. The menu was *kofta, tandoori chicken, korma, and Bombay aloo,* cooled down by some *kulfi* and an assortment of Indian desserts.

As usual, there were few in the crowd who moaned about the food. They complained that the dishes tasted as if they were prepared as per the "Al Qaeda Cookbook." The hip male crowd drooled over their glamorous *premikas* (dates). Others planned their exit strategy to their favorite piquant restaurant after the party for late-nite entertainment with their soul-mates and away from the glare of their ma-bap (parents) and the ever watchful "aunties." After a few Scotches, one FOB (fresh of the boat) fella recounted how he called the front desk clerk at this hotel and said: "I got a leak in my sink." The front desk clerk replied: "Go ahead."

A *begum* (classy *devi*) was overheard complaining, "My daughter-in-law's idea of housework is to sweep the room with a glance."

Dinner was followed by a buffet table laden with a variety of Indian desserts. There were some diners whose definition of a balanced diet was "a plate of *laddoos* (sweets made with lentils) in one hand, and a plate of *peddas* (sweets made with milk) in the other." However, most of the crowd worked off their calories with a lot of jiggin' (dancin').

In Houston, the Texan crowd was in their summer best. More than a third of NASA's scientists are ethnic Asian. As a result, there was a big representation of workers from "outer space." A few *babus* wore their cowboy boots and hats. For the ladies, casual cowboy attire was not good enough. They chose to appear in the latest Indian fashions, their hair done in the New-do, and a strut which demonstrated an "I'm the perfect gift" attitude. Pakistanis, Bangladeshis and those from the Near-East and Far-East all joined the Ind-o-US for the festivities.

Their attire included *farshi* (wide-legged trailing pajama) with richly embellished *gote* (bottom part of a *farshi pajama*) all from the *jamakhana* (the name given to the storehouse for garments in the Mughal and other royal courts). The ladies' attire included their *jamavar* (woven or embroidered Kashmir shawls) and *jhoomar* (jeweled ornament worn on the head). The women glittered with diamond-studded necklaces, bracelets and earrings.

Santosh, one of the guests, drew her middle-aged husband's attention to a couple seated at the far end of the room. "Do ya see them? How caring *dono* (both) are, no? He kisses her about every fifteen minutes. Why don't you do that?" she asked. "I'd love to, honey. But I don't know her well enough," her *pati* responded.

Maya criticized Usha for being cranky and always criticizing her *bichara* (poor) hubby. Maya said, "Look at me, my shri (hubby) is stupid, lethargic and a coward; have I complained about him?"

The curling world went completely gaga over the success of the

American team and their new techniques. The Canadian curlers "went bonkers" trying to understand how a game that takes three years to be proficient in and five years to be an expert at could be mastered in such a short period. Yes, it was true that Atul Reddy had played ice hockey for some time and that as a physician he had knowledge of anatomy and ergonomics. Those facts still did not justify his unparalleled expertise.

Audiences in India raved about curling even though this was an unknown sport to Indians. There was singing and dancing in the streets when Team USA won the Continental Cup. AR's praises were sung in English, Hindi, other languages and the new lingo, Hinglish. There was also a sudden interest in curling among a people whose general knowledge of seasons was limited to warm, hot, monsoons and the "dog days of summer." Most of the one billion people analyzed the game, play-by-play, in the bus, taxi, train and *rickshaw* (2-seater scooterized taxi), in coffee shops and barber shops, and under every *peepal* tree. The people had their own theories about the moves and about better ways to curve the stone or do a peel. Television stations, viewers with VCRs and TiVoites repeatedly re-played the game in digital-slow-motion.

Among the masses watching the TV was one soul named Joseph Fernandes. When he saw AR on the tube, he recognized his long-lost boyhood friend and neighbor. Joe's mind worked overtime on how he could meet his buddy. The Indian government wanted to honor AR and invited him to Mumbai, the city in which he had grown up. The state Governor and Chief Minister wanted to present AR with an award and accolades on behalf of the fifteen million Mumbai-*wallas* (residents).

AR had to do a lot of soul-searching before accepting the invitation to visit India. He had patients to take care of. The American celebrations had taken a big slice of his allotted vacation time. A trip to India for ten days would be all that he could spare and it would be a return to his roots. He felt this step back in time might relax him. Clearly, there was more than one reason to make that pilgrimage. He could then return home to close the chapter on curling and end the celebrations. Grandma Reddy did not want to undertake that hectic schedule herself. AR decided he'd be gracious and make a doctor's visit to the land of his birth.

Hero's return to Mumbai
> 15 <

Atul and his family flew to India at the invitation of the government and the people of India. The national airline, Air India, provided the Reddys a first class flight from JFK Airport to Mumbai, on the west coast of India. A trip to Asia involves losing a day in travel time and several changes in time zones. The day lost is partly regained on the return trip. The Reddys flew from JFK Airport on a Thursday night after a full day's work. Upon their arrival in Mumbai on Saturday morning, they received a *Maharaja's* (Royal) welcome. AR could have spent a month, nay, an entire year in Mumbai basking in the adoration of the crowds. The days and evenings for the Reddys in India - the largest English-speaking country in the world - were packed with social events, big and small.

Mumbai is the true convergence of East and West in thinking, life style, music, people, art and architecture. Mumbai has been and continues to be at the crossroads of Old and New India. At the airport, the central government, state and city officials and throngs of people, all greeted the Reddy family – their home town hero. There were fresh flower garlands galore. As the Reddys stepped off Air-India's 747, christened "Ashoka," the *desi* crowd was both overwhelmed and ecstatic to see their *nava* (new) idol in the flesh. Until then, they had just watched him on the tube. There were plenty of *"Namastees"* – a word in Hindi that means both "hello" and "goodbye," similar to "Aloha" in Hawaii. The theory of six-degrees of separation was proven again. Among the fifteen million residents, every Mumbaiwalla knew a cousin or a friend who knew a cousin or an acquaintance who was related to, or knew Atul or Anita. Many knew the complete life-history of the Reddys and re-discovered the theory of "six-degrees of separation." There was the usual *tamasha* (ruckus) and expressions of joy *aajkul humko bahut happiness hai* (today I am very happy).

Arrangements were made for the Reddys to stay at the Mughal suite - meant for an Emperor - at the Taj Hotel. Here the parents would enjoy "sweet dreams," and the kids would have "suite dreams" after they had gotten over the day's culture shock. The hotel had stunning views of Mumbai Bay and the Gateway of India, as well as the blue green and royal blue waters of the bay (Arabian Sea). The Gateway monument was completed in 1924 to commemorate the visit of King George V and Queen Mary to India in 1911. Ritzy hotels, clubs and restaurants all vied to have the Reddys visit their nightclubs some time during their stay.

Early in the morning, the Reddys saw beach-side yogis, yoginis and yogi wannabes; quite a few guests enjoyed a shiatsu massage. In the bay, they saw ships 'n clips and others taking to the water as a wonderful sea-escape. The Reddys caught sight of the harbormaster at work and boats returning from crabbing. Their suite had fresh flowers and Turkish bathrobes imported from the Denzili region of Turkey, and special hand-embroidered "*slippahs*" for each Reddy. The hotel had a fully equipped spa with masseuses, electric neck massagers, and hand and body lotions, among other pampering devices. The décor and the ambience were truly reminiscent of "the Raj (colonial India)." All the bellboys were decked out in traditional turbans and colorful uniforms. April offered perfect days of sunny weather. The Reddy boys found this a picture-perfect setting to write about to their friends back in Utica. In his letter to Grandma, Ajit wrote, "It's a 'relax to the max' vacation! We have fresh mango smoothies for breakfast and a daily "meltdown" massage and then watch the sunset from the verandah." There is no better or more luxurious hotel in the entire city for tourists to stay in than at the Taj.

The boys stepped into the world of the Orient and soon discovered that if they wanted to sit in the front seat of a car as a passenger, they had to enter on what is the driver's side in the U.S. This is because in India, as the kids observed, "They drive on the 'wrong side' of the road." Most of the world drives on the right side of the road. Britain and its colonies follow the ancient Roman tradition of driving their horses and carts on the left – "The Left Rule." That tradition began when drivers of horse carriages held the reins in their left hand so that their right hand was free to shake hands with passing horsemen or to defend themselves with a sword. The rules of the road changed in the U.S. during the 1700s.

On Saturday evening, the prestigious Bombay Gymkhana honored the Reddys at a gala affair. Here, the Reddy family mingled with Mumbai's crème de la crème. The crowd was Old Money a.k.a. Brown *Sahibs* and *Mem-sahibs!* This was the suave collection of contemplative high-brows, half of whom now claimed they had taught

Atul in St. Xavier's College and G.S. Medical College, or Anita in Sophia College in "them-good-old days."

The men were sartorially suited in luxurious pin-striped, cashmere or gabardine three-piece suits, with gem-studded cuff-links and suede shoes. These were men of discerning taste who lived in the lap of luxury. The silver-haired, distinguished-looking seniors were reinvigorated just to be part of this historic occasion.

Their "Divas" wore dream designer's outfits, gold embroidered saris or evening gowns. These femmes were well-traveled "both in and out of India", well-read and could be called "culture vultures" with a passion for preserving history. They certainly had quite a job at hand in dealing with India's five millennia of history. There were groups of gal-pals and clusters of the very-oldest friends for whom style was ageless. Their chit-chat could best be described as Devi-2-Devi and Diva-2-Diva. These *padma devis* (padma goddesses) had also found the secret cure for wrinkles and they were not about to share it. When in a relaxed mood, they would share other all-time favorite tips whether their listeners liked it or not. After all, these *memsahibs* lived the life of "been-there and done-that." Some had been through the School of Hard Knocks and had countless experiences to share. This was Old Wine, very confident in itself with no attempt to be repackaged in new bottles. Theirs was a life well-lived, and the Gymkhana was their private fiefdom.

The younger crowd was clad in figure-hugging pants and alluring multicolored tops embellished with sewn-on "bling"; their hairstyles were well-coiffed. The menu was Mumbai's best, topped with North Indian sweets, mango and cheese desserts. The favorite drink was Scotch – a Parsee peg on the rocks!

The parking lot at the Bombay Gymkhana was filled with chauffeur-driven Rolls, BMWs, Mercs, Lamborghinis, Aston Martins and Pajeros. Some couples arrived in classic Mustang convertibles with the top down, while others showed up in antique classic cars from the time of the British Raj. These vehicles were personally babied and kept polished by a team of specially hired mechanics and chauffeurs, all under the watchful eyes of the maharajas and the maharanis (kings and queens) of the estates.

Dr. Ank was an outstanding local ophthalmologist who was by nature usually reserved. On this special evening, he was outspoken in exercising his prerogative as a distinguished member of the club, requesting a photo-op with the Reddys. He said, "I am 'The Eye' of the Bombay Gymkhana."

Several families in Mumbai have last names that represent the profession of their ancestors: Doctor, Engineer, Daruwalla (wine merchant), Narielwalla (coconut merchant), Bootwalla (cobbler), Topiwalla (milliner / hat maker), and Paymaster.

AR's visit was a unique opportunity for the "Who's-Who" of Mumbai to interact with their special guest. In return, Dr. and Mrs. Reddy credited much of their personal and professional success to their professors and dons. All these Old Timers had set the benchmarks for originality, creativity and diversity, and had transformed the next generation of "free Indians." Respect befits these experts who organized post-independent India by working in the trenches and from the ground up. Their efforts have led to India's present success.

The emeritus professors commiserated with one another on their "senior status." They lamented, "We've reached the age when the 'Happy Hour' for us is a nap." They were clearly the old fogies basking in the reflected glory of their protégés. A few competed with each other about who could take more credit for the Reddys' success. They finally settled on, "*Acha,* (OK). All of us can take the cred." These seniors had reached that point in life where they agreed to stop lying about their age, and start bragging about it. Without a doubt, like the World War II generation of the west, these folks were all battle-tested and only recently "tossed it in." Membership had its privileges!

On Sunday, the Reddys woke up to the warm morning sunshine. They were scheduled to greet the masses of Mumbai at an open-air celebration at the *Azad Maidan* (playground). The huge *mamuli* (Joe-six-pack) crowds were dressed in their Sunday best which ranged from chic and classy to suave and sassy. The clothes made all the *Bindu-bhens* and *Sita-bhais* (Jane Does) appear slim and elegant. For the visiting Reddys, this was Mumbai – alluring, brilliant and charming.

Long before the event started, the blue-and-white-collar crowds, *gharwallas* and *gharwallis* (husbands and wives) appeared charged with the cocktail of big-city imbibing. This event even took the curl out of men's mustaches. At one time, Asian men believed that the size of a man's mustache reflected his manhood. As a result, long mustaches were common among the elders and military types. Today most men know that something has been lost in that translation.

The celebration was also Joseph Fernandes' opportunity to reunite with his neighbor and childhood friend, Atul. Joe arrived early to get a front-row seat at the celebration, so that he could get a close look at his boyhood mentor.

At the event, their eyes connected. After all the ceremonies were over, Joe met AR, embraced and said, "*Hey Atul koso asa tum?* (Hey Atul! how are you*?) Poilea suater tuka Dev borem korum mhonnttam, tuvem Goeant ani Bombaim mhaka khub adhar dilo.* (In the first place thank you and God's blessing on you; you helped me a great deal in Bombay)." Atul flashed his characteristic, broad smile, hugged his long-lost friend again and said, "*Sodd ti ghozal. Ixtt mhonnttat te kiteak re?* (Cut the talk! What are friends for?). *Hota hai!* (It happens!)".

The conversation lasted for quite a long time, even though it was an unscheduled chance encounter happening in a packed audience. At the end of their visit, the Reddys invited Joey to visit them at the Taj. Joey told Anita, "Because my polio affected my arm and hand, I had some chips stacked against me when I was a kid. Atul help flip the odds."

The Reddy and Fernandes families grew up in the same building complex in Bombay. The families in the building had different religions, (Hindus and Catholics) but shared the similar cultural backgrounds and values. The two men did not disappoint each other when the families met the next day at the Taj. They reminisced about their encounters and growing up in Bombay; and then caught up on news about their family members. Joey was a college graduate, partly because of the tutoring he received from Atul, as well as the correspondence and night courses he had taken. Atul was delighted to know that Joey was a bank official.

After a long and enjoyable visit, Atul invited Joe's family to join his at the beach resort of Juhu "just for old time's sake." Joey and his family were delighted to accept the invitation.

During the rest of the week, the Reddys enjoyed a royal tour of the city, its government buildings, modern skyscrapers and the grand architectural structures of colonial Bombay. The city saw an economic and building boom after the Suez Canal was opened in 1870. The family visited the city's landmarks such as Bombay University, built in

1857, and the nearby 280-foot-high Rajabai Clock Tower, erected in 1880. And there was the inescapable view of Chhatrapati Shivaji (formerly Victoria) Terminus (1887) which handles more than half-a-million rail passengers daily. These and other buildings, with Gothic structures, are adorned with exquisite stained glass windows and figures carved from Porbander stone. Bombay's colonial buildings can best be described in the words of its most famous creator and designer, John Begg. According to Begg, "The structural designs are meant to reflect the city's energetic, exuberant, sparkling character with building stones of many kinds and colors." The architectural styles of these majestic buildings were Venetian-Gothic, Neo-Classical, Renaissance and Indo-Saracen - a blend of Indian and Westerns designs. The façades and interiors reflect the styles of Victorian Britain. The commonest colors are yellow and blue from the basalt stones quarried from Bombay's surrounding regions.

Residents in the building complex where Atul grew up had keenly followed his progress through life. Most of his neighbors had proudly graduated to the status of *chacha and chachi, nana and nani* (grandpas and grandmas on the father's and mother's sides). The building had scores of elderly relatives, friends, and lots of imperial papajis and the imperious mamajis. When Atul arrived at his old home, his family had to endure showers of hugs given with enthusiasm and exhilaration. And the "aunties and *mauxis* (grandmothers)" had to plant a uummcchhh kiss on both cheeks of each of them. Many residents of this building complex who came from Goa had conversed in the Konkani language. So Atul picked up the language as a child. Some residents of the building who still clung to the Portuguese mannerisms of their ancestors said: *Olla senhor doutor... moghall Atul ani Anita...zaite diss zalet tumchi khobor nam!* (Hello doctor...Atul and Anita dear...it's been a long time since we heard from you).

Mauxis: *Arre Atul baba tum khoim? Kitloch kall zalo tuji khoboruch na mu rre*? (Grandmas: Our son Atul where have you been? For a long time there's been no news from you)

Atul: *Borem mauxi, Mog asundi* (I am ok, grandma), as he embraced them lovingly.

Neighbors: *Sozmotam tumim borim saudin passar zatat mhunon zosim amim angasor assaum.* (We hope you are keeping good health, just as we are doing here).

The charming Pitu: *Boro motto zalai murreh! Borem khatai, beefe, chicken, ani steak besides Kentacky bazzlelem chicken. Ani tumi amkan sangtai cholesterol, tantiam ani mass khanakai munnon?* (You've gotten real fat! You guys eat beef, chicken, steaks and Kentucky Fried Chicken, and then tell us to watch our cholesterol and avoid eggs and meats.) The local comedian was introduced to AR as, "Our Roads Scholar."

Old friends: "Bravo! Whaada guy!" (showing their pride). Then they said to each other, "Look who has returned! *Bapuji* (Old) Reddy's *baccha* (boy), Atul is back with his family. Amazing, Amazing!" Other residents said: "Congrats! *Aniek Kor! Tumcho khalto ixtt murre. Asli Goemcar.*" (Congrats, encore! We are your good friends and Goan buddies).

The whole building became the scene of an impromptu get-together, with people meeting old friends, and making new friends and in the process creating more bonds. Ajit and Anil received offers from girls to be their "lovable sidekicks." The girls yelled out to the boys, "Hey! Good looking!" When Atul bumped into the *lulus* (women) he didn't marry, some reminded him of his boyhood antics. Many neighbors lined up to be photographed with the famous couple. Some advised Dr. Reddy, "You should thank your parents; especially your father and mother."

The Reddys graciously accepted all the congratulatory messages and good wishes. At times, the Reddys' experiences were a mix of one part humor with two parts of grin and bear it. On the whole it was sunny-side-up with fun photo shoots. Atul's favorite reply was the native, "*Dev borem korum ani borer bachen ravat* - God bless you and y'all stay well."

Traveling through Mumbai gave the Reddys the opportunity to meet other locals – one-on-one. The college students were always the "smart alecks." They knew the statistics of the whole world and had no qualms about showing off. They recounted that today's Bombay, unlike the good old days, had become believable, beautiful and the best. The comical types, referred to as "four-o-four" (without common sense), were usually hushed by the kind and hospitable crowd. One of them caught Dr. Reddy off guard with his unique definitions of various medical terms: "Impotent is for distinguished people" and "labor pain reflects getting hurt at work" etc. The jostling crowd realized that Dr.

Reddy was not used to this silliness. An elderly man advised the Reddys to ignore the antics; while the next guy clarified, "This chappy has a Degree in Bottomology." Another *pundit* (wise man) said, "What to do, no? In India, we're like that only." Yet some of the aspiring stand-up comedians took the remark, "*vo samko pagal hai* (he's real nuts)" as a compliment.

As it happens in every crowd, there were also the know-it-alls and "smartie-pants." One asked Ajit, "In the U.S. why do y'all ship by truck and send cargo by ship?" For the doctor-sahib's benefit, one told medical jokes: "Did you hear about the guy whose Viagra tablet got stuck in his throat? Now he suffers from a stiff neck."

Dr. Reddy responded to the light-hearted banter with a riddle of his own. "If someone with multiple personalities threatens to shoot himself, is it a hostage situation?" One student gave it the typical Mumbai response, "Maybe, Definite!"

The Reddys had fun reconnecting with the youth and reciprocating their smiles and handshakes. Mumbai allowed the family the chance to go wild over Indian cuisine, meet and greet the locals and bowl them over with charm and humor. One topic of conversation was the observance of the Indian festival of Holi – the festival of colors. Atul asked the audience if they still remembered, "the holies - hole-e-crap, hole-e-cow, hole-e-moley, hole-e-mackerel and hole-e-Moses."

At times the encounters were a riot, filled with comic chaos. The crowd included the usual supply of *swamis* (philosophers) who could tell listeners how to balance their *doshas* in life; the gurus who could talk about the power of dreaming; and the palm readers and the mystics who interpreted dreams and foretold the future. One sage divulged his theory: "First the world was flat; then it was round; now it is crooked."

The Reddys explored Indian culture and cuisine. They had a whole smorgasbord of culinary delights to choose from – vegetarian, non-vegetarian, North-Indian, South-Indian, and from the traditional thali (vegetarian buffet) to a-la-carte. They had a field day sampling popular local delicacies especially the faluda bar which served tropical refreshments. There were also the nostalgic small, "corner diners" called *Iranis* which are operated by former immigrants from Iran. Irani restaurants are an integral part of the city's cosmopolitan heritage. Their owners are Zoroastrians – believers in the oldest practicing monotheistic religion, started around 1600 BCE. Typical of these diners are the straight-backed wooden chairs, small cubicles for families, and red and white checked tablecloths, (akin to a trattoria), along with the aroma of freshly baked bread, sweet cakes, spiced tea and savory snacks.

Posh restaurants overlooking the Bay served banquets which were gastronomic and aesthetic feasts in an atmosphere of elegance and fragrance. The Reddys' favorite orders included the hors d'oeuvres: samoosas and mutton patties followed by *Chat* which is an assortment of Indian snacks with potatoes and vegetables, all served with authentic Indian sauces. The other dish of choice invariably was the native *pav-bhaji* – Bombay's vegetarian version of the hamburger, all washed down with *lassi* (a native yogurt drink) and falooda. Then there were the decadent treats that come loaded with the guilt of calories.

After watching the west-coast sunset from their room with a view at the Taj suite, the Reddys joined the "movin' and groovin' set" at several avant-garde clubs, restaurants and bars. There was a world of entertainment available at every turn. The clientele comprised Mumbaiwallas who had achieved balance and success.

The night was for those in pursuit of renewal of mind, body and spirit, romance and pleasure. The adult Reddys were swept up in the fun, the food and the dancing to feel-good music. Live bands filled every place with the sounds of Bombay's best sounds. There was a party every night. The native view was: "After the day in the sun, it's the night - for relaxation, fun and to work out your frustrations."

It was a "good time" atmosphere and the dancing extended to the wee hours of the morning. With the Reddys, the crowds went wild doing the conga-line; they were swept away with groovy moves of fancy dancing. The adult Reddys were invariably served Mumbai's signature cocktails - the Monsoon and the Mango Mojito (rum mix).

For the young and not-so-young crowd, Mumbai's night life was the ultimate in recreation after a hectic day with lunch "pelican style - eat on the fly." Mumbai offers some of the hottest tropical night life. For most, it was an evening to "dress to impress." This was a well-heeled, chic and eclectic crowd. When the young met AR they all told him, "We watched the curling game on our TiVo (digital video) recorders and you made it look arree sooo veery eazy. We all were confident that the U.S. would win." Then they gave the Reddys the highlights and the lowdown of the city - what's hot now and the "make over" of the month.

AR told them what a wild year he had had. His response to these TiVoites: "Nothing beats the winning feeling! For now, Mumbai is the Night-Life-Mecca!" While the Reddys had to leave the party early, most of the young crowd danced the night away at the fancy clubs. The Reddys were warned, "Friday night parties don't end until Saturday morning." But for the Reddys, late to bed and early to rise, makes a healthy person "socially dead." The Mumbai newspapers described Dr. Reddy as "handsome, witty and charming with plenty of self–confidence." The papers added advice for the Mumbaiwallas: "Believe everything you read about him during the Continental Cup games, and then double it."

Midweek, the Reddys attended a big awards ceremony and reception at Sachivalaya - the Government House in Mumbai. The state governor, chief minister, cabinet and elected representatives were all present, as were the U.S. consul and the consular staff. AR was awarded the "Star of Bombay" in an ornate red-carpet ceremony, where everybody was dressed to impress everybody else. The government speakers' comments reflected the pride of Mumbai's residents - Mumbaiwallas - in their former, now "honorary citizen." Dr. Reddy was introduced as the "*Raja* (king) of *Kurl* (Curl)" and the mayor presented AR with the keys to the city.

These politicians were proud to call themselves Gandhiji's *betas* and *betis* (sons and daughters). The men wore the *topi* (cap) and some had the *pagri* (turban). That's where the connection between the "Father of the Nation" and the politicos ended. None of them wore clothes made from *khadi* (homespun cotton fabric - the symbol of the struggle for freedom). The women were dressed in *paithani* cotton and silk saris, *odhani or patka.* The p*allavs* (borders) were extensively decorated. Some had *Chikankari* (white embroidery with floral patterns, fine cotton with untwisted threads of cotton or silk) and *Kanchala - Kundal* (earrings).

The men wore *kurtas or kameez* (tunics) of silk, *tussar* (wild silk from eastern and central India), *mulmul* cotton (muslin woven in Bengal) and different styles of p*aijama* (trousers). These hot-shot men and women were proud of their "Boo-ti-full and Beautiful Bombay" and their "*Maha* (Very) Magnificent Mumbai." After the award presentation, there were cultural performances which included temple dances - *Araiyar sevai, Kathakali* and other dance routines.

That evening, a dinner function was held at the Cricket Club of India, an event favored by the "nouveau riche" - a glamorous party sponsored by the entrepreneurial set. The guests were predominantly babalicous Bombay-wallas who did not have a cash crunch. Scores of them had risen from the lower rungs of the economic strata through hard work and perseverance. They were affiliated with the Bombay Stock Exchange (BSE) a.k.a. Mumbai's Wall Street, aptly called Share Bazaar. This crowd was a heart-beat away from being "beyond Bombay" and closer to Wall Street, New York City, or St. Paul's, London.

These guys and gals were well-heeled "scud studs" with chicklet teeth and assorted yet expensive outfits. During the cocktail hour there was a lot of laugh, talk and sip, since this clique had the "Midas Touch" with a business package to pursue. Some were smooth-talking rakes, led by their imaginations. The *babus* loudly voiced their opinions "Woulda, Coulda and Shoulda" on a myriad of topics. Some were overheard pleading with others, "Work with me, please, on this... Now!"

In the groupies milling around, the most popular guys in the clusters would talk, gawk at and applaud one another. This was no popularity contest as the most admired guy was prejudged. The loudest, wildest applause erupted when the honored guest of the evening was introduced. He was, "The Maharaja of Curl;" and "India's Beckham," (David Beckham, Europe's soccer mega-celeb).

The *biwis* were in matching mind-numbing bling bling (flashy jewelry) glamour to show off their man. Each woman wore one-of-a-kind handmade designer jewelry decorated with diamonds and other precious stones. They were living the good life - wine, dine, recline and whine about sumpin'. In the crowd were mainly baby boomers in their 50s and baby boomlets (the Google Geeks) in their 30s. Many were computer jocks looking for ideas on how to spark their creativity. This group belonged to blogosphere and spoke blingo. They had their own iPod and biPod shuffle. There was a lot of advice being shared among the crowd: "Experience is a wonderful thing. It enables you to recognize a mistake when you make it again," and "The dumb and foolish make money while the smart and cautious go broke."

The youngsters had their boos (boyfriend or girlfriend) and most in the crowd were PHAT (pretty hot and tempting). Most of them rolled in on some nice chauffeur-driven wheels. Unless one was planning social suicide, one couldn't be caught arriving in a Maruti – India's mini-car built for the masses.

One young twit asked Atul about America and remarked, "How come you guys choose from just two people for President and from fifty for Miss America?" Atul was about to respond with his own humor when the youth's mother cut the kid short. "*Shanna keya*? (Are you being smart?)," she asked the flustered teenager.

The clique, called *babalog,* was a western social group. Nobody here was cutting grass (just lying around). Rather, they were confident and thriving creatures of the urban jungle. Most were aiming to captain a business team, if they had not already done so. Yet for now, they were ready to rock 'n roll.

On the weekend, a reception was held at a Bollywood movie studio with Mumbai's socialites and Bollywood celebs in attendance. The Reddys did not disappoint the rock-star crowd and vice-versa. The alpha males, including actors, producers, directors, dancers and vocalists arrived on the scene dressed in *Sherwanis, Churidars, Jodhpuri* and *Kaliyondar* paijama. They were called *Diwan Saheb* and presented a smooth appearance with their diamond-studded rings and shirt buttons. They had the flair of mega-giants of the silver screen.

The alpha females, including actors, producers, directors, dancers and vocalists wore *Kanchipuran* silk *saris, meghana, odhini, moti, minakare* and *jumka*, made of wool and silk embroidered with metallic thread and semiprecious stones. The younger divas were clad in their *salwaar* and *kurta* or *kameez* (tunic), *lachaas, lehengans*, or outfits of lace, chiffon, silk and satin - all from celeb designers' boutiques. They also wore r*ani kada*, pearl necklaces and other expensive jewels.

In short, the celebs - including all the Grande Dames of pop vocals - looked bee-yoo-tiful and exuded expensive perfume. The stars who were studded with lux ruby red and hot diamond stones around their petite necks were "stoned-out." The round bindi on their foreheads matched their rocks. A few stars made a cameo appearance just to show respect to the world-champion curler and to rub shoulders with their younger co-stars and other who's-who of the Bollywood world. These were the heroes of Bombay's movie blockbusters from the last three decades and were demigods to the average Indians.

While the inside crowd had a buzz of its own going on, out in the parking lot their chauffeurs were busy polishing their sizzling Rolls,

Jags, Pajeros, Caddies, Solara Convertibles, Ferrari Testarosas, BMWs 850iL, Mercs 560SEL, as well as many classic antiques.

In true Bollywood style, this was a fashion-show experience, with the Indian divas in their cleavage-baring outfits. Everyone bore the "I'm the perfect gift" expression. The stars also wore luxurious footwear - jutis and mojirs - of exotic leather. And the *Umas and Mayas* (women) in Marvel-land had an array of accessories to give them the fresh and uninhibited look. The ritzy families and extended relatives were all lined up to have their pictures taken with the honored guest of the evening. For the Reddys, this "Bombay Bash" was a mini-version of what it's like at LIFW - Lakme India Fashion Week – India's Academy Awards for fashion.

The celeb wannabes were a well-heeled chic crowd with cool looks in hot fashions. Ninety-nine percent of Indians could only dream of being here in Wonderland. Yet, for these Belles of Bollywood there was more to fashion than hot chicks and hot cheeks! These pretty dudettes and hopefuls were more socialites than fashion plates, even though they had trendy wardrobes. Their careers were at stake! They had to show off their staying power in a fiercely competitive market of one billon fans. This was their platform of expression to break through the stronghold of a few. There was no *faltu* eye (candy flakes) in this fresh blood of aspiring actors and actresses, singers and other entertainment professionals. Their philosophy of "a life well lived" focused on the need to dig in, look healthy, stay fresh and bear all with grit and a smile.

In the crowd of new-dos there was a collection of romantic duos milling around. This was also a *shaadi* (marriage) showcase. The Reddy boys were pleasantly surprised to see the *desi* girls with shoulders bared or with spaghetti-strap dresses, low neck lines, bare backs and outfits with the retro look. The music and songs at the event were a blend of "oldies 'n goodies." There were lots of schmoes with super-cool cell phones who suddenly appeared when the stars arrived, and then it was the usual: "Wazz-up; Yo y'all (hello); Wassup (what's up); Sup, Hello; and what's new? Kia ora? Kea rre? Chalta hai!"

The guests were humorous with charming demeanors to match their "hanging-out image." This throng was made up mainly of Gen-Xers in their 20s. There were a lot of hook-ups (introductions) with the hotties (attractive persons) in their bolero pants. Many owned built-in compact digital cameras; those who had camera phones e-mailed digital images to all their cousins, friends and relatives both near and far. While there was plenty to eat in this "movie capital of the world," everyone there was weight and figure conscious. This was a banger (extremely impressive) kind of crowd. There were no salad-dodgers (over-weight persons) in this horde. "Fat free and sugar free" were their diet mottos.

The banter was sprinkled with buzz words and clichés: "I wouldn't touch him with a ten foot pole," "she's beau," "nice hair and eyes...very shapely...good looking."

Some guys lamented, "No response - hard to talk to...her parents are not so pretty liberal." More commonly heard phrases included the new Hinglish (Hindi and English) terminology such as: "Bolo kiss miss... love Yua...hungry kya...*chamcah* (hanger-on)." Romantic pick-up lines and their responses went something like this:

I could make you *bahooth* (very) happy!...Then why don't you leave?
Can I have your name, *bhen* (sister)?...*Kea rre*? Don't you have one?

The evening's entertainment began with lights and dazzle. There were no technical glitches during this non-stop pop show - after all, this was the real thing, being broadcast live. The Master of Ceremonies proclaimed, "Thank you in anticipation of your consideration." Then he went on to introduce the "Rock Star" to wild applause! The show opened with a parade of pros and wannabe performers in eye-popping and mind-dazzling outfits which sparkled with semi-precious stones. The entertainers presented a Salsa India Fiesta consisting of a collection of *desi* dances, *ghazals* (poetry recitals), and solo performances. There was a retinue of dance performances whose choreography reflected the new "Bombay Blast of Filmi dancing" and "Shah Rukh shimmy." They danced while the orchestra played *Hum Kissise Kum Nahin* (Who's Out In The Cold) and *Kaisa Jadoo* (the Magic Continues) among other songs.

Fortunately for Dr. Reddy, his audiences were different each night and so he gave the same acceptance speech at each event. His friends' and neighbors' children back in America had offered suggestions after they had researched acceptance speeches delivered at the Oscars and at other Hollywood ceremonies.

There was the obligatory, "Excuse me while I kiss the stars; I thank my parents, without whose unfailing support and guidance I would not have made it to these heights. I've been fortunate. I played the odds and won." Then he encouraged those in attendance, "You don't need the next person to believe in you. You've got to believe in yourself and feel confident that hard work and talent will deliver the best. Don't be fenced in by circumstances." He always concluded his speech by thanking the attendees. "I thank you, my devoted well-wishers and fans who have come to convey your greetings and best wishes."

He persuaded them to try curling even though India was not familiar with this sport. In this shrinking world of rapidly spreading technology, a curling arena in India's premier city of 15 million people would be a great draw for the young and not-so-young. The arena could become a place for families to enjoy a sport together. He ended with, "*Hum tumhe pyar karte hae,* and (for the benefit of the Chennais in Tamil) *Nan unnai kathalikaraen* - I love you all." This invariably sparked a high impact standing ovation and Dr. Reddy loved it as it recapped the thrill of his victories in America.

The Reddys went on a frenzied shopping spree in Mumbai. They were loaded with "bargains" (something one cannot use, at a price one cannot resist). In addition to these, they picked up some great inlaid wood-work and other carvings of teakwood, mahogany, sandalwood and soapstone done by artisans who learned and mastered the art that has been passed down for generations.

Atul and Anita also visited their alma maters. The city of Mumbai and its suburbs have four medical colleges and numerous major private health facilities, making it a powerhouse of medical technology. Some physicians are so well-known that their peers refer to them merely by their initials, such as Dr. KKT or Dr. PPD, which would refer to only one person in the entire city of 15 million. Some physicians get their *bhav* (reputation) bolstered by being appointed to some high-level positions such as cardiologist to the president of India or surgeon to the governor or gynecologist to the *maharani* (queen) of No-Where Land. There is no longer royalty in India, yet some hold on to their beloved titles.

The staff at medical colleges includes examiners, professors and emeritus-professors of one or more universities in Mumbai and across the country. Most of these professors, on being appointed to a medical college, volunteer to see patients and teach medical students at the "public facility" for four hours each morning. These hospitals provide free medical care to the indigent. This practice is termed "honorary work." At noon or later, chauffeurs drive these consultants to their private practices where they work until 7:00 or 8:00 in the evening.

As a result, a visitor with a health care problem who wishes to see a consultant will be encouraged to see the "world famous expert" who has a waiting list of six months to see patients - even those with "connections." Further inquiry may direct the tourist to another "very famous doctor" who is a double-professor at two medical schools and has a waiting list of one year. The third physician recommended might be a professor who is the physician to the Prime Minister of India and is so great that five universities in India and abroad requested him to join their faculty. Yet, this doc could accept only two; he had to turn down the other three. This cardiologist had a waiting list of eighteen months. A patient "with pull" (influence) might "stand in line" to see the doctor for eighteen months, and for three years if he has "no pull."

One visitor in obvious distress asked the patient in line before him about his medical condition. He responded, "Right now, I'm fine! I am in line because I know by the time my turn comes to see this universally acclaimed cardiologist, I will need a stress test or have a heart attack!"

The Reddys spent a few days at Juhu Beach. While on the beach, some tourists from England said, "By golly, these tots look posh. Wish we could mmwwaah the two boys!"

Some U.S. vacationers were proud of the Reddys. Their teenagers described the two boys as "wicked-sweet." A lady from Georgia said to her family, "Yo' Mama! Yo' aren't gonna believe this. We are sooo very lucky baby, to see the curling champ." AR had some words of advice for the Americans, "Mumbai has got you covered; check out the scenery; enjoy the unique ambience; savor it; join the fun and share my Mumbai!"

A group of Aussies met AR and recounted the litany of compliments they had uttered as they watched the curling game. And they also added the terms used by the Local Area Network in Australia, "the LAN down under": Ya blood's worth bottling!; Ya kicking them; Hooley-Dooly!; Dem boys think of ookin' every thing!"

Juhu Beach has miles of golden sand and a promenade ringed with palm trees. Wherever water meets land in tropical Asia, there are millions of crabs scurrying on the sand, much to the delight of the children. These crabs include: the robber, hermit, land, ghost, amphibious and soldier. Common to all of them are their movable eyestalks, a hard shell and five pairs of legs - the first being claws and the rest used for walking or swimming. The million-dollar Juhu Beach was further bedecked with *mamuli desis* (everyday guys and dolls) and *bintus* (kids) in chic swimsuits. The adults wore capri pants, Bermuda shorts and cropped pants in a painter's palette of colors and prints. People were dressed in stylish clothing with matching sunglasses made of polarized lenses and unsinkable frames. No one on the beach wore an unhappy face. There was a noticeable "cheer factor" in the air and a few were in beach nirvana. The "hot numbers" milled around in beaded thong sandals, tropical fashions, and trendy beach wear.

Anita said, "I don't have to shut my eyes to imagine that I am on Cloud Nine." Dad replied, "This is ecstasy itself! Like a South Florida beach, Juhu Beach stretches out for miles in a friendly atmosphere of people and numerous delightful bars and grills."

And the crowd of *bablis, sweetus, bantis and petites* who were showing off their toned and tanned physiques would support his opinion. Most of them had see-worthy outfits; a few could have been calendar girls. Beach lovers and sun worshippers stretched out along the golden sands and basked in the warm rising or setting sun. Others played in the water as it kissed their toes or lapped at their feet and washed away their fatigue. This was truly a lover's delight, whatever one's love might be. Yet, if needed, there was always the option of blissful solitude. Many in Mumbai had mastered the art of having the best of both worlds and could reverse the scenario as needed.

AR sent greeting cards and e-mails to his teammates, staff and well-wishers back home in Utica with the words, "Wish you were here." Anita's greeting cards, snail-and e-mails to her pals in U.S. contained the messages, "Missing You - From the Silvery Sands" and "Thinking of you in Magnificent Mumbai."

Mumbaiwallas and foreign tourists alike flocked to Juhu beach en mass for DaLife and in their quest for inner joy. In the warm morning sun, countless health-conscious men and women practiced yoga - the basics and its *Kundalini, Iyengar, Ashtanga, Svaroopa, Anusara, Vinyasa* variations while enjoying the soft, salty ocean breezes. The different types of yoga make up the world's oldest holistic self-development system. It includes a blend of yoga postures with breathing methods, self-awareness and practice routines. This age-old

Indian ritual awakens the *charkas* (the spiritual energy centers in the spine). The yogis and yoginis found their balance and tuned into their inner peace. After the yogis and the non-yogis completed their exercises, they "took a mo" for themselves and their families. They enjoyed the beaches of the picturesque fishing villages which dot the north Mumbai coast.

The Reddys planned to picnic at Juhu Beach the next day with Joe and his family. Anita wore capri pants and Atul and their two sons slipped into Bermuda shorts. AR had fond memories of childhood days spent at Juhu and he expected that the day would be fun for his family, too. The adults and children reveled in the gently lapping waves, the balmy breezes and the warm sunshine. This is what the locals called "intense leisure activity," walking or jogging a few feet from the surf. This had been the routine when Atul and Joey were children. Once again, the two men walked the beach, spotted seashells and crabs, and examined the different colored rocks that washed ashore. They tried to decipher the magic and mystery of the Indian Ocean.

When Atul and Joe were growing up, the radio was a luxury. In the span of one generation technology had advanced by leaps and bounds. Now on the beach, the two men traveled back. There was no television with VCR or DVD, no CDs, no telephone, no computer or e-mails. It was like old-times when there were no excuses for not experiencing good vibrations with family and friends. While the beach crowd boogied to the music or stretched out on the sand and basked in the warmth of the sun, the families took a stroll, hugging the water line along the white sand. In the midst of their hectic lives, Juhu Beach was a place for quiet reflection to float away stress and soothe the soul. While the friends walked on the beach, the sand served as a natural exfoliate, skin smoother and a foot massager, pressing on those reflexology points.

As Joey and Anita walked on the beach, Joey recalled his memories of young Atul. "When we were growing up, schools were not equipped to deal with students with disabilities. I had to drop out after the sixth grade when I was afflicted with polio. Atul stepped in as a surrogate teacher." Joey related how he eagerly waited for Atul to come from school. As Atul did his assignments, he would revise the language, math and science skills he had been taught that day; in the process, Joey learned them from Atul.

Joey continued, "While I was waiting for Atul to return from school, I would spend my time playing traditional games using fruit seeds, marbles and pebbles." These games were most popular during the summer holidays before the onset of the monsoon season, which coincides with the beginning of the new school year.

Atul and Joey reminisced about their childhood pastime of tossing pebbles and sand dollars to make them skip over the waves. The one whose pebble skipped the most number of times was the winner. Atul seized the opportunity to ask the question that had long baffled him. "How were you so good at the game even though your forearm and hand were affected by polio?" Joey replied, "I'm not sure I am good; it may be not in spite of but due to the disability that I got skilled."

"Is it possible that I subliminally learned the skillful wrist movements from you as we were playing pebble hopping and *Biyani* (cashew seeds game)?" Atul asked.

Before Joey could answer, they were joined by their families. Atul was eager to have his burning question answered. The adults and children compared their hand and finger movements. They realized that the men had similar thumb, index and little finger movements which were different from those of the rest. The men also had a recoil motion of the arm after delivery. Joey explained that the delivery with a recoil spring action delivered a greater control on the stone. These intuitive movements combined with Atul's reading of the ice learned from the time he landed in New York made him an artful curler. The secret to Atul's skill at curling the stone was discovered as the holidays were coming to an end! Everybody previously had got it wrong!

Before the Reddys left Mumbai, they created a shared journal with many friends. For the final act, they had to submit to a native ritual. The superstitious believe that because the Reddys had garnered worldwide adulation they ran the risk of suffering the effects of the *disht* or "evil eye." Such a belief is also common among southern European and Middle Eastern cultures. Aunt Sohini proceeded to perform "the *disht* removal rites" on each of the Reddys to "remove the evil eye." The aunt recited special invocations while holding three dried red whole chili-peppers and salt over their heads. The sons, now Americanized said, "Oh mom! Do I HAVE to do this?"

Bye-Bye Bombay - Hello New York
> 16 <

The Reddys left Mumbai with a restored sense of the basic kindness of people and with the thrill of experiencing beauty in an urban jungle. They were exhilarated, a term which combines a relaxed body, radiant spirit, contented mind, all created by Mother Nature and the native ambience. The family was leaving with mixed feelings and sweet sorrow.

The Reddys flew back to the U.S. on Air India's Jumbo 747. As with any international flight, the Reddys experienced the usual, "hurry-up and wait" at every step. AR observed, "The good news is that as one flies west, we are constantly moving along with the sunrise and gain time. We'll arrive in New York the same day that we leave Mumbai!"

As usual, security was tight with the screening of check-in luggage, carry-on baggage and shoes. As the plane finally took off late that night, the travelers could take in the illumination of magnificent Mumbai and its shoreline. It was as if the city was bidding the flyers Bombay's "Best of Good-Byes." The flight was peaceful, except that the Indian travelers and the crew on board were proud to be traveling on the same flight as the world-renowned curler. Each admirer was eager to get AR's autographs. They assured him they would treasure the memento and tell their children and grandchildren how they got it.

Once they settled down for the flight, AR advised the kids, "You've heard about Mumbai and now you've experienced it. You have the photographs to remember it and you have explored your cultural roots." Anita felt it was a healing vacation for her, one which allowed her to breathe in deeply the warmth of family and friends. For AR the trip was exhilarating and exhausting, relaxing and rejuvenating. The family and other passengers on the flight returning to the U.S. remarked, "The city is a vibrant mix of new and old."

The airline menu gave the travelers the choice of broiled yogurt-ginger chicken breast or baked crisp Parmesan-Romano chicken with braised cabbage. For dessert, they could choose either lemon crepes or mango ice-cream topped with fresh mangoes.

As they relaxed after dinner, they analyzed their culture shock. Ajit, the 15-year-old asked his dad, "Is it true that in India men get to know their wives only after they get married? "

Dad replied, "Son! That's true all over the world. Everyone appears amiable and alluring until you know them."

Morning broke as the plane was flying over Greece. The El Grecos were served breakfast. The Reddys and other fliers were enjoying the flight and as the plane flew over the Alps, they were in "Swiss Bliss."

Later, some *desi* kids traded their insights on Indian culture:

A Mumbaiwalla drinks to his wife's health so often, it ruins his own.

A Delhi-walla doesn't have to tell his wife anything - their neighbors do.

Indian girls marry men like their dads. That's why the brides' mothers cry on the wedding day.

Anita realized that she would have a hectic time after returning to the States. So, she spent some of the long in-flight hours writing out her "thank you" cards to the relatives and friends they had just left behind. She concluded each note with "thanks for the memories."

To help the travelers pass the long hours, AR recounted a funny story: A Goan called Keni was attending a meeting of automotive executives in Japan. They were reviewing a new model car which was just off the drawing board. Everyone was very happy with the car's engineering and design. There was major discussion concerning the naming of the model. While the discussion was in progress, Keni received a call on his cell phone from his wife in Goa. He excused himself from the meeting. After 20 minutes, the chairman of the board approached Keni for his opinion. To end the conversation with his wife, Keni said to her, '*Tho Yeta, Tho Yeta*, (he's coming)'." The chairman overheard the words and liked the way they sounded. He decided to name the car 'TOYOTA'."

Other fliers followed with similar *kaneos* (stories).

Relaxing on the plane, Anita decided to get over the "India blues" by thinking about her upcoming spring garden and imagining the options. New York is a four-season state and her neighbors show-off their gorgeous flowers in their front and back yards. She planned to get a jump start and take advantage of the remaining April showers which promise great May flowers. Every time she walked into her Florida room she felt as if she had just taken her morning tonic. She and grandma considered the room their personal space where they had fun and could relax, surrounded by bouquets of flowers in a rainbow of colors. Anita envisioned how she would drive her husband crazy by presenting him with flowers, each signifying a specific message: Pink carnation for I'll never forget you; red poppy for pleasure; red rose for passion; red tulip for love; stephanotis for happiness in marriage; primrose for I can't live without you, and ivy for eternal fidelity.

She evaluated the varieties of roses that would be right for her outdoor garden, selected a few and visualized the ideal sites for the temperamental flowers. She revealed to Atul, "In the shade, let's go for the red roses and use the fence for the climbers."

Atul replied, "This year, let's make a special effort to take the time to stop and smell the roses in our La Rouge Galleria." In addition to the fragrant roses and honeysuckle vines, Anita's garden had the usual marigolds, coreopsis, zinnias, black-eyed-Susans and clematis. To brighten the summer, Anita also wanted to plant colorful tuberous begonias among the hostas along the porch. Her garden, active with hummingbirds and butterflies, would be a happy place.

This year, their annual crop of prolific colorful daylilies would need some springtime care and attention with compost and grass clippings. The Reddys always looked forward to that dazzling and feisty burst of color occurring later in the summer and fall. Each daylily, as its name suggests, opens for just a single day and then dies. This routine lasts for three weeks. The daylily family consists of about fifteen species which originated in Asia, and reflects the earth's great bounty. For the Reddys, daylilies have a special significance because they are also used in cooking and for medicinal purposes.

Anita continued, "In the shade we'll plant coleus and impatiens. This will be our spring fling." During the twenty-hour-long flight across the North Pole, she also thought about her organic garden (a.k.a. gardening with a conscience). She wanted to maximize the benefit of the compost that she and AR had been working on all winter. Anita was a savvy gardener who aimed for balance and serenity in their garden. AR cut short her trend of thought by saying, "When we get back, I've got to clear the yard of dead leaves and winter's worth of ice-felled branches which will have littered the garden floor."

Meanwhile some chic "Venitas" shared with each other stories of the treasures they had found in Mumbai. "You know us girls are shop-aholics," one explained. Another recounted how her *beti* (daughter) was getting married in Chicago; so she had to "hit the top-line Indian gold and other jewelry stores daily, like a heat-seeking missile."

The "Monicas" had humorous observations about men:

If you want a committed man, look in a mental hospital.

A sensitive, caring man is: An oxymoron or a moron.

What do you do if your boyfriend walks out? Shut the door.

On the flight, AR met Dr. Naik, another BUMA (Bombay University Medical Alumni) member who lived in Dallas, Texas. The two physicians reminisced about the good old days and the old-times. Several years earlier, they had played host to a visiting distant friend named Laloo. Dr. Naik recounted how Laloo was very impressed with upstate New York when he visited AR.

As Naik recalled, "What impressed Laloo most was that everything in the upstate region was big compared to Mumbai. The cars were big, as were the houses and the streets." When Laloo visited Dallas, Texas, he found everything was huge compared to New York. According to Laloo, "Texans do not wear baseball caps but Texan hats. Their boots, belts, cars and homes are all very large."

Naik continued, "We went for dinner one evening at the Cowboy Bar and Grill. Laloo was impressed with the decor, the beer that was served in a foot-long 'Texas boot' and the 20-ounce sirloin steak."

Before digging in, Laloo said, "Things in Dallas are indeed large, very large." Midway through the dinner, after downing the beer, the visitor wanted to use the facilities. He was directed to the restroom.

Fifteen minutes, then half an hour later, there was no sign of Laloo. Naik went looking for his guest. He checked the restroom with no success. After fifteen more minutes of frantic searching, Naik spotted Laloo thrashing about in the hotel swimming pool, two hallways down from the restroom. When Naik approached him, Laloo wildly waved and screamed, "Please don't flush! Please don't flush!"

The boys unwound after their hectic trip to the west coast of India. They could only relax for so long and then they found themselves bored. They began to track their flight on the in-cabin monitor as the plane passed several countries and made several changes in altitude, and then in longitude and latitude as it flew northwest to the North Pole. This led the brothers to play the game of capitals of the various countries, but they had no luck with the international scene. So Anil suggested, "Let's play the game of the capitals of the various states in the U.S. and its territories." While Anil took the big and well-known states, Ajit named the capitals of smaller states and territories: "Puerto Rico - San Juan; Guam - Agana and American Samoa - Pago Pago."

All the partying for the last two months forced the Reddys to review their diets and choose foods which would allow them to "eat what they loved and yet lose the weight they hated." Anita shared with the rest of the family two e-mails from her Utica friends. They were all determined to "be thin by spring and have flat tummies before summer."

A passenger asked the doctor-sahib, "What got you into curling? You were never exposed to the sport as a child in Bombay!"

AR responded, "That would be a long story. Yet, looking back I realize that, as they say, 'The journey of a thousand miles begins with a broken fan belt and a leaky tire'."

To another traveler who asked how it felt to be on Team USA, AR said, "It is a once-in-a-lifetime chance to experience it up-close."

When they finally landed at JFK Airport, the brothers inquired, "Are we there yet?" Mom replied with a sigh of relief, "No! But we are not far from home sweet home."

This, of course, was just the first leg of their trip back to their home in upstate New York - Utica. The Reddys began longing for all the comforts of home in spite of the enjoyable visit they'd just had with their extended family. They cleared Immigration and Customs and made their way to the connecting flight to Syracuse where they would re-check their baggage. The more the Reddys traveled outside the U.S., the more they loved the country on their return.

At JFK Airport, they met a disheartened old Indian passenger.
He whined: "I've lost *mera* (my) luggage," as he wandered around the terminal with tears streaming down his cheeks.

An airport aide: You're already homesick?

Old Timer: No, I've lost all *mera* (my) luggage!

Airport aide in his New York City twang: How'd that happen? You have two suitcases and a few other parcels with you!

Old Timer: "*Arre*, the cork fell off the *garrafao* (three liter bottle) of home-made feni (alcohol)!" This old soul was carrying two pieces of luggage, *khatli-potlis* and everything but the *ponos* (jackfruit). Anyone making a big trip or taking a long vacation would take along a three-month supply of provisions. This tradition was followed until about two generations ago in the U.S. and one generation ago in India.

The Reddys had an eight-hour layover at JFK Airport before they caught their late evening flight to Syracuse. They decided to tour the Big Apple and take in the charms of the city they knew well from the time they had lived there during AR's residency. They enjoyed a gourmet meal at their favorite restaurant, visited the Twin Tower Memorial, and then took the City Tour bus from the 9-11-01 site. The parents reminisced about their arrival in the city as newcomers and their first experiences of living in the Big Apple on the salary of a young physician-resident at the hospital.

They admired the architecture and beauty of Flatiron Building (1901-1903), Penn and Grand Central stations (built 1902-11 and 1903-13) and then Chrysler (1928-30), Empire State (1929-31), Seagram Building (1954-58), Rockefeller Center (1931-40) and Guggenheim Museum (1956-59) among others. They decided to return soon to visit the must-sees of this great city. The New York sights and sounds were in many ways comparable to the ones the Reddys had enjoyed in Old Bombay and New Mumbai. These were similar experiences but at different ends of the world. In their own way the New Yorkers - creatures of the urban jungle - were no different from Mumbaiwallas; both population groups demonstrated their fast-paced determination to get to their destination, their tenacity and zest to try the new and be on the cutting edge of fashion and style.

In the evening, the Reddys stopped at their favorite restaurant which was acclaimed by the cognoscenti and included in the city's Gastronomic Heights. They ordered Greek salads and appetizers. For their main courses, the family dined on lemony chicken with capers and Kalamata olives, petite filet with chicken Francaise, pasta pomodoro and Green Beans Almandine. Their feet back on U.S. soil, the kids reverted to their Utica lingo. This first generation of Indian-Americans described the entrées as *"Just Delicioso."*

The Reddys made their way to JFK Airport to board the Cessna for the short flight to Syracuse in the upstate countryside. When they took off, they called out, "*arrivederci* (see you again) New York City!"

A big "Welcome Home" banner held high by friends and fans awaited the Reddys at the Syracuse Airport. The Reddys could smell the fragrance of the upstate region! They could almost feel the comforts of home! They could smell spring in the air! When Anita saw so many of her friends at the airport she exclaimed, "That's *Amore*."

When the Reddys crossed the threshold of their Utica home they felt enveloped in the loving arms of "Home, Sweet Home." The house was filled with the warmth of Grandma Reddy's presence and the *diya* (oil lamp) burning brightly.

"When my time comes to die,
I don't want to discover that I have not lived."
Henry David Thoreau, American Naturalist and Writer

Shield of Faith Eph 6:16

Jesus is the object of my Faith

1 source of Faith - Jesus is the author + finisher of our faith

2 strength of Faith - exercise an act of Faith. - ~~exerc~~ practice having Faith envision victory

We will be conformed to the image of His son.

We must consistently practice an act of faith.

Do what His Word tells you to do - Look up verses on fear - stand strong in what God tells us in His Word. Practice His Word and act in faith to what comes against you

Printed in the United States
39681LVS00005B/151-201